Stamps, Vamps & Tramps

EVIL GIRLFRIEND MEDIA

Published by Evil Girlfriend Media, P.O. BOX 3856, Federal Way, WA 98063
Copyright © 2014

All rights reserved. Any reproduction or distribution of this book, in part or in whole, or transmission in any form, or by any means, electronic, mechanical, photocopying, recording or otherwise, without the written permission of the publisher or author is theft.

Any similarity to persons living or dead is purely coincidental.

Cover photo by Sabelnikova Olga.
Cover design by Matt Youngmark.

"Easy Mark," copyright © 2014 by Rachel Caine
"The Whole of His History," copyright © 2014 by Barbara A. Barnett
"Mungo the Vampire," copyright © 2014 by Sandra Kasturi
"The Lightning Tree," copyright © 2014 by Carrie Laben
"Follow Me," copyright © 2014 by Christine Morgan
"Only Darkness," copyright © 2014 by Paul Witcover
"Flies in the Ink," copyright © 2014 by Megan Lee Beals
"The Hungry Living Dead," copyright © 2014 by Nancy Kilpatrick, reprinted from *The Vampire Stories of Nancy Kilpatrick,* Mosaic Press, 2000
"Josephine the Tattoo Queen," copyright © 2014 by Joshua Gage
"Stabilization," copyright © 2014 by Daniels Parseliti
"A Virgin Hand Disarm'd," copyright © 2014 by Mary A. Turzillo
"Summer Night in Durham," copyright © 2014 by Cat Rambo
"His Body Scattered by the Plague Winds," copyright © 2014 by Adam Callaway
"From the Heart," copyright © 2014 by Kella Campbell
"Sideponytail," copyright © 2014 by Lily Hoang
"His Face, All Red," copyright © 2014 by Gemma Files

ISBN: 978-0615970783
ISBN-10: 0615970788

Dedicated to those eternally tattooed,

By soul-sucking vampires,

Damned to wander the night,

And to only know darkness.

Table of Contents

Introduction 7

Easy Mark, *Rachel Caine*..9

The Whole of His History, *Barbara A. Barnett*......................29

Mungo the Vampire, *Sandra Kasturi* 41

The Lightning Tree, *Carrie Laben* 49

Follow Me, *Christine Morgan*..71

Only Darkness, *Paul Witcover*...87

Flies in the Ink, *Megan Lee Beals*..103

The Hungry Living Dead, *Nancy Kilpatrick*.......................127

Josephine the Tattoo Queen, *Joshua Gage*..........................135

Stabilization, *Daniels Parseliti* 141

A Virgin Hand Disarm'd, *Mary A. Turzillo* 161

Summer Night in Durham, *Cat Rambo*..............................175

His Body Scattered by the Plague Winds, *Adam Callaway*......179

From the Heart, *Kella Campbell* 201

Sideponytail, *Lily Hoang*..217

His Face, All Red, *Gemma Files*..229

Biographies..265

Introduction

Stamps, vamps, and tramps: from three little words have come sixteen compelling, beautifully crafted stories. Among them, you will find the work of award-winning authors and fan favorites, as well as exciting new talent. In editing this anthology, I was delighted to encounter such a diversity of style and subject matter within the shared triptych of themes.

Across the stories, the "stamps"—that is, the tattoos—are variously protective, punitive, parasitic, totemic, cryptic, funny, and even figurative, making narrative cameos or taking center stage. And yes, two stories feature a classic "tramp stamp." The "tramps" include the homeless and the restless; the trashy and the titillating; travelers and transgressors of sexual boundaries. And lastly, the "vamps" are a variety of blood-seeking creatures, ranging from a classical, caped seducer in Nancy Kilpatrick's "The Hungry Living Dead," to the gherkin-sized fumbler of Sandra Kasturi's hilarious "Mungo the Vampire," from femmes fatales to winged monsters, manifesting in psychosis-fueled grotesquerie in Daniels Parseliti's mental-ward tale, "Stabilization," and in allusions to pop-culture icons in Lily Hoang's "Sideponytail," whose protagonist prefers sexual role-play.

As befits a volume that includes "tramps" in the title, the stories' settings range widely. "Follow Me," by Christine Morgan, centers on the risky freedom of street-walking prostitutes in ancient Greece; Mary Turzillo's "A Virgin Hand Disarm'd" tells of a Renaissance man whose almost-literally burning passion leads him to London. Barbara A. Barnett's "The Whole of His History" takes place in eighteenth-century America, where a man tries to elude his illicit desires. Rachel Caine's "Easy Mark," follows a Depression-era "boxcar boy" (or rather girl, in disguise) in search of a decent meal. "Josephine the Tattoo Queen," also set in the 1930s, begins in a dark circus side-tent—and where it ends is definitely unlike *Water for Elephants*. Adam Calloway's "His Body Scattered" takes us far away, to a lyrical, alternate world named "Lacuna," where paper can be sacred, magical, sentient… and dangerous.

Two of the stories transpire in tattoo parlors—Cat Rambo's playful, modern misadventure, "Summer Night in Durham," and newcomer Megan Beals' eerie "Flies in the Ink," set in Tacoma near the end of World War I. Both feature tattoo artists who are reluctant for different reasons in the face of an insistent vampire. Other struggling artists are the protagonists of two sharp urban stories, "From the Heart" by Kella Campbell, and "Only Darkness" by Paul Witcover, which depict, respectively, an exotic dancer in Toronto and a sidewalk portrait-sketcher in New York City, each drawn unwittingly into contact with the supernatural. Carrie Laben's superbly wry narrative, "The Lightning Tree," takes place in a rural Northern town that is far from any metropolitan diversions, yet the place is cursed with something far deadlier than just boredom. Gemma Files' novella, "His Face, All Red" closes the anthology. Hers is a story with relentless momentum: a story of hunting, pilfering, and murdering; of witches, vampires, demons, and family—with some intriguing overlaps in identity.

We at Evil Girlfriend Media are really excited to have brought these stories together for *Stamps, Vamps, and Tramps*, and we hope that you enjoy reading them as much as we did.

Shannon Robinson, Editor
Baltimore, Maryland
January, 2014

Easy Mark

by Rachel Caine

The sticks arranged close to the back fence were a message Danna could read as easily as printed words: two twigs, arranged like a sideways T. She shifted the bindle on her shoulder in a familiar, automatic gesture, one that had developed over the first week since she'd caught the first boxcar and started developing calluses where the broomstick rubbed—and considered what it meant.

Easy mark.

Even though she was still pretty new at being a Boxcar Boy—and you *had* to be a boy if you were on the road, like she was—she knew you couldn't always trust the signs left by other hobos. Tramps were just as good and bad and indifferent as regular folk, and they could be mistaken, or just plain mean. She'd fallen for a false sign on one house that said it was a *sit down feed* only to find a man with a gun and vicious dog ready to use both on her. So *easy mark* bothered her. Usually it meant a soft touch, someone kind who'd hand out a good, hot meal and some casual talk, maybe even a bath and a bed if you were real lucky. Luck didn't hold, though. Things went bad fast, and stayed bad for days or weeks or months or years.

Like it had for her pa.

Danna hadn't wanted to leave her family, but she hadn't had much choice. Her father's job had been blown away in the dust storms in Oklahoma, where just about every farm had been reduced to desert and sticks; her ma had sickened and died on the road while they'd been trying to make it to California to pick crops. Better she had, really; they'd been told the jobs were in California but when they got there it was nothing but lines of hungry faces waiting.

Someone had to do something if what was left of their family was going to survive.

Her younger brother, Clarence, was too young to be on his own, but she was a solid seventeen, built strong and tall, and flat-chested and thin-hipped. Only natural she'd be the one to go off on her own, so the food would stretch better between her too-thin dad and little Clee. Her father had been stone-faced about it, but she'd seen the tears at the corners of his eyes, and he'd given her some threadbare old pants and a belt to hold them up, and a shirt too big for her but still sturdy enough. She'd had to use her own shoes, but they were farm shoes, built plain and none too girly. Once she'd taken a razor to her hair and reduced it to a short fluff, she passed for a boy just fine. She'd never had nice-girl manners anyway.

She'd had a vague notion of earning some money and sending it for Clee's care, but she didn't know where they were now, and anyway, money was powerful hard to come by out here. Today she had a dollar hidden in her shoe, and nothing else but the bindle on her shoulder and a thin, piercing cramp in her stomach.

She had to chance it, this *easy mark*. She'd been without solid food for three days now; the last hobo jungle she'd tried had been ruled by a cruel old buzzard who'd demanded she go steal a chicken from a farmer down the road if she wanted any mulligan stew. She'd lost the bottle for it when she'd seen the thin, desperate face of the farmer's wife, and the pathetic skinny chicken—their last one, probably—scratching at the dirt in the yard. Besides, she was no good at catching chickens anyway.

Danna hoisted herself over the wood fence—it wasn't too tall, and she had long legs, lean and strong from all the wandering—and dropped down on the other side in a crouch, eyes darting all around. No signs of a dog; no lumps of shit on the ground, no bowl of water or food (though she'd known tramps hungry enough to eat the food right out of a dog's bowl. Many townsfolk wouldn't even put it out at night anymore for fear of attracting them). The yard was mostly hard-packed dirt, but there was a small vegetable garden growing in the corner, well-tended, and the smell of herbs like rosemary and lavender drifted on the still night air.

Seemed like a nice enough place.

Could dig up a couple of the vegetables and skedaddle, she thought; the idea of a fresh carrot or tomato made her mouth water, and her eyes too. But she wasn't built to be a thief. Same reason that poor farmer still had his chicken.

It was dangerous, but she walked up to the back door and knocked softly. There was soft light inside behind the lace curtains, but nothing moved for a long moment, and then the curtains shifted aside, and a face looked out.

Danna took a step back—not out of fear, but out of something else she couldn't really name at all. The man—was it a man that she'd seen?—was big. Big enough to blank out her mind and make her hand shake and grip the bindle-stick tight enough to hurt.

The curtain dropped again, and it was peculiar, but she couldn't rightly say whether that face had been a man or a woman, old or young, ugly or pretty. Her brain said *face* and that was all. Like it didn't know how to deal with it at all.

She was ready to turn and flee when she heard a lock click back, and the door creaked open, and a little old man shuffled out on the step and looked at her with a kind, sad smile.

not him not the face I saw

It was a snatch of nonsense that ran across her mind, and Danna dismissed it firmly like she'd shut away night terrors and so many other things over the years. He was an old man with a kindly, lined face and a shock of unkempt white hair, and light brown eyes the color of the dirt that had swallowed up half the Midwest.

"Hello there," he said. He had a quiet, Southern voice, deeper than she'd expected. "You lookin' for a handout?"

"Yessir," she said, and nodded a little too hard. Somewhere out in the dark, she could hear someone weeping. Far off and very quietly. She knew the sound of despair, and that was it, all right. Didn't come from inside his house, though. His house seemed like the only sign of warmth and light and kindness in the world, right now.

"Well, come on in, then, you're lettin' all the dark inside," he said, and shuffled back into the house. He had on an old checked robe, one pocket torn and flapping, and under that a well-worn pair of old Levi's and a work shirt that had seen better days. Slippers on his feet. "I got some stew I can put in a bowl for you, maybe some stuff you can take with you. How you fixed for clothes?"

"Pretty good," she lied, and came over the threshold into a fairyland of warmth and glimmering light, of clean floors and a polished table and the rich smell of bubbling stew with real meat in it. Her eyes filled with tears, and she felt wrong here, wrong and bad and dirty in this beautiful kitchen. She hadn't had a wash in so long she knew she smelled like feet and sweat, and her clothes had so much road dirt on them she could almost see it smoking off of her to cloud up the room.

"Make yourself at home," he said, and waved a palsied old hand at the table and chairs. Three chairs, which was an odd number; most people had two or four, but three seemed uneven. Still, it was a round table and chairs set at a triangle, and maybe it just made sense for him. Maybe he only needed three.

She took one point of the triangle and eased herself down, putting her bindle down on the floor by her feet. She instinctively put a boot on it, as if she was still in a hobo camp where someone might steal it out from under her, but he ignored her as he puttered around the fresh-painted green cabinets and took out a china bowl in dusty pink for the stew. He set it down in front of her with a big, heavy spoon, and as she stared at the hot, steaming meal, thick with fresh carrots and peas and potatoes and chunks of meat, real meat, he cut some slices from a loaf of bread and poured her a china cup of coffee, too.

Danna burst into tears.

She didn't mean to, but the place, the food, the kindness just overwhelmed her. The tears gave her right away, because however much she looked like a boy she cried like a girl, and she hid her face in her dirty hands as he patted her awkwardly on the shoulder.

"C'mon, gal, let's get you clean before you fill your stomach. Come on with me, now."

She stood up, still gasping back sobs, made use of the bar soap and water at the sink. She did her hands and face and neck and arms all the way to the elbows, and the tingle on her skin made her want to weep again. It felt so good to be clean. To be cared for.

He handed her a dish towel, embroidered with little blue flowers at the corner, and she dried herself off and pulled in a full, shaking breath. "Sorry about that," she said. "I—"

"No need," he said. "My name's Riley. Folks 'round here call me Grandpa Riley. Now, you sit yourself down and get some food in you, you're shaky as a willow tree. Thin as one, too."

She took the first bite of the stew and the tears almost came back, because it brought back so much—memories of her mother puttering around the warm little farmhouse kitchen, baking bread, cutting fresh vegetables out of the garden, bestowing kisses on Danna's head as she stirred the pot. There was love in this stew. She could taste it.

When the old man reached out for his cup, she saw something under his sleeve—a tattoo, maybe, blue ink like old sailors carried on their bodies. It looked strange. Her hunger was making her dizzy, she thought, because it almost seemed to move against his skin.

He wasn't eating. She stopped long enough to ask, but he waved it aside. "Already did," he said. "Always keep a little extra on the hob for those in need. You just tuck in."

She tried to eat slowly, savoring every rich, meaty bite, but all too soon the bowl was empty, the bread reduced to a thin dusting of crumbs on the teal-blue plate, the good strong coffee drained. She sat for a moment in silence, just taking in the fact that she no longer felt hungry or thirsty or *unwanted*, and then reached for the plate and the bowl to take them to the sink. He took them first and shuffled over to dunk them in some water. "I'll wash 'em later," he said. "You need more coffee, girl? Hey, what's your name?"

"Danna," she said. "Danna MacKay."

"Out of Oklahoma, I expect. Maybe Texas?"

"Up around Norman, sir, in Oklahoma."

"How long you been on the road?"

Forever. "About three months or so, I guess."

"Smart of you to pretend to be a boy, Danna. Too many bad men out there on the road—not that being a pretty young boy'll always save you either, you know that?"

She did. She'd had a few bad moments; one had been stopped by an older hobo who'd seen it coming, but the other she'd had to get out of on her own, at the point of a knife.

She didn't want to talk about that. She changed the subject. "You feed a lot of tramps, sir?"

"Grandpa, call me Grandpa. I do what I can. Most fellas are just down on their luck—good folks, just bad circumstances. Ain't had but a few who thought he could take me for something more than a hot meal and a soft bed." Grandpa Riley smiled, and for the first time, Danna felt a shiver go up her spine. "Bless their souls."

"Grandpa—" She started, but then she stopped, because she wasn't sure what she was asking, really. He seemed to know, though.

"You can stay the night, if you want," he said. "Got a bathtub for you, and I can get you some fresh clothes. Might be a tad too big on you but girls don't generally wear the right size on the road, do they? A night in a bed won't hurt you none. Maybe two, if you want to do some chores. I ain't as young as I was. Could use some help patching the roof."

"I can do that," she said, and tried not to sound as eager as she felt. "My pa always said I was more mountain goat than girl."

"Then let's get you a hot bath drawn and your bed made up, and you'll be up on that ladder tomorrow, lickety split."

As they went down the narrow central hall that ran from front door to back in an unbroken line, she studied the things on the walls. Some old-time photos of people in stiff black coats and high-necked dresses, nobody smiling. Some old stitched samplers that said GOD BLESS THIS HOME and PEACE TO THOSE WHO ENTER HERE.

There was one more, smaller and hung in a darker spot, and she only had time to glance at it before Grandpa opened up a door and flicked on the light. It was odd, but she could have sworn it said EVIL TO HIM WHO EVIL DOES, which wasn't something girls generally embroidered onto their samplers and pillows.

She forgot it when she saw the room. It had once belonged to a girl, she thought; there were feminine touches in the curtains and the colorful quilt, and a big hope chest of polished cherry wood sat at the foot of the four-poster bed.

She had the oddest feeling as she put her bindle down in the corner of the room that it was *still* a girl's room, though there was no trace of someone living in it now. No frillies on the clean dresser top, no perfume or jewel box. Not even a picture postcard.

Grandpa Riley must have sensed something, because he said, "Was my granddaughter's room. Lila Mae. She's gone now. Consumption—TB, they call it now. She's been gone a few months now."

Tuberculosis took a lot of folks. There were plenty of hobos with it, and she'd tried to stay well away from them as they hacked and coughed. Most died hard and slow. Her ma might have died of it, too; they hadn't been sure what had killed her, in the end. Just too much sickness and too little comfort.

"I'm sorry," she said.

"God gives and takes. Ain't no use asking why. I'll start your bath across the hall. You sleep tight, now. There's some gowns in the drawer there."

He shuffled away again, and she sat down on the edge of the bed, staring after him.

Easy mark, the signs had read, but she didn't think he was. Not at all. For all his kindness and his good food, there was something steely underneath all of that. Something that wouldn't be fooled, or shoved.

She had a flash of that face again, the face framed by the curtains in the window. The face that wasn't his, or anyone's; wasn't even a face, exactly.

She shivered, and when she heard the hot water running in the tub, she grabbed a nightgown from the drawer and went across the hall to wash up for bed.

※

Being on a ladder again felt good to her. Danna balanced herself easily, swung the hammer hard. Driving in the shingles felt like making a home again, even though she knew she couldn't stay here. Shouldn't even think about it. *Just a kindness for a kindness,* she told herself, and wiped her sweaty forehead. She felt strong today—stronger than she had in months. Grandpa Riley had fed her breakfast of eggs and thick ham steak and buttered biscuits and more coffee, and she felt she could hammer all day long and half the night. She could build a house if she had to, all by herself. Amazing what food and sleep and safety could do for you.

Grandpa had gone inside to fetch her some lemonade, and she'd clambered up on the pitched roof to rip away some old damaged tar paper and put down some new when she heard a new voice from below in the back yard say, "Hey, you the man of the house?"

Danna looked down. She was wearing old, baggy pants and a thick man's shirt and a peaked cap, and climbing around up there she supposed anybody would have thought she was a young man. She crouched at the edge and stared at the man looking up at her.

Like her, he was a tramp. Unlike her, he was big and burly. Life on the road hadn't been too tough on him; he still had muscle and bone, though he was dirty enough she could smell him from here. Lazy, too. She saw it in his mocking grin that thought all that hard work she was doing was for suckers.

"Naw," she said, and kept her voice rough and low in her throat. "I just work here."

The back door banged open, and Grandpa came out with a thick glass pitcher filled with cloudy yellow, lemons still swimming in around the ice cubes. He had two glasses.

The hobo standing in the yard looked over Grandpa Riley and kept that mocking grin firmly in place. "Don't mind if I do," he said, and held out his hand. "Ain't had lemonade in a coon's age."

"Ain't having it now," Grandpa said. "It's for my handyman up there. Dan, you come on down, now."

Dan was the name she'd asked him to use—it was the one she needed on the road, and it fit natural enough. She didn't want to get too used to being called Danna anymore.

The hobo standing in the yard reached out for the ladder, and for a second Danna thought he meant to steady it for her to come down—but as she reached for it, he tipped it sideways. It topped over, slamming hard into the ground and tearing up a tomato plant in the garden. "You just stay up there, handyman," the hobo said. "Me and the old man got things to talk about."

Danna caught herself, balanced on the edge. She didn't know what to do. Grandpa Riley wasn't looking at her, wasn't looking bothered by this either. He just put down the lemonade glasses, poured one, and handed it to the man who'd knocked over her ladder. "Drink it and go," he said. "We don't want no trouble, mister."

The hobo upended the glass and drank it in one long rush, dirty throat working as he glugged. When it was just ice cubes and a lemon slice, he handed it back. "Nice start, mister," he said. "Gonna want some dinner too. And whatever cash you got to spare."

"Ain't got no dinner for you. And no cash either."

"You have to be paying your handyman something, and I can smell that food from out here. You just fork it over and there won't be no need for trouble."

Grandpa poured him another glass of lemonade. "You drink it and go."

The hobo poured the lemonade—perfectly good lemonade!—on the thirsty ground, tossed the glass aside, and grabbed Grandpa Riley by the shirt. "I ain't playing games with you, Pop," he said. He was still smiling, but it was a nasty sort of smile, something that made chills crawl up Danna's spine despite the warm sun. "You, kid, jump down. Do it now."

"It's a long way, mister," she said.

"Fuck I care? Jump or this old man gets hit. You know I'll do it."

She knew. He had the look, and the big scarred hands of someone who hit often and for no reason at all. But she also knew that if she jumped now, things would go worse, not better.

She still would have jumped, even knowing it, except that Grandpa Riley suddenly threw himself to one side, hard. "Now!" Grandpa yelled. "Get 'im!"

She threw herself off the roof and landed on the lug feet first, driving down hard and feeling bone break. Collarbone, most like. The hobo yelled in shock and fury, and twisted as she was knocked to the ground. She hit hard, and the wind got knocked out of her. He loomed over her the size of a mountain, dark against the sun, and she saw the white slice of a knife in his undamaged right hand.

"Shouldn't have done that, kid," he said. "Last thing you'll ever do."

Grandpa hit him in the kidneys from behind with a sucker punch, and Danna watched in horror as the hobo turned, snarling, and drove that sharp knife in a hard, shining arc… right into the old man's stomach.

Grandpa made a sound like a squeak, as if his throat had closed up tight to stop any scream, but his mouth was wide open and dark as the grave. He grabbed the hobo with palsied old hands, but the man pushed him contemptuously away.

Grandpa fell into a sitting position, both hands pushing against the wound in his stomach as if he was trying to remove a knife that was no longer there. The hobo hadn't given it up, of course. He was holding the blood-streaked blade in his hand and glaring at Danna, and she could see the thoughts crawling through his muddy, mean eyes: *the kid saw me. Kill him, too.*

Only Grandpa wasn't dead.

Grandpa was *laughing.*

Danna rolled to her knees and grabbed for the old man, but he turned and looked at her, and his face blurred as if she was seeing it through tears, and she stopped before she touched him.

Him? No. That was… that was…

It was what she'd seen in the window, framed by the quaint old lace curtains. That face. That face that… that…

"You shouldn't have done that," Grandpa said, and she distantly realized he—*it*—was mocking the hobo with his own words. "I try to be nice, you know. I try to be what he'd want me to be. But there's always enough like *you* that I don't have to go looking."

Danna saw it move. It had the unsettling, *wrong* feel of watching a spider scuttle—fast, but all joints and angles. The hobo stabbed it again, and again, and it kept laughing. One pale hand—no longer old and shaky—grabbed the place where the hobo's collarbone had broken and squeezed, and the man let out a howl like a wounded dog that froze her in place.

"Let's do this inside. The neighbors may get nosy," the spider said, and took the fly into the house.

Danna sat in the dirt, too weak to move, too scared to run. She knew she should, but she also had the awful, awful idea that if she did, it would come after her, and having it come at her from behind was worse than facing it.

After a long, silent few minutes, the back door opened with a creak, and Grandpa Riley stood there looking at her. He looked just the same as before, except there was blood on his shirt, fresh and red. There were holes in his worn blue shirt.

"You'd better come in, Danna," he said. "I ought to explain."

Come into my house, said the spider to the fly.

He saw her hesitating, and she felt like—crazy as it was—that the look on his old, seamed face of regret was real. "I won't hurt you, girl," he said. "You done me good, and I'll do the same for you. You come and go in peace, just like before. My word on it."

How could she take its word? In what Godforsaken world did any of this make any sense at all? She didn't believe in fairytales, never had; she believed in people, good and bad and indifferent. People did the good in this world, and they did the evil. She'd never needed angels or demons to credit for the one and blame for the other.

But she didn't know what to make of this. Not at all.

Her mother came back to her again, a smell of sugar and apples and cinnamon, and Danna closed her eyes just for a second to savor the memory.

Curiosity killed the cat, Danna, she'd laughed, and whacked Danna's chubby little hands playfully with her wooden spoon. *You are the most curious creature I've ever seen. You watch that, now.*

But she couldn't just leave. Maybe it was that cat-killing curiosity; maybe it was a feeling that the thing that wore Grandpa Riley's face really didn't want to hurt her.

Well, she thought, *everything I own is inside tied up in a bindle and leaning in a corner.*

She'd lost a lot, the past few years. But she wasn't prepared to run away from everything she had left.

Danna rose to her feet, dusted off, and limped on into the spider's house.

It was no different inside. She'd expected it to be; she'd expected to see rot and mold and darkness ruining the well-scrubbed home, but instead it was exactly the same as when she'd walked out this morning with the hammer and nails and a leather tool belt strapped on her hips. Her morning plate with the remains of the scrambled eggs still sat on the counter.

As she sat down at the kitchen table, Grandpa sat her thick chipped mug in front of her, full to the brim with steaming hot coffee. She sipped. It tasted fresh.

There was no sign of the hobo in here.

Grandpa looked down at his shirt, sighed, and poured his own cup before he sat down across from her. "I'm sorry you had to see that. I wanted to spare you if I could."

That didn't sound good. Danna took another mouthful of coffee. If she was going to die, she figured to do it on her own terms. "What are you?" she asked. "You're not Grandpa Riley."

"I can be," it said. "I like being Grandpa Riley. He was a nice man. I miss him. He took care of me when my parents sent me here. He didn't have much, but what he had, he shared. Not just with me. With anybody who needed it."

The voice changed just a bit, sliding into a higher register, something not quite male, not quite female. Neither. Both. Grandpa's face was getting slowly younger, slowly thinner. His shock of white hair was darkening and falling flatter around his head.

Her head. There was something of Grandpa in the features, but they were softened, made young and feminine, with wide brown eyes and soft curls framing her cheekbones.

She wasn't that much older—at least she *looked* it—than Danna herself.

"This is what I looked like," she said. "When I was myself. This was where I lived, with my grandfather." There it was again, that indefinable look of regret, of loss, of loneliness. "My ma and pa sent me out here because they thought the air would be better for my lungs."

"You had TB," Danna said. "You were a lunger?"

The girl nodded. Grandpa's clothes fit her about as well, in this form, as Danna's clothes did her. The two of them, passing for something they weren't, out of necessity.

"I've been sick a long time, but I was so bad they thought I wouldn't make it all the way here on the train. I did, though. I guess they were sending me away so they didn't have to watch me die." Lila Mae—that was the name Grandpa had used, Lila Mae—stared out the window for a moment. Her pretty round face had grown still and serious. "My grandpa was a sailor, when he was younger. He traveled the world, and he said he knew things that could help me. He went all the way to Asia when he was younger, and that's where he found out about *her*." The girl's throat worked, as if she struggled to swallow a bad taste. "They had a lot of names for her, but mostly they call her Lilith. She's old, real old, and my grandpa said it was told that she could suck the sickness out of someone who was dying. Make them better."

It sounded crazy, but Danna didn't say so. She was into something that was crazy already. The girl rolled up Grandpa Riley's shirt sleeve, and there Danna saw the one thing that hadn't changed from the old man's body to the young girl's form.

The tattoo.

It still gave her a queer feeling, looking at it, as if her whole body vibrated. She couldn't make it out, any more than she'd been able to understand the face at the window. She just knew it was ink, blue India ink, and full of swoops and curls. It made her head hurt to try to understand it.

Danna looked away and sipped coffee to settle her unquiet stomach. Lila Mae rolled the sleeve back down. "Hurts, doesn't it?" she said, and pulled a sympathetic face. "I can't look at it either. It hurts all the time, like thorns under my skin. I was too sick to say no when he got the needles and the ink and started drawing it on me, but I would have said yes anyway, because he said it would make me better. Make me well."

The girl's eyes were haunted now, staring into a memory. Danna shivered just a bit. "What happened?"

"She came in the night," Lila Mae said. It was just a whisper. "She sucked all the sickness out of me, just like he said. But she left something, too. Something—" Her fingers brushed and rubbed restlessly at the fabric that covered the tattoo, and she snapped back to the present and gave Danna a quick, guilty smile. "I woke up well for the first time since I was just a kid. Grandpa died a few weeks later in his sleep. Maybe she came to get him, life for a life, I don't know. All I know is that while this thing is still on my skin, she can come and go any time she wants in me. Mostly she leaves me alone, but sometimes—when I meet somebody who's like *him*, the one outside—sometimes, she comes in. And when she does… it's like she's hungry. So hungry."

"Where is he? Is he dead?" Danna asked. She wasn't sure she wanted to know, but she'd rather know now than stumble on some horrible corpse in the dark.

"Gone," Lila Mae said. "She took him, body and soul. Took him down to hell. You know your Proverbs?"

Danna shook her head. "I never was much for reading. My ma was always despairing about how I never learned the Good Book."

"In Proverbs, it says, *Her house sinks down to death, and her course leads to the shades. All who go to her cannot return and find again the paths of life.*" Lila Mae looked down at her hands, clasped around her mug, and swallowed hard. "He's with her now. Somewhere."

"Why do you pretend to be Grandpa Riley? You don't need to. You can't—"

"Die?" Lila Mae shook her head. "No, I can't. She won't let me go. I guess I pretend to be Grandpa because it's easier than… being me. Because he was a nice man, a good man, and I loved him. I try to *be* him, as much as I can. I try to help people who come, if they're like you. But sometimes…"

"Sometimes they're like that other man," Danna said. "And they deserve what they get." *Her house sinks down to death.* "I wouldn't lose any sleep about him, Lila Mae." She'd seen too many like that on the rails, in the camps—willing to cut a throat for an extra slice of bacon, or a good pair of shoes. Willing to do anything for their own comfort and pleasure. "Does it hurt?"

"When she comes?" Lila Mae fussed a bit with the hem of Grandpa's shirt, and nodded without looking up. "More when she comes, but it hurts all the time. I go half crazy when I'm alone with it."

"You want it out of you?"

Lila Mae's eyes, when she glanced at her, were wide and surprised. "It's a *tattoo*, it's permanent, like the one Grandpa had from crossing the equator on the ship that looked like a turtle. It doesn't wash off no matter how hard I scrub it."

Danna took in a deep breath. "Skin comes off," she said. "If you cut it."

There was a clear, ringing silence in the warm lemon-scented kitchen. Outside, a bluebird took up a melody. The sun drifted warm through the lace curtains.

Lila Mae looked uncomprehending at first, then scared. Her lips parted, and her eyes grew round. But she didn't say anything.

"If it's—some kind of magic, maybe it'll come off," Danna said. "Or maybe you can disfigure it somehow. Do you think that would work?"

Lila Mae got up, opened a drawer, and took out a butcher knife. She handed it to Danna handle first. "You do it," she said. "I'm not very brave. I've never been very brave."

Danna wasn't either, but she'd seen things, done things on the road. She'd ridden the rails with murderers, thieves and rapists. She'd seen men die and men maimed by the rolling steel wheels of boxcars. She'd helped cut off a man's leg once that had been hanging by some stretchy tendons; she'd held the knife while the other hobos had pinned him down, screaming and thrashing. A lot of it came back to her now, with the knife in her hand, and she shook some. "Needs to be hot," she said. "Red hot, so the wound doesn't fester."

Lila Mae took the knife back and opened up the lid of one of the burners on the old cast-iron stove; she laid the knife over the flames and watched it as it heated up. When it started to glow on the edges, she wrapped a knitted potholder around the handle and brought it back to hand it to Danna. Even through the wrapped fabric it felt hot enough to scald her fingertips.

Lila Mae skinned up the sleeve of the worn old blue shirt and put her forearm flat on the table, turned to show the tattoo. It was moving now, a tangle of curls and swirls that seemed like some snake beneath the skin now.

As if it knew what was coming.

"Try to hold still," Danna said. "I'm sorry. It's going to hurt a lot." She hesitated again. "You know it could kill you, don't you? Maybe this thing is all that keeps you healthy. Maybe once it's gone…"

Lila Mae managed a shaky smile. "I was dying before," she said. "Might as well get it over with if it's coming. I don't think I want to go on like this."

That was, Danna thought, good enough. She pinned Lila Mae's wrist to the table with her own forearm, and the girl's fingers curled warm around her skin.

She readied the hot knife over the tattoo. It was thrashing now, and the motion made her head hurt, her eyes water. She could hear a thin howling sound now, like a distant wind. It grew louder and louder like a siren, and she had to fight the urge to drop the knife and cover her ears. *No.* Danna gritted her teeth until her jaw muscles ached. *No I won't. I won't.*

"Danna."

She made the mistake of looking up, and her mother was looking back at her, her *mother*, and her heart broke and her breath caught and she wanted… wanted…

"Danna, my dear girl, don't do this. Don't make me go away again.

Don't make me leave you."

That wasn't Lila Mae behind those dark eyes now; there was nothing there but cold and darkness and hunger. The voice was warm and kind, but the dark was merciless. The fingers wrapped around Danna's forearm tightened, and they felt like talons.

"It's lonely here," her mother said. "I miss you. I miss you so much. Please don't make me go."

"I'm sorry," Danna whispered. "But you can't stay."

She brought the knife down—not the edge, but the flat of it, still smoking hot and shimmering red at the edges. She hit the center of that writhing tattoo, and smelled burning flesh, heard the sharp sizzle. The arm she pinned down twisted and tried to pull free but she grimly held on, thinking of that hobo on the tracks, his leg dangling from threads that had to come off, it had to be done, had to be…

She was dimly aware of the screaming, and whether it was the memory of the mutilated hobo or the shriek of a train whistle or her mother crying out or Lila Mae, she didn't know. Maybe it was all of that. Maybe it was her own voice.

Lila Mae's hand went limp.

Danna gasped and dropped the knife, and as it fell away she saw that the tattoo was clear now, easy to see… the face of a woman. The knife blade's burn had seared away the center of it, but the eyes looked dark and savage, and the open mouth had fangs like a snake's.

Lila Mae slipped bonelessly out of her chair to thud on the wooden floor of the kitchen.

Danna hurried to her side and pulled the girl into her arms, and put her ear to the thin chest under the bloodstained shirt.

She heard a heartbeat. Slow, but strong.

Lila Mae was alive.

It took the whole afternoon and into the night, but Lila finally woke up. She seemed feverish and in pain, but Danna had bandaged up the burn and put some salve on it, and she hoped it wouldn't turn bad.

"It's better," Lila said, when she asked her. The girl looked pallid and sweaty, but she smiled. "She's gone. She's *gone*. I can tell."

Danna hugged her. "I'm glad. You look—"

"Sick?" Lila said, and laughed. "I'm all right. Just tired. I'll be better in the morning. You'd better get some rest, you look tired too." She coughed, just a little. "Promise me you'll stay, Danna. Promise me."

They shared the bed, and come morning Danna woke up feeling rested. Better than she had in a long time, actually. The sore ankle she'd earned coming off the roof seemed totally healed now, and the only thing that hurt on her seemed to be a sore spot on her arm, where Lila's hand had gripped so hard. Bruised, she guessed.

She rolled over, and found Lila looking at her with a faint smile on her face. A sweet, peaceful smile.

It took her a moment to realize that it was the last smile of Lila's life. The brown eyes were open and fixed, ever so slightly filmed. *Life for a life.*

It wasn't until Danna had closed the dead girl's eyes and arranged her peacefully that she thought to push up the sleeve of her own nightgown and look at her bruise. It *was* a bruise, already turning a dark, ominous, storm cloud blue.

She could already see the eyes, though. The mouth. The teeth.

Life for a life.

There was a whisper in the back of her mind, one she knew came from far, far away. *Plenty of bad men to take, Danna. You will be doing them a service, all those honest, poor men and boys riding the rails. Taking away those who deserve to suffer.*

She took a deep breath, and nodded slowly. The voice sounded like her mother's, soft and comforting. She could almost feel the gentle stroke on her hair.

The strong did what they had to do. That's what her pa had always told her, what he'd told her when she'd put on his spare set of clothes and set out on the road to find her own way.

The strong survive.

In the early morning light, she bathed and dressed and made herself some breakfast. She walked down to the church and told them about Lila Mae's death, and the pastor was full of sympathy, and promised he'd come with the undertaker to get the girl. "And who are you?" he'd asked her, as an afterthought.

"Her brother," Danna said. "Dan. Our grandpa left us the house." *Promise me you'll stay,* Lila Mae had said. She would. It was a good place, a warm place, and eventually, it would be home.

Last thing she did, before going into the house, was to go to the back fence and make sure the sticks were still there.

A simple sideways T shape. *Easy mark.*

The tattoo was almost formed now on her arm. She knew she could get rid of it any time she wanted, banish Lilith back to the pit she'd come out of, but for now... for now, her mother's voice was right. There were good men to be fed. Bad men to be stopped so they wouldn't hurt anyone else.

And she was fine with that.

She knew the exact moment the image was complete; she felt the hot pricking of thorns, and felt her face and body go fluid and warm and pliable. She would be what she needed to be, for anyone who came. The welcoming Grandpa or the sweet Lila Mae or the strong Danna.

Until it was time to let go and be someone else.

Her house sinks down to death.

There were always people looking for an easy mark.

The Whole of His History

BY BARBARA A. BARNETT

Frederick has made the journey between Boston and Philadelphia so often that his horse seems to know every turn without his prodding, every ditch and old fallen tree limb to avoid—the memory of the road absorbed to the point of instinct. But though familiarity governs the horse's steps, Frederick is certain this is the first time he has laid eyes upon the town of Hawthorne. At first, the town strikes him as the sort of unremarkable place he would not expect to recall, with its rough, stony dirt road leading past shops and small boxy houses, some of brick, others of wood. But little by little, Hawthorne's peculiarities begin to reveal themselves. Frederick spies neither church nor stock and pillory, the mainstays he is accustomed to seeing in such towns. The people are an even odder matter. Frederick worries that his very presence has somehow proven offensive, for not a single soul meets his gaze. They all pass him with bowed heads, the men's faces obscured by the shadows of their tri-cornered hats, the women's hidden behind veils. Frederick is accustomed to loneliness, even among those who call him friend, yet the way these strangers avert their faces makes his isolation seem a tangible thing, a great stone-like mass weighing him down.

In the town square, Frederick calls to a figure ambling ahead. The man turns with a graceful spin worthy of the ballerinas Frederick saw during his brief time in France. Unlike the other people of Hawthorne, this gentleman meets his gaze, presenting him with a disarming smile. Frederick feels a flush in his cheeks that makes him wish he had called to someone else. He has prayed for God to rid him of these sinful feelings, yet still they come. This man in particular possesses a preternatural beauty that rouses an unwanted attraction with sudden and surprising force. There was a time when Frederick wondered if God had abandoned him, deeming him too unworthy to save; now he wonders if God was ever there to begin with.

The gentleman draws closer, an expectant look on his face. He appears no older than Frederick's own thirty years, trim and broad-shouldered. His jacket and breeches, though clean and neat, have the well-worn look of travel about them. His skin is pale, almost luminous. A turn of his head toward the sun, though, and Frederick at last notices an imperfection—a reddish mark on his neck, some type of scar or birthmark obscured by his ruffled cravat.

Frederick swallows to moisten his drying throat. "Would you be so kind as to tell me if there is an inn where I may find lodgings for the night?"

"Of course," the gentleman replies. He speaks with a musicality that Frederick finds far too alluring. "I was heading there now myself if you care to follow."

Frederick thanks him and prompts his horse into a slow walk to keep pace with his newfound guide. With each step, he feels an irrational yet growing urge to burst into a gallop and see if he can reach the next inn by nightfall. Frederick tells himself there is something unnatural in the way no one but this man has looked him in the eye, but in truth he knows that his apprehension has another cause: this man has made him fear what is unnatural in himself.

"Samuel," the gentleman offers by way of introduction. "Samuel Warren."

Frederick doesn't want to know the man's name, but there it is. Civility leaves him no choice but to offer his own in return, for it takes only one glance at the sky's ominous hues of darkening purple to know that he will find no safe shelter beyond this town tonight.

The inn to which Samuel leads him is called The Wayward Tramp, a modest brick building with a weathered sign that features the silhouette of a man with a walking stick and a sack slung over his shoulder. While Frederick secures his horse to a post outside, Samuel bounds toward the entrance, promising to let the innkeeper know that he has a guest for the night. Only when the door closes behind Samuel does Frederick realize how tense he has been since meeting the man. His breath comes easier now; a dozen knots seem to unclench in his stomach. So unnerved by a stranger, he chides himself, by barely more than a smile. Frederick considers a new possibility: that God—if He exists—has not abandoned him, but has put before him a test in the form of Samuel. A test he has failed before.

Once inside the inn, Frederick is greeted by the hum of conversation, the familiar kitchen scents of boiled meat and freshly baked bread, and a lively tune played upon fiddle and fife. In the main room, the fireplace sits unused—no surprise with such a warm spring. Tables and chairs of all shapes, shades, and sizes are scattered throughout the wooden-pillared room. The patrons occupying them are just as eclectic. Frederick has never known of an inn or tavern where men and women mingled in the same room, or where the Indians native to the colonies were permitted at all, and yet here he sees them all sitting and talking together. Unlike the people he passed on the street, these individuals do not hide their faces with veils and tilted hats. Yet there is something shadowed about them that Frederick cannot make out from where he stands.

A burly man emerges from the kitchen. With a deep, boisterous voice, he greets Frederick and introduces himself as the innkeeper. His vigorous handshake is accompanied by cheerful words about providing feed and water for Frederick's horse and the rare pleasure of being able to offer him a room to himself, but Frederick does not hear all of it properly. His attention is fixed on the innkeeper's skin. The man's face and hands are covered with an odd array of red-inked tattoos: figures and portraitures, a feast spread upon a table, a child playing with marbles, a hound chasing after some unseen prey. Every image is impossibly detailed, like miniature paintings upon his skin. They conjure memories of a Lenape warrior Frederick once encountered; depictions of the man's every feat of bravery were inked upon his body. But for all the fascination such markings inspire in Frederick, he is well aware that most people regard the natives and their painted skin as unsightly at best, at worst an affront to God—mutilations of bodies made in a divine image. The innkeeper, though, displays not the slightest hint of self-consciousness about his uncommon appearance.

Frederick stops gaping long enough to secure his room and ask for a hot meal and a mug of ale. He takes a seat in the main room, apart from the other patrons. As much as he longs for conversation, he fears the questions that will inevitably be asked, particularly the ones about why an established young man of his years has yet to marry, for surely he must have prospects.

At first, Frederick is relieved not to see Samuel among the gathered patrons—perhaps he has his own lodgings here and retired to them straight away. But that brief thought is quickly pushed aside as Frederick takes in the faces around him. They are all tattooed like the innkeeper, men and women alike. Some bear only a few visible marks; others are like a living gallery of miniature paintings. A serving girl sets a pewter mug before Frederick, and his eyes trace the markings on her exposed skin, so numerous that they bleed into one another. It is all so extraordinary that Frederick marvels at the fact that he has never heard stories of this peculiar town before; he can't possibly be the first traveler to have passed through.

"May I join you?"

Frederick looks up to find Samuel standing before him, his own mug of ale in hand. The man's dimpled smile stirs an unwelcome flutter in Frederick's stomach. As rude as it would be, Frederick knows he should say that he prefers solitude, but curiosity wins out. Who better to ask about the painted people around him than the person who led him to this very inn?

"Please," Frederick says, gesturing to the chair across from him.

Samuel sits. Frederick starts to ask Samuel what he knows about the markings, but his voice trails off as his gaze falls on the man's neck. What from a distance Frederick had thought to be a birthmark or scar is actually the same type of dark red tattoo the others have. Frederick can make out a tree and what might be the top of someone's head; the rest is covered by Samuel's cravat. It should not be surprising that Samuel is marked like the others, Frederick knows, yet the fact of it catches him off guard all the same.

Samuel laughs, a teasing tone that says he knows exactly what has left Frederick speechless. He tugs his cravat down to reveal the entire tattoo—a man sleeping with his back against a tree.

"We're encouraged to hide our markings outside," Samuel says. "Everyone is afraid we will frighten off visitors if we reveal ourselves too soon."

Everyone, Frederick marvels. He has heard gossip of the occasional man allowing a native tribe to mark him as a sign of trust or alliance, always in a discreet and easily covered spot so as not to invoke public scandal. But an entire town? And these tattoos differ from those of the natives. There are no patterns invoking the elements of nature; they are not limited to representations of battles or other great feats. Nor are they like the brandings of criminals, the only other inkings of this sort Frederick has ever seen. Instead, these tattoos are strangely mundane in their depictions, mostly faces and events one might encounter in everyday life. The ordinariness of them makes Frederick uneasy. Commemorating the extraordinary with such an ostentatious display is something he could understand, but with the people of Hawthorne, he can't help feeling as if unremarkable lives like his own are being mocked, scarred onto skin so as to distort them.

"I've barely enough markings to hide," Samuel says. "But I still believe we should display them as proudly outside as we do in here. I'm much more interested in those visitors who would choose curiosity over fear."

Frederick downs a mouthful of ale. He *is* unsettled by the markings, and he thinks Samuel must know it, for his words sound like a challenge.

"Allow me to inquire then," Frederick says, choosing to meet that challenge. "Why does everyone here have such markings? I have never seen their like."

"To remember," Samuel says, as if that is explanation enough.

Frederick regards the image on Samuel's neck with a short laugh. "To remember what, exactly? A nap by a tree?"

"Each other." Samuel brushes his fingertips over his tattoo. "I never said this was my memory."

There is a wistfulness to his voice and to the way he touches the tattoo that sparks jealousy within Frederick. It's irrational, he knows. Samuel is a stranger. And as for the tattoo, its detail and artistry does not change the fact that it is a primitive practice to be frowned upon in the civilized world—at least that is the reaction Frederick knows he is supposed to have. Instead, the intimacy implied in Samuel inscribing another person's memory onto his skin leaves Frederick trying to fight off envy as well as attraction.

"Whose memory is it then?" he finally asks of Samuel.

"A lawyer passing through Hawthorne on some boring bit of business or another. I'm sure he is safely ensconced back in Richmond by now, once again resting against that tree and doubting his entire life." Samuel takes a long drink from his mug. When he at last sets it down, his expression is rueful and distant, fixed on the table yet seeming to see past it. But as soon as he returns his attention to Frederick, his easy smile returns. "He would have been better off staying here. Once I found Hawthorne, I couldn't imagine ever leaving."

Frederick has been wondering if Samuel hailed from some other part of the colonies. He stood out as different the moment Frederick first laid eyes upon him, bounding down the street with his head high while others shuffled past with ducked heads.

"Where do you come from originally?" Frederick asks.

"A small village in Virginia. No place anyone has ever heard of."

"And how long have you been in Hawthorne?"

"Two months? Maybe close to three now." Samuel laughs. "It's easy to lose track of the days here."

"This place is a curiosity to be certain," Frederick says, casting a look around him. The Painted People would be a more apt name for the inn than The Wayward Tramp, he thinks. "Why the markings? What is it about them—about Hawthorne—that made you choose to stay? To abandon whatever life you had before this?"

"The life I had before this abandoned me. My father…" Samuel takes a swig of ale, then follows it with a bitter laugh. "The golden-tongued preacher, they called him. Only his tongue was not so golden when it came to me. His last words to me were that I was no son of his, but of the Devil, and that he would see me driven from his home. So I left. I traveled about for a good many years, and then I found Hawthorne." Samuel's smile returns, though the unmistakable weight of sadness leaves it not so broad as before. "A wayward tramp found himself welcomed at The Wayward Tramp."

"I'm sorry," Frederick says. He almost asks what made Samuel's father disown him, but stops himself. He wants too much for the answer to be the very secret he himself hides. To know that Samuel harbors those same kinds of feelings would be too great a temptation; to know that he doesn't, too great a disappointment.

"If you want to know what is so remarkable about Hawthorne," Samuel says, "it's this: This is a town of good people, the kindest people I have ever known. Yet anywhere else, each and every one of them would be an outcast for some foolish reason or another. We all have stories the world isn't ready to hear. But here... here we can live more honestly as ourselves, without shame. Here we can share our stories on our very skin."

Samuel speaks with a passion that suggests he has inherited his father's golden tongue, despite whatever differences drove them apart. Frederick glances around the room and, for a moment, permits himself to entertain the fantasy of living among painted people who tattoo themselves with stories and memories. What would it be like to dwell in a place where he could finally share all the longings he has kept secret, where he would not have to beseech a dubious God to make him other than he is?

"Such a place sounds too good to be true," he says at last.

A solemn look passes across Samuel's face. "Living in Hawthorne is not without its price."

"The markings," Frederick says. "Are they the price? They must involve a great deal of pain, I imagine."

"Only for a moment."

Frederick has his doubts about that claim, for he has heard how some of the native tribes tattoo themselves. They mix the ashes of burnt straw with water, and with that inky mixture, the desired image is drawn upon the skin and then pricked with needles. The blood and the ash combine, leaving an imprint on the skin that can never be removed. Using such a process to achieve the detail in Samuel's tattoo—to portray the minutiae of individual leaves and the crevices in the tree bark—would have to require far more than a moment's discomfort.

"You seem curious," Samuel says playfully. There is suddenly something ominous about his dimpled smile, something calculating in the glint of his eyes. "Perhaps you'd like one of your own?"

"No," Frederick says. He shivers, overcome by a fear disproportionate to Samuel's question, a fear he can find no rational reason to feel.

A serving girl appears with Frederick's meal—a tureen of peanut soup and a plate overflowing with boiled pork and chunks of bread and cheese. The food is barely upon the table before Frederick is downing a mouthful of pork, hot enough to burn his tongue. His chill quickly passes, and with it his fear. There is nothing in Samuel's gaze now but nonchalance and charm. The ill effects of travel, Frederick tells himself as explanation for his burst of anxiety. Merely hunger and fatigue masquerading as dread.

As he eats, the conversation turns to matters far less strange than memories inked on skin. Frederick tells Samuel of his work for the wealthy and insufferable Benjamin Hutchins, whose business interests frequently have Frederick traveling throughout the colonies. After another tankard of ale, Frederick speaks of losing his parents—his mother during the birth of a stillborn child, his father to a shipwreck off the coast of New Jersey. Another then another, and he is admitting how lost he has come to feel in Philadelphia with no family left, how those who call themselves friends cannot truly be so; they know too little of what is in his mind and heart.

"And what is it you're keeping from them?" Samuel asks.

Frederick lets out an incredulous laugh. "Why would I tell a man I've only just met when I cannot even tell those whom I've known since childhood?"

"Because I have no expectations of you. Because Hawthorne is a place of no judgments."

Frederick stares at Samuel for a long while, unable to speak for fear of what might escape his lips. He wants nothing more than to reveal his every secret to Samuel, yet the desire to talk so freely feels as shameful as the longings to which he would confess.

"I should turn in for the evening," Frederick says, standing. "I have a long day's journey ahead of me tomorrow."

The impact of how much he has drunk reveals itself in his unsteady steps. Samuel is standing as quickly as Frederick is staggering, grabbing him by the arm to steady him.

"In your condition, you'll have a long journey to your room as well without some help."

Frederick can feel the eyes of the inn's other occupants on him. Not wanting to leave Hawthorne with a fine for public drunkenness—if the town's unorthodox residents even impose such things—he nods and allows Samuel to help him toward the narrow staircase that leads up to the guest rooms. The stairs creak with every step, and Frederick finds himself lulled by the sound. He sags against Samuel as they reach the upper landing and start down a dark hall. Frederick hates that Samuel doesn't pull away, that he was so foolish as to have drunk so much, that he ever stopped in this accursed town to begin with. He can't help but wonder if, deep down, he has put himself in this position on purpose.

"Here we are," Samuel says, stopping in front of a door.

Frederick mutters a quick word of thanks and opens the door, ready to shut it quickly behind him. Before he can, Samuel is cupping his face in his hands, kissing him deeply. What little resolve Frederick has left departs him in a rush of desire. He and Samuel stumble into the room, mouths still locked even as Samuel pulls the door closed. Their arms entangle in a hurry to undo clasps and slip off garments.

"Would you leave me something to remember you by?" Samuel whispers as they sink down onto the bed. His skin feels surprisingly cool, the earthy scent of him intoxicating enough to overpower the sour odor of every traveler who has slept there before them.

"Yes," Frederick answers, so breathless that the word barely makes it past his lips.

Samuel's mouth trails down his neck, but the gentle brush of his lips soon stops. Two sharp pricks, and then Frederick is crying out as pain sears its way across his neck. For a moment he is paralyzed, aware of only heat and the pounding of blood through his veins. Then the pain fades, leaving only the feel of Samuel driving into him, teeth still buried in his neck. Frederick cries out again, this time in pleasure, and the already darkened room goes black around him.

ⓥ

In his first moment of wakefulness, Frederick is certain he has dreamed—at least the bite, if not the entire encounter. But as his eyes adjust to the morning light, he sees small splatters of blood on the mattress, then Samuel asleep beside him, his mouth smeared red. Frederick touches a hand to his neck and flinches; the skin there is sore to the touch. He shudders, not sure which frightens him more—Samuel, or the fact that he recalls more pleasure than pain when he stares at his own spilled blood.

Frederick tries to slip away quietly from the bed, but stops when he notices the half-formed image on Samuel's bare chest. Impossibly, blood-red lines appear on Samuel's skin, twisting and turning themselves, each adding to the image's completion. But there is already enough there for Frederick to know with dreadful certainty what this marking portrays: a top he played with as a child, exact in its representation, down to the chip near its point and the jagged scratch down its side.

Frederick leaps from the bed. This is impossible, he tells himself, yet he cannot deny what he sees before him: his own memory, one he never shared with Samuel, forming on the man's chest.

"Frederick?" Samuel, now roused, quickly gets out of the bed. "Don't be—"

"What are you?" Frederick demands, his voice quavering as he backs away. His heart pounds so fast that he feels sick.

"I know you're afraid," Samuel says, taking slow steps toward him, hands held out like one trying to convince a snarling dog that he means no harm. "I was too, at first."

Frederick looks to the door. He could run, but what then? He is naked, his clothes strewn about the room. And the other people in the town—they're all like Samuel. Would they attack him, try to stop him from fleeing?

"What are you?" Frederick demands again.

"Yet one more thing in this world that is wrongly feared. Like everything and everyone that comes to Hawthorne. Like you."

"You are nothing like me," Frederick says, though he can hear the tinge of doubt in his words. For all his fear now, he never struggled against Samuel the night before, and part of him yearns to endure it all again. Frederick grabs a candlestick from the mantel of the room's fireplace and brandishes it like a weapon; if only he could fight off his own desire with it as well as Samuel. "Stay away from me."

Samuel stops. His face falls, a look of such genuine-seeming hurt that Frederick half-lowers the candlestick.

"You're free to leave, Frederick. But if you stay..." Samuel starts toward him again. "Imagine no secrets. Imagine not having to deny what you feel."

What Frederick imagines is the night before. The pain was so brief, so fleeting. And the rest of it—more than any carnal pleasures, he longs for the simple act of sitting across from Samuel and talking, knowing he can reveal what's in his heart without fear.

"But at what cost?" Frederick asks, knowing such freedom cannot possibly come so easily. "You said last night that living in Hawthorne is not without its price."

"The choice to stay is one you can never take back. And the memories—you will always hunger for more. But..." Samuel closes the space between them, strokes a hand across Frederick's cheek. "Imagine you and I knowing everything there is to know about each other."

Frederick's gaze strays to Samuel's chest. The image has fully formed now—his childhood top, as scarred on the outside as he has always felt inside.

"I want to stay," he whispers, letting the candlestick fall from his hand.

Samuel kisses him softly, then looks around the room, clearly searching for something. He rummages through their discarded garments until he at last finds a knife he must have had somewhere on his person. Frederick feels a flare of panic. Before he can question what the knife is for, Samuel pulls the blade across the spot where Frederick's memory has formed on his chest.

"What are you—"

Samuel hushes him with another kiss, then gently pulls Frederick's face toward his bleeding chest. The blood moistens Frederick's lips and trickles into his mouth, sweet on his tongue. For reasons his rational mind fails to explain, he is overcome by the desire to taste more of it. He sucks at the wound, swallowing blood while Samuel's fingers run through his hair. Frederick's body suddenly goes rigid, his mind a canvas of blackness. A spasm of pain follows, as if fire is shooting through his innards. When the pain subsides, Samuel is kissing him again. Frederick's lips stray to Samuel's neck. He feels a tingle in his mouth, the strange sensation of his teeth elongating. A hunger deeper than any he has ever known rises from within him. Overwhelmed, Frederick sinks his teeth into Samuel's neck and swallows blood as sweet as any wine. Then Samuel feeds from him in turn, each of them again and again, drinking until the whole of each other's history is spelled out on the other's skin.

Mungo the Vampire
by Sandra Kasturi

Once there was a tiny little vampire whose name was Mungo Cheswick. He was no bigger than a pickle. Mungo was terribly in love with film star Annabel Cartwright, former "Scream Queen" of many beloved horror films, and now a Serious Actress, who lived in San Francisco and sometimes Hollywood. This was not helpful, as Mungo lived in London and was not a film star. Also, Mungo was a thousand times smaller than Annabel, which made the pursuit of love somewhat troublesome.

Mungo thought carefully about how he could make Annabel Cartwright into his vampire bride. First, he had to get to "the Colonies," which is how he still thought of the Americas. Mungo's archaic nature was somewhat charming; he had certainly charmed his way into the graces of other ladies, mostly fairies and small elves, even a less-homely-than-usual gnome or two. They had all succumbed to his whispers and mosquito-like buzzing, which, as one of the fairies had said, tickled a bit, but was otherwise quite pleasant. Of course this didn't last, as eventually Mungo would drain them dry and leave their desiccated corpses (now even smaller) in various gardens, under the shrubbery or in beds of perennials.

But what Mungo Cheswick, miniscule vampire, really wanted was a red-blooded American girl, an enormous (to him) actress. His mother had always warned him against taking human blood—it caused drunkenness, freewheeling and general bad behavior amongst tiny vampires. Mungo had been a good son and followed Mother's edicts. Until he'd spotted Annabel Cartwright on a film poster in Piccadilly Circus and was instantly smitten. Happily, Mother came afoul of a fly zapper by the kitchen door of a vicarage and Mungo was finally free to pursue his dream.

☙❦❧

Getting to America did seem problematic. Mungo thought about stowing away on a boat, but he didn't really take to the sea. His one excursion to Brighton for an evening cruise in a Barbie Party Cruise Ship™ had resulted in terrible seasickness that was only alleviated by Mungo eating most of his guests, and then he couldn't show his face in polite vampire society for fully six months.

Mungo then considered an aeroplane, but was worried that, being so tiny, he might get sucked into some sort of unpleasant intake valve and be irreparably smoodged. He could always burrow into a human's pocket, but he was nervous that he might be tempted by the heady scent of blood from non-celebrity *Homo sapiens* and cave in to its lure, when he really wanted to save himself for Annabel.

Finally he hit upon the perfect plan. He would post himself to America. Straight to Annabel herself! He'd still travel by air, but would be safe inside his little coffin, itself stuffed into a fat, padded envelope. Mungo would also take several ticks bloated with fairy blood to sustain him on his journey. He felt quite bursting with cleverness at this plan. None of the other little vampires in England had ventured as far as he was about to go. Now, he just needed to find a way to get his parcelled-self deposited into a post box, with "fragile" and "handle with care" written on the outside of the parcel.

After much thought and the bullying of a few brownies and dwarfs with nimble fingers, Mungo managed to have his wee coffin (with himself inside it) bundled into the bubble-lined envelope that was guaranteed to be light-proof by the photo supply shop he ordered it from. He even had a small witch he knew hex the postman into bringing the appropriate stickers and postage. Appropriately enough, the somewhat befuddled postman showed up with commemorative Christopher Lee stamps, which Mungo felt boded well for his upcoming venture into world travel and romance. Excitedly, Mungo settled himself and his blood-filled ticks in for the long journey to the New World.

◊

Things didn't go exactly as planned. Who could have known that Mungo didn't travel well? His lurching journey to the post box in a dwarf-sack left him terribly seasick—worse even than on his ill-fated cruise—and he wasn't able to have a single sip of supper that night. Even more unfortunately, the dwarfs, early risers all of them, had dumped him in the Royal Mail first thing in the morning… which meant that the entire weight of the day's post rested right on top of Mungo's coffin. As the letters piled up, the coffin creaked alarmingly, warped out of true at the joints, and then squished into a tiny trapezoid, Mungo and his ticks similarly flattened inside. It was most upsetting.

Mungo's parcel finally arrived in California, croggled, mashed, and much the worse for wear. Mungo himself was not the jaunty little vampire he had once been. The only upside was that the envelope was indeed light-proof, as guaranteed, so poor Mungo did not suffer the indignity of bursting suddenly into flames after being touched by sunlight. Unfortunately, he still hadn't reached his beloved, but had been redirected to the office of Annabel Cartwright's agent, where all the star's post was automatically sent.

But here, after his terrible journey, Mungo finally had a piece of luck. The day after he was deposited at Stephen Bram & Associates, Annabel herself came to the office, and, on a whim, swept all the post they'd been saving to answer on her behalf into a bag, saying, "I need to be more in touch with my fans," and then swanned down to her waiting limousine.

Mungo's second piece of luck in the Colonies happened right in Annabel's kitchen—she decided to open her post at night. When she withdrew the squashed coffin from the padded envelope, she dropped it onto the coffee table, thinking it was just another piece of horrible homemade "art" sent by some demented movie-lover. She went back to her third gin and tonic and sighed. But then she saw something move.

Mungo, still somewhat flattened, crawled out of the remains of his wooden coffin. Annabel took one look at him and shrieked, dropping her drink.

And there, because all good things come in threes, Mungo had his third piece of fortune. Annabel's glass smashed on the tile floor, and pieces flew up, cutting her bare legs. The scent of her blood was more than poor starving Mungo could resist.

He gathered the last of his strength and latched onto Annabel's calf. She shrieked again and tried to shake him off, but he clung tighter than even one of his ticks would have. Annabel gathered breath to shriek again—she wasn't the "Scream Queen" in those early films for nothing, after all—but she realized all of a sudden that whatever was happening on her leg felt quite pleasant.

She looked down, and saw—what on earth *was* it?—it looked like a tiny person in a *cape* sucking the blood from a cut on her leg.

Mungo stopped drinking for a moment and looked up. "Hullo," he said. "I'm Mungo Cheswick. And I love you."

Annabel vowed then and there to quit drinking. Tomorrow.

"Uh… hello." She noticed that where Mungo had been sucking her leg, the cut had almost entirely healed over. And… she couldn't be sure, but didn't her skin look creamier? Mungo moved onto another cut, and began licking the blood from there. The sensation felt even better to Annabel. "Ooooh," she said.

By the end of half an hour, all of Annabel's cuts had been licked to healing, and she was pretty sure that most of her varicose veins had disappeared. Not that she would have admitted to having varicose veins to anyone.

Annabel made herself another gin and tonic while Mungo explained his tremendous passion for her after seeing her film poster in Piccadilly Circus. Annabel couldn't help but feel flattered, even if her gentleman caller was no bigger than a pickle. She wondered how things could work to her advantage. And then Hollywood's "Scream Queen" thought faster than she'd ever thought in her life. Which usually wouldn't be saying much, but when it came to her own beauty, Annabel Cartwright was practically Mensa-level.

Maybe she'd get Mungo to use his tongue on her face? He might be the best cure for wrinkles she'd ever found. And that dreadful unicorn tramp stamp she'd gotten in her late teens! Annabel had never felt confident in laser removal or plastic surgery—she shuddered at the thought of the awful scars and mangled facial messes she'd seen on some of her contemporaries. No one was going to film *her* in soft focus! She'd get Mungo to take care of the tattoo, those little lines around her eyes and mouth—everything. And if she had to give up some of her own blood, so what? Actually, given how good that awful Meryl Streep had been looking lately, she wouldn't be a bit surprised if Miss I-Can-Do-Any-Accent-in-the-World didn't have her own tiny little vampire at her beck and call.

☥

Annabel and Mungo settled down to a mutually beneficial existence. He'd nibble on her neck or her cheek, or, if he was feeling really frisky, on the curve of her breasts. He never left any marks, and Annabel's skin grew simply remarkable. Mungo sucked the terrible unicorn tattoo right out of her skin. Everyone commented on how she looked twenty years younger, and other actresses muttered about how she must have found a *really* great plastic surgeon. Annabel just smiled smugly.

Everything was going swimmingly until the inevitable happened. Annabel asked Mungo to "turn" her, make her into a vampire like him, so she could be immortal and (somewhat) young forever.

"If only I had met you earlier," Annabel sighed. "But it's not too late. I still have my looks, and I look better than ever after your attentions, Mungo!"

Mungo, in response, gently nibbled on her earlobe. Annabel giggled.

"So… when do you think you can 'turn' me?" she asked. Annabel had seen this sort of thing as part of the plots of many horror movies, some of which she had starred in, and of course on that sexy vampire series on HBO.

"I'm not sure I can do it, darling," buzzed Mungo in her ear. "You're so big and I'm so small. I'd have to drain you entirely, and then give you some of my blood… I don't think I have enough."

"I'm not that big! Well… maybe we can start with a few drops at a time? Please?"

Mungo could deny Annabel nothing. That very night when he drank some of her blood, he gave her three drops of his own. Annabel woke the next morning feeling better than she ever had in her life, better even than when she was still a little girl and full of gumption. She looked thoughtfully over at the kitchen cupboard where Mungo's coffin was hidden for the day.

If this keeps up, I'll be a hundred before I get enough tiny vampire blood to turn me, thought Annabel. *And God knows how I'll look by then.*

The next night, Annabel begged Mungo to drink as much of her blood as he could, just as an experiment. Mungo sipped at the vein in her elbow for a good hour and a half, until his belly was distended and he staggered woozily to her knee, where he collapsed in a stupor.

Quick as anything, before Mungo could fly away or come to his senses, Annabel snatched him up, popped him in her mouth and bit his head off.

Then she swallowed the rest of him (mostly) whole and belched in a genteel fashion.

Now I'll really *be immortal*, Annabel thought. Would she miss Mungo? Well, certainly, but she'd soon get over that—once she was an even bigger star. She toasted herself with a gin and tonic.

🦇

Things did not go exactly as planned. Annabel couldn't sleep for the terrible stomachache she got. It was as if her guts were literally turning inside out. Even when she stuck her finger down her throat, in hope of expelling the tiny little vampire, it didn't help. The only thing that came up was a bit of his cape.

After a dreadful night, Annabel fell into a fitful sleep in the early hours of the morning. When she woke, the clock showed it was almost noon. But her stomach had finally settled down. In fact, she felt quite marvelous!

She got out of bed and was on her way to the bathroom when she almost fell onto her face—her pajama pants were loose and she'd tripped over the legs.

"I'm getting thinner," she whispered in ecstasy as she staggered back to her feet. Mungo's body and blood were working even greater miracles than she'd expected. She lifted her pant legs and ran to look in the bathroom mirror.

Annabel could barely see over the bathroom counter. She shrieked in horror. It wasn't possible… was it?

Yes, it was. Annabel was shrinking.

She grabbed the powder-puff stool from her dressing table and stood on it to look in the mirror. Annabel looked like a three-foot tall miniature version of herself. Even as she watched, she grew smaller. As she shrank, she leapt for the edge of the dressing table—and found she could fly. She hovered over the dressing table and managed to land back in front of the mirror. Her face was very pale.

As Annabel opened her mouth to scream her last scream as a Scream Queen, she saw that she had grown fangs, too. Eating Mungo whole had worked. She was, in fact, "turning"—into a tiny little vampire. No bigger than a pickle. And not even a very large pickle.

The news was full of the headlines—"Former Scream Queen Annabel Cartwright Disappears!" and "Hollywood Horror Show: Annabel's Gone!" and "Vanishing Actress Mystery Puzzles Police."

Annabel's mansion eventually became known as the "Cartwright Mystery House" and was bought at auction by another film star, then quickly sold and resold several times. There were rumors of strange noises, bedbug infestations, perhaps a haunting? No one ever stayed in the house for long, and its mystique increased.

Finally, the place was bought by a real estate mogul, who would sometimes hint to his guests at drunken parties that he knew the *real* secret behind Annabel's disappearance. He didn't. But he did eventually put his home on the market, just like everyone else, after numerous complaints from his family—they all had very peculiar dreams involving *something* nibbling on them in the middle of the night, which no amount of fumigation seemed to help, so they concluded it was probably psychosomatic. The mogul's children eventually developed anemia, but everyone was sure this was unrelated. The kids did say they could hear a strange buzzing near their ears just before falling asleep. Sometimes it sounded just like shrieky little words.

The Lightning Tree

by Carrie Laben

So Adriana's doing porn now?

A cursor sat blinking just below the instant message; I'd been staring at it, trying to decide whether to even bother responding, when I saw that Scott was typing again. I tabbed back to my work and waited to see how he was going to try to dig his foot out of his mouth.

… that's what Emily said. She made me delete Adriana from our Instagram feed. She seemed pretty upset.

You mean the tattoo picture. Our Instagram *feed?* I wondered what had happened to the man who wouldn't dog-sit for me lest we "get too entwined." *That's the memorial tattoo she got for Cody, judgeypants.*

He hadn't replied by the time I was finished with the latest batch of essays. I could only do three or four before I had to take a break; each of them reminded me of the dreams I'd had back when I thought I was getting out of this town for good. A lot of them also reminded me that if I'd had even half the brains and my family had twice the money, those dreams might have come true.

Or if Cody hadn't died. If my stepdad wasn't already dead, and Mom wasn't in jail, and Grandma wasn't almost eighty and inclined to forget all of the above every morning. If Adriana didn't only have me.

You can't do good editing when you're that angry, not even when the material is as trite as some half-wit rich kids' college papers. And the last thing I wanted to do was lose this gig making sure that half-wit rich kids had every advantage over people like me.

I needed to get up, get away from the computer. Otherwise I'd just give into the temptation to go over to Facebook and feed the rage more. Anyway, I'd already edited—rewritten, actually, but we didn't call it that to let our clients save a tiny bit of what they pretended was dignity—enough for today. The pay was high for the effort involved, and the checks showed up fast. And I got to work from home. It was a good job. I should be grateful. If I didn't remind myself, Grandma would for sure.

I grabbed a jacket—it might cool down as the sun set, or the mosquitos might come out, or both. I slipped out the side door, out of Grandma's line of sight as she watched *Wheel of Fortune*. I set out for the lightning tree.

There was going to come a day when we would lose the back forty to back taxes. There was going to come a day when someone was going to bulldoze the lightning tree and the rolling pasture around it and the little creek and put up, probably, a Walmart or an apartment complex. But I was trying to calm down, and I made myself do the deep breathing my therapist had taught me during the brief window of time when I could afford a therapist through the school's counseling center, when they'd tried to offer me "bereavement support." It had been kind of nice, to be honest. Someone whose whole job was just to listen to me bitch about the fact that my baby brother was dead and everyone was pretending it was an accident. Beat Grandma's lectures on Attitude. Beat dumping on Adriana and making things worse for her. Beat trying to find friends in this Godforsaken town. Must be fun to have insurance all the time.

Breathe. Calm down. Let it go.

I'd taken Cody and Adriana on this walk about a million times. With Mom and my stepdad—Cody and Adriana's dad—when he was alive. By myself after his motorcycle accident, to try to keep things kind of normal for them. I was sixteen when they were born and people were always mistaking me for their mother, partly because Mom had had me when she was nineteen and people just expected bad shit to happen to everyone in my family, partly because I was the one running around picking up diapers and Flintstones Chewables and Dr. Seuss books from the library a lot. Especially after the accident. If that hadn't happened, Mom probably would have stayed clean and she probably wouldn't have gone back to jail. People expected bad shit to happen to our family at least partly because bad shit did happen to us a lot.

It was only about a quarter of a mile out to the lightning tree, but it was over a rise and not visible from the house or the road. I could hang out there as long as I wanted, or until Adriana came home—she'd know where to look for me. But that was okay. She'd be hours yet.

It was called the lightning tree because it had been struck by lightning, years ago, when my stepdad was a kid. He'd seen it happen. It was one of the last live American Elms in the whole county, and he'd been playing underneath it when he heard thunder in the distance and headed for home. He was only a couple of yards away when lightning struck out of the clear sky. He'd said that he felt the air buzz on his skin as it happened, and his hearing never was exactly right again—you'd be talking right to him and suddenly he'd be paying attention to something else, a sound inside his ears. Maybe that was why he didn't hear the fire engine and get out of the way in time.

When he told the story—Adriana and Cody used to beg to hear it over and over, that was why Adriana'd gotten a picture of the lightning tree as her memorial tattoo—he'd always shake his head and say "I was lucky I decided to head for home. I wouldn't have thought lightning would strike there, with the trees on the rise so much taller."

Now, standing under the tree, I looked back towards the rise and tried to measure in my mind. Most of the trees that were there when he was young were gone now, rotted and taken down by the weather. The lightning tree, dead, had outlived them all.

I heard a sharp crack and turned my attention up. There was a bird on the tree. Not the hawk that sometimes sat up there to scan the pasture, but something I'd never seen before. It was huge and mostly black and white, with a red crest. Judging by its bill and the sound it made when it hammered against the trunk again, it was a woodpecker. I'd just never seen a woodpecker that big.

It looked at me once, then went back to work. I wondered if it was something rare. It was certainly beautiful, and I felt like it was important not to disturb it. I lowered myself to the ground.

Maybe it was building a nest, I thought, and leaned back in the grass to watch it. The idea of a nest in the lightning tree pleased me. Maybe there would be baby birds to watch all summer.

The woodpecker made its way along the blackened scar that creased the trunk, pausing every few hops to drill at the bleached wood on either side. It wasn't taking breaks, and it wasn't getting paid either. It seemed to be on a mission, and on the brink of success. I could remember when I'd felt like that. Now I was just tired.

I woke up in the dusk. How the hell had that happened? I hadn't felt sleepy. I'd been watching the woodpecker. It was gone now, though it had left a large dark hole where a low broken limb had once been.

I heard a voice, almost in my ear, say "Go home, now."

I felt my skin prickle.

As I came over the rise, I saw that all the lights in the house were blazing. That meant that Grandma was having a freakout and had forgotten to worry about the electric bills. I started to run.

Grandma took a swing at me with Grandpa's old cane as I shoved through the door, but I managed to catch it—she really wasn't strong enough anymore to be a threat with a blunt object. She knew it on some level, too. She tried to wrench the cane from my hand for another shot, but I gripped the worn wood and held on until I was able to make eye contact.

"Grandma. Grandma! Listen. It's me, Katie. What's going on?"

"They're trying to get in the house."

"Who are? Why?"

"They are, the sons of bitches."

"They can't get in while I'm here." I let go of the cane, but kept my hand raised until she dropped it to the floor. "I won't let them in. I've got it under control."

"Do you now. Likely story." It always marked the return of regular, sane

Grandma when she started taking digs at me, so I was pleased. "They got Cody, what makes you think they won't get you?"

I led her to the living room, flipping off lights along the way, and got her settled on the couch with a blanket.

It was only then that I realized what else was wrong with the picture. "Where's Adriana?"

Grandma looked up. "You were supposed to watch her. You're always supposed to watch her after school."

Well, shit.

I glanced out the window—no sign of Adriana's car, so she'd never come home. Checked my messages. Exhaled when I saw her name on a text, and then wished I hadn't let myself relax.

Went 2 Fun Land. Back late or maybe 2morrw.

It was good that I'd slept when I did, because the rest of the night was going to be a washout on that front.

Why would she go there? Why would she tell me that she went there? It wasn't that I wanted my baby sister to lie to me, but just like that, in a plain declarative sentence with no justifications? Back to the place where her twin brother died a few months ago? We'd agreed never to set foot there again, after a late-night discussion that had involved only enough whiskey to get the tears going, not enough to forget what we'd said.

I let Grandma fall asleep on the couch—once she got agitated like that it was lucky if she could get to sleep at all, and I wasn't going to rouse her— and sat at the computer, resisting the urge to jump up and look out the window every time a car went by from the direction of the theme park.

Fun Land was a strong contender for being the worst place in America at living up to its stupid generic name. It had been a Six Flags for a little while just after I graduated high school, but they'd sold it off again less than three years after they acquired it. Official word was that modernizing it was just too expensive to make sense, and I kind of believed that. The only people who ever showed up, besides people from town and the city kids that the Baptists bussed in when the washed-up Christian rock acts played, were antique rollercoaster buffs who wanted to photograph the rickety wooden monsters that still rattled through the summer. When they weren't down for maintenance after yet another "accident." How many times could someone get maimed or killed there before they were no longer allowed to use that word? An accident was something you didn't expect, but we'd come to expect our allotment of death and dismemberment from Fun Land every summer.

But the whole local populace flocked to it anyway—partly because everyone in town was related to someone who had a summer job there and got the discount coupons, partly because there was damn little else to do. Was that what had driven Adriana back there? Pure boredom? If so, I had to be sympathetic.

I glanced down to check the time. One in the morning. How the hell had that happened? Fun Land had been closed for hours, and though I knew what kids Adriana's age did after it closed—there were plenty of places to park out in the boonies in that direction, plenty of fields to party in when the weather was this nice—I was still starting to get the brain weasels. If she had died, the police would be here by now for sure, though. Right?

By the time I heard the car pulling into the driveway, I wasn't sure if I was going to hug Adriana until she couldn't breathe or chew her out, or do both at the same time. That's probably why I didn't register that the car had come from the wrong direction until the knocking at the door started.

Shit. Cops. The bad news again. I felt like my brain left my body and went to hang out on the TV stand while I walked to the door.

So when I saw Scott and Emily on the porch in their matching down vests, my brain wasn't there to help me figure out what the hell to say. I just stared.

"Hey," Scott said. "Did we wake you up?"

"No."

"Good, good. We were trying to go up to Toronto and we got turned back at the border. I was wondering if we could just stop over for the night."

"Scott, this is stupid," Emily said. "We can get a hotel room."

"No, no." Like an idiot, I smiled and stepped back from the door, waving them inside. "We have plenty of room."

Scott had been here half a million times, but Emily stared at my stepdad's hunting trophies as though she were in a wax museum.

"Do you guys need a drink or anything? We've got beer, Jack Daniels, Dr Pepper."

"Water's fine," Emily said, and followed me into the kitchen.

"I have to warn you," I said as I turned on the tap, "we have well water. It tastes a little funky. You might want to go with the Dr Pepper."

Emily shook her head. "I don't really drink soda."

Of course not, I thought. Scott had trailed us into the room by now and she took the glass and scooted back to his side. "I'll take you up on the beer," he said.

I pulled two Labatts from the fridge. We'd both drunk classier stuff in college but this was what I could afford now, and at least it wasn't Genny.

"So you got turned back at the border? How'd that happen?"

"It was the weirdest thing. The computer pulled me up as having been deported in 1997 for trying to work in Canada without a visa. So now apparently I'm a no-go."

"Mmm-hmmm." I sipped my beer. "Bummer about that. What were you headed up there for?"

"Going to Montreal," he said, and had the decency to look uncomfortable for a minute. "It's our anniversary."

"Staying at Angelica Blue?"

He nodded. Emily shot him a look.

"It's a nice place."

"Yeah, it is." He stared down at his beer for a moment, then made a show of looking around the room. "Say, where's Ronin?"

Goddamn it. "He got run over. About a month after I moved back here."

"Oh, that sucks." To my surprise, Scott sounded genuinely sorry. He'd always complained about the dog fur that would get on his clothes when he stayed over, back when Ronin was alive.

"My mom had my cat put to sleep a month ago," Emily said. "She had diabetes and wouldn't stop peeing on the couch. The cat, not my mom."

"I'm sorry," I said, and slugged more beer.

"So yeah. Losing a pet is terrible. Their lives are too short."

Platitudes reminded me that I was tired. "Let me get the air mattress for you guys. If you need to use the bathroom, remember to jiggle the handle after you flush, or it'll run all night."

While I was digging the air mattress out of the back of the closet in Grandma's room, I heard Adriana come in. She slammed the door and crossed the living room floor as though she were a herd of elephants, not a 98-pound teenage girl; I braced myself for Grandma to wake up and start flipping out again, between the hour and the actual strangers now in the house. But she didn't.

When I came back downstairs, she'd found Scott and Emily in the kitchen. She'd opened herself a Labatt, which I was pretty sure she didn't need at this stage of the evening. The halter top she was wearing exposed about half of the tattoo, and the red streak in her hair was freshly dyed. She must have touched it up this morning before work. Emily was clinging to Scott's arm like she was in a horror movie.

"You're all set up in the guest room," I announced, and Scott and Emily headed for the stairs at the fastest walk they could manage, tossing "goodnights" and "thank yous" over their shoulders. I grabbed another beer and took the seat where Emily had been, across the kitchen table from Adriana.

"Fun Land, huh?" I tried to keep my voice neutral but that had never worked before and it didn't work now.

"Stop being a bitch," she said. There was a bit of a slur going but not as bad as I had expected. "How do you expect me to investigate if I don't go to the scene of the crime?"

"It won't do any good," I said. "Even if you find out what actually happened, we'd have to be able to afford a lawyer to…"

"We don't need a lawyer, we need an exorcist."

I tried to take the beer from her hand, but she was gripping it tight. "I met this guy at the Alligator while I was working, he was telling me that there's a curse. On Fun Land, on the whole town. He was super cute, too." She giggled. "So I said I'd go on a date with him when I got off work, if he'd explain the curse thing to me. And I did. And he showed me."

"A curse." I tried to get a look at her pupils; they looked normal.

"Yeah. Why do you think people are always dying?"

"Because Fun Land is a dilapidated shithole run by irresponsible, greedy bastards?"

"Yeah, but they don't just die at Fun Land, do they? Dad died on Route 20, and Grandpa electrocuted himself fixing the pump, and Erik Anderson died in that barn fire, and Mrs. Gowalski fell down the stairs in the library, and those are all just people who lived on this stretch of the road."

"Those are all things that could've happened anywhere. Do happen anywhere."

"All the time?"

"Pretty much, yeah." But I'd always wondered myself why it wasn't enough that this place was poor and insular and full of morons, why we had to be plagued with bad luck, too.

Adriana shook her head. "I know he's right. I can feel it. Laugh if you want. But I'm going to figure out a way to stop it."

"Okay, Buffy," I said. But she rolled her eyes at me and took another swig of beer.

"I should go to bed. He's coming to pick me up super-early tomorrow, like before-sunrise early. He wanted me to stay at his place, but I said you'd lose your mind if I didn't come home."

"That's not fair. I've never interfered with your love life, have I?"

"You kept leaving condoms in my room every time you were home from when I was thirteen to when I got my own driver's license."

"And was I wrong to do that?"

"Well, you don't have any nieces or nephews. But it kind of counts as interfering."

"Someone had to give a damn, and Grandma only would have given you a lecture."

She reached across the table and pulled me into an awkward hug that almost made me spill my beer.

"That said, I don't think you should go with this crazy curse-guy any place that's not public. And I think you should take your own car."

"I have to go, if this is for real, it's important. It would mean no one else would die like Cody."

After she went up the stairs I poured myself a whiskey and wondered, until I couldn't stay awake any more, how I was going to get her off this particular crazy train before she got her heart broken in a way that a tattoo needle couldn't stitch together—again.

⚜

Normally, I believed Adriana when she said she was going to get up early almost as much as I believed her when she said she was going to get her act together and finish her GED. But sure enough, when I finally got out of bed she was gone, though her car was still in the driveway. Scott and Emily's car was not, but their bags were still in the guest room. Grandma was in the living room, eating Frosted Flakes and watching her talk shows. She seemed entirely back to normal, and oblivious to the fact that anything had gone on last night. I didn't bring it up.

Scott and Emily were the first to get back, before I even got sick of editing rich-kid papers. Scott said that the border guards were looking into his problem and might have it fixed by tomorrow, could they stay one more night? Emily elbowed him, but I said sure. Then he dragged her off to show her around town. Apparently she'd never visited home with him before. Lucky her. Five minutes after they left, Grandma asked if that wasn't the boy I used to date. Something about her voice seemed even more disconnected than usual.

Adriana returned just after lunch, looking shaken—in fact, she was so rattled that Grandma looked up during a commercial and told her that she'd better take a vitamin, but still in that slow, checked-out voice that almost made me miss her lectures. I tried to talk to Adriana, too, but she told me she was tired and went up to her room. Just before she slammed the door she yelled down to me that I was right, she should have taken her own car, but she was fine. The slamming door should have brought on a lecture, too.

I spent the afternoon with a sense of impending doom that made it hard to even edit.

Towards dinner time, Emily got back. Her mascara was blurry and she had gigantic sweat-stains under her arms, and Scott was nowhere in sight.

"Are you okay?" I asked, looking up from the stove. It was a dumb question.

"He took me to see Fun Land."

"And?"

"And we ran into this guy in the parking lot. Red hair, kind of pale, on the scrawny side. Never took his sunglasses off. Scott said he didn't know him, but the guy talked to Scott like he did."

I racked my memory of high school, but I couldn't think who would have met that description. "And then they left together, and I waited and waited, and now I'm really scared."

"Left together?" I glanced out the window. Scott's car was in the driveway.

"In the other guy's car. Thank God I have my own set of keys to Scott's."

"Indeed." It seemed out of character for Scott—for anyone, really—to go off with someone like that. I thought of Adriana's tall-tale-telling stranger and his insistence on using his own car.

"Has he ever done anything like this before?" Emily looked at me for the first time as though she was really interested in my answer.

"He stood me up on a date once in tenth grade. But that was because his dad had to go to the hospital."

She didn't seem to see the humor. "He wasn't acting like it was an emergency. Should we call the cops?"

"Scott's a grown man. I think we have to wait twenty-four hours."

"No point calling the police," Adriana said from the top of the stairs. "You guys, we need to take a walk."

Emily stared at her like she thought Adriana was on crack, but I started putting on my shoes. If nothing else, it would be better for all the nervous breakdowns that might potentially happen to happen outside, and not disturb Grandma from her game shows. It was a miracle of deafness and dementia that she wasn't up and yelling already. I turned off the burner under the Kraft Dinner and left a note on the table on the off chance she would get up and start wondering where we were, but she'd probably just fall asleep in front of the TV again.

Once we were outside, I headed towards the lightning tree just by force of habit. Adriana was ahead of me before long—she'd gotten taller than me over the past couple of years, and had legs that made thoroughbreds feel dumpy. Emily had a harder time keeping up and I dropped back to make sure she knew where she was going.

"I thought the dangerous part was going to be having him sleep in a house with his ex and her hot baby sister. Not the boring tour of his hometown crap."

I glanced at her sharply, but it didn't seem like she was trying to be mean. "We broke up for a reason," I said. "I'm not after him."

She stared at Adriana's butt and didn't say anything.

The woodpecker flew up and away from the trunk as we approached. It had been working along the scar some more, and now there was a basketball-sized hole, dark against the dark of burned wood, which I only saw as I got close.

Adriana stretched up and grasped the bottom edge of the hole, almost beyond her reach. Almost effortlessly, she ripped off a chunk of flaky, rotting wood nearly as big as the phone book.

"What are you…" Before I could finish my question, a snake slithered out of the hole in the tree and down the trunk. It was huge—as big as the boa constrictor that Adriana had owned for a while after she dated a Goth kid in twelfth grade—and like the woodpecker, it was black and white and red. I was pretty sure it wasn't native to the area, or maybe the world.

That suspicion was confirmed when it reached the ground, coiled up, and transformed into a redheaded woman in a black dress, taller than Adriana and far curvier as well. Emily gasped, and the next thing I knew, I was holding her up because she had slumped against my shoulder.

"All right," Adriana said, sounding not nearly surprised enough. "Here we are."

"Took you long enough," the woman said. "If your sister had gotten the tattoo I could have been out of there weeks ago."

"No, you couldn't," Adriana said. "She can't reach that high."

"She pays more attention, though."

"Anyone up for explaining what's going on?" I asked as I settled Emily on the ground with her head between her knees.

"Oh, I'm so sorry," the redheaded woman said, mock-graciously. "I'm Calla. I'm here to help you avenge your brother, lift the curse from your hometown, drive off the vampire prince, and just generally be a hero."

"Why?" Yeah, I could have asked for an explanation of the curse or the vampire prince but honestly, the first rule of life is don't just take favors from talking snakes without checking for strings attached.

"Oh, you are the smart one. *Cui bono*? The reason, as it happens, is because the same person—if you want to call him that—responsible for Cody's death also shut me up in that tree, and I have my own scores to settle with him. Also, I rather resent them taking out a member of what I've come to think of as my family." She smiled at me like she expected me to be flattered, and that silly grin did more to convince me that she was telling the truth than anything in her actual words. I figured that at this point, additional skepticism would just be pissing into the wind anyway.

"Not just one," Adriana said. "He got my dad, too."

"Oh, the little boy who was here when I arrived? That's a shame. I wish I had known, but until recently I was more or less asleep."

Emily lifted her head. "He's also got my boyfriend. At least, if he's a guy who looks like he could be your sickly cousin."

"Good," said Calla. "Then we're all on the same page."

Emily frowned, and struggled to her feet. I let her grab my arm to help. "We should go get him before something awful happens."

Calla laughed. "Yes, we'll just walk right into Fun Land and challenge a vampire prince on his own turf. I'm sure that will work out just as well as it did the first time I tried it."

"Well, what do we do, then?"

"We get his heart."

"Oh, that'll be a piece of cake," I said.

"Well, he doesn't keep it on him. Someplace he has access to, obviously, some place he can feed it easily when he has new victims, but not inside his chest where just anyone might look for it. We get hold of that, he'll be in the mood to talk."

"Is that a normal thing for vampires?" No wonder Adriana hadn't taken my Buffy crack to heart. Whatever curse-boy had told her, she was way ahead of me and Emily.

"Only the ones smart enough to see that when you're staked, having your heart elsewhere gives you the last laugh."

I nodded. "That still seems like it involves a fair amount of challenging him on his own turf, though."

"Not if we use bit of trickery, I think. He'll have gotten spoiled, all these years. Who here doesn't mind snakes?"

Adriana raised her hand. She was smiling in a way she hadn't since Cody had died. I felt like a bit of revenge might cheer me up, too.

When Adriana stepped out of the car wearing her short-shorts and Calla-the-Snake coiled around her neck, every male gaze in the parking lot snapped to her, and the girls weren't exactly ignoring her either. It was like something out of a music video. Emily and I might as well have been invisible behind her, which was annoying when we tried to pay to get in, but once we were inside, it worked out exactly how we wanted.

"Have you ever tried talking to her about the way she dresses?" Emily whispered to me as we slipped behind the amphitheater where the bands played on weekend nights.

Really? Now? "It's not my business."

"Yeah, but she seems to look at you as a mother figure."

"It's still not my business. She can have her fun."

"It seems like people might get the wrong idea, though. I did."

"Your idea. Your problem."

She looked like she wanted to say more, but I'd spotted the trap door right where Calla had said it would be. It was a little rusty, and it shrieked when I opened it—no, that was whoever had been caught in a shaft of sunlight and turned to ash as I lifted the door away. According to Calla, there were plenty of weak little minor vampires like that hanging around, but they wouldn't really be a problem so long as we hit them with sunlight or silver. It was the Overlord we were after. And with any luck he wouldn't be in.

I'd put on every ring I owned, and borrowed Adriana's big chunky death heads and poison rings as well. All Emily had was her silver Star of David pendant. But she jumped out in front of me as the next vampire approached, a strange creature that looked like a long-dead Don Knotts, and swung the pendant in his face even as he tried to lean in at her. She was pissed. She let out a little yell when the vampire crumbled and punched the air, and this unexpected side of her distracted me until it was almost too late—another rat-faced vampire was coming at me from the left. I clipped him across the ear.

Once we got the hang of it, it was like we were in a video game, mowing down stooped corpse-looking things. I kept an eye on that shaft of sunlight, though. Calla and Adriana were supposed to join us as soon as they could, and I didn't like the thought that maybe they couldn't.

We made our way to the main room, huge and full of old books and papers and an incongruous fish tank full of plecos along the back wall. The other walls were lined with doors, which I wasn't very happy about.

"How do we check all of these without exposing our backs?" Emily asked, echoing my thoughts.

"I'll check. You cover me. It'll take a while"—I thought about Calla's reassurance that we'd recognize the heart as "something odd," which didn't seem at all helpful—"but these guys aren't so tough. If more show up, we can handle it." I didn't say anything about what we'd do if the big boss showed up before Calla and Adriana did, because I had no plan for that.

"No." She looked over at me, and I must have frowned, because her voice got more insistent. "I have some range with this pendant. And I've studied jiu-jitsu. I should take point."

I wanted to argue, but I had to hand it to her. She really did love Scott. Also, she had scored more vampire kills than I had in the corridor.

Emily opened the first door to the right. It was your basic walk-in closet out of an episode of *Hoarders*—filled with a pile of tangled scarves and jackets, ball caps and single shoes. A cheap promise ring fell out and rolled towards us, but it didn't look odd at all, it was one just like all the churchy girls in high school wore. It would have been funny if the whole heap hadn't smelled like rotten meat.

Emily looked back at me, grimacing. "Do we have to dig through all of this? Forget vampires, we'll die from the stench."

"It can't be buried in there if he's getting it out every time he kills someone. Try the next one." She shut the door in a hurry, and I was glad, because I thought I'd seen the brim of a familiar hat—the one I'd given Cody for Christmas two years ago.

The next door was more of the same, and the next. When I spotted the singed sleeve of Eric Anderson's old Grateful Dead hoodie, I started not looking into the closets at all.

As Emily opened the sixth door, I heard a noise behind me and spun. Adriana caught my fist without any trouble. Grandma's cane made for good practice.

"Where's Calla?"

"Still being a distraction. Half the park employees seem to be keyed in specifically to keep her from getting here, like they're programmed or something. So I dropped her and she turned back into a human to lead them away." She rubbed her neck wearily. "She's heavy."

"That's funny," someone drawled. "You'd think that with all the time she'd been locked away, she would have lost some weight."

The redheaded man had gotten between us and the exit in the brief time that I'd been focused on Adriana. I raised my hands but I knew that silver wasn't going to cut it here.

"Where's Scott?" Emily asked. As if that was going to help.

"The fellow I grabbed from the parking lot? I'm still working out what kind of accident he's going to have when I'm done with him. I've gotten bored with traffic and fires, and we've already had a nice dramatic beheading this season. As I'm sure you remember," he said, turning to Adriana. I was afraid for a second that she'd jump him right there and get killed. If she did, I would too.

While he was busy being an asshole, I scanned the room. He wasn't actually paying a lot of attention to us—I'd noticed that with Calla, too: that when she started talking, she sort of got lost in her own voice. He'd even shifted so he wasn't between me and the door any longer.

If we made a run for it, though, he'd catch us in a second. And we wouldn't get what we'd come for. Either of the things we'd come for.

"I suppose with so many of you I could make it look like a serial killer is on the loose. That would really stir up the local yokels. Your fear and anger are better than your blood, you know. Even when those stupid rides actually do malfunction, it's all to my benefit." He laughed. "Do you remember that fellow with no legs who insisted on riding the log flume and fell out and drowned last summer? Lap bars don't work without legs, you see. Entirely his fault and none of my doing, but it was *delicious*."

"Why are you telling us this?" I wasn't sure that Emily was trying to keep him talking on purpose, but I had to admit, she'd hit on an excellent question.

"Oh, since I locked Calla away, there's basically no one to talk to, and I'm so bored. I'd hoped to take over a real city, you know, or at least someplace interesting. Now I'm stuck here. One grows weary of bottling it all up."

I did not, by any means, want to feel like I could relate to this vampiric asshole. I just wanted to find the damn heart. Was anything odd? Aside from a vampire keeping tropical fish in an otherwise ridiculously gothic lair?

"Honestly. I mean, why do you think someone two hundred years old is still going to places like the Alligator Bar and Grill to play mind games with tawdry, gum-chomping waitresses? Is that the behavior of a man who's satisfied with his life?" I slipped my heaviest ring from my hand. Then I glanced across at Adriana and saw how tight her fists were clenched.

"Have you tried deep breathing exercises?" I asked him. "They really do help."

"I don't breathe anymore," he said, deadpan.

"My bad." I tried to make it sound like what Adriana would have called a sick burn, but it didn't seem to help.

"But back to the subject at hand, yes, I think serial killer for you three. Well, you two. I can't really feed on you thanks to your stupid tattoo," he said to Adriana. "And I won't get much out of your new friend since she's not from around here. In fact, you're all going to die, but Miss Deep Breathing here is the only one who is going to be at all satisfactory."

"Thanks a lot," I said, and hurled my heaviest ring at the glass of the tank.

It barely cracked. The vampire laughed. "You small-town girls with your tempers! It's like my own private Jerry Springer set."

I watched the crack. If it was as full as it looked… yes. It began to get bigger. Dickhead vampire would have noticed if he hadn't still been laughing.

I pulled off another ring. He saw that, and the laughter stopped, but by the second throw it was too late—the new crack joined the widening one and the entire front shattered. Fish and water and gravel spilled out on the floor, a plastic castle, a bunch of plants.

One of the fish looked… odd.

If I was frustrated with Calla for that description, I couldn't be any more. My first impression was that it was an albino, but it was the same color as all the others. It was the same size, the same basic shape. It flopped the same, only perhaps a bit less randomly, a bit more in the direction of the vampire.

I didn't have time to analyze much more than that. I grabbed the fish, squeezed it with my ring-clad hand. The redheaded man lurched towards me, but Adriana grabbed him long enough for me to really clamp down. His face went somehow even paler, and he began to pant.

Emily squeaked and turned her eyes away. I kept telling myself it wasn't a real fish. That was the part I felt bad about.

When the fish stopped squirming, so did the vampire. And that was around the time that Calla strolled in.

"Everyone trying to stop me from getting here suddenly dropped their guard and looked confused. I figured you'd found it."

I held out the dead fish to her. As she held it in her palm it transformed back into a heart, oozy and deep red. She dropped it to the floor and squashed it beneath her shoe.

"Excellent," she said. "And now, to look over the papers and see what I've just become overlord of."

"Like Hell," Emily said. "Like Hell you get away with that." She held up a bug, like a cicada before it molted but huge and pale. "His isn't the only heart that's breakable. I found this at the foot of your tree."

Calla frowned and reached out her hand. "Come on now. Don't be silly."

"Why should we let you wreck people's lives any more than we let him?"

"Because if it's not me, it'll be some other vampire in a few months. Towns like this draw us. I mean, I'm sure he gave you a good line of talk about how in charge he was, but let's face it, no one could work up a level of slow carnage and popular indifference to all the accidents if there wasn't a pre-existing curse."

"That's such a load of crap."

"No, I'm pretty sure it's true." Emily wasn't looking at me, and it was easy to snatch the bug from her hand. She looked at me as though she'd been betrayed, but I had other things on my mind.

"He said he wouldn't get much good out of Adriana because of the tattoo. What did that mean?"

"Well, just that she's one of mine now." Calla smiled. "He knew what the tree meant, of course, but even with vampires I've never met it should serve as pretty good protection from now on. Because I could always talk to and through anyone near the tree, and now she's always near the tree."

"One of yours to protect. Not to eat yourself." Please say yes, because otherwise I just made the biggest mistake of my life.

"Of course not! That would be like eating your poor dog."

I looked down at the bug in my hand. It was chitinous and yellow and gross enough that I really would have wanted to squash it even if I hadn't known what it was.

"Just one more thing, then. Where's Scott?" I stared at Emily. She stared back, but she didn't say anything or move towards me.

"Probably tied up in one of these closets." Emily hesitated a moment longer, shrugged, and started opening doors again. The smell billowed out, and Adriana gagged.

"So. Never fuck with my family."

"I wouldn't dream of it."

"Look out for them?"

"Of course."

"And if you get so bored that you start wanting to turn serial killers and things loose, just call me to chat or something."

Calla nodded. I crossed the room and handed her the bug back.

She smiled. I could see the tips of fangs, but it looked genuine.

◊

Scott recovered fast enough to start complaining about losing his deposit at Angelica Blue by the end of the night. I had a feeling when I watched him and Emily drive away that she'd never, ever be spending any holidays at his folks' place.

Adriana looked at the back of my head as I watched them go, until I had to turn around and talk to her. "We didn't lift the curse," she said. "We're not heroes."

"Of course not. But we made things a little better for everyone. And a lot better for us."

"Do you think she'll actually call you, ever?"

"I think so. Vampires seem chatty." I didn't want to admit, even to Adriana, how much I hoped she would.

"Well…" Adriana shrugged. "We did avenge Cody." She was holding the hat that we'd retrieved from the closet—it still stank, but out here in the open air it didn't seem so bad. "So there's that."

"There is that." I put my arm around her. We didn't say anything else as we walked to the back forty.

It wasn't much of a ceremony—I would have felt goofy about that, and we'd already gotten through one funeral—but I stood with Adriana as she flung Cody's hat high into the lightning tree, to catch on a snag. We leaned Grandma's second-best cane against the trunk, too, just in case it might help. One of Adriana's hemp necklaces, an old pair of my glasses, a letter from Mom. I even added a lock of Ronin's fur that I'd saved.

Then, as we watched, the black-and-white woodpecker landed on the tree. After a moment, a second bird joined him.

Follow Me
by Christine Morgan

Cool blew the breeze from the wine-dark sea. Rosy-fingered Dawn touched her fingers to the sky. In Piraeus, port of Athens, the marketplace awoke.

This was the great agora, the city's bustling heart. Here, shopkeepers displayed their wares and artists hawked their trade. Here, priests, poets, and politicians orated, displaying their wares and hawking their trades as well.

As did the prostitutes, Euterpe among them, though morning was not the best time for their particular business.

In the early hours, men were more concerned with commerce. Once they'd made their money, they'd be more eager to spend it. Conversely, those who'd done poorly in their dealings would seek solace to forget.

She walked nonetheless, walked through lines of sun and shadow in the marble colonnade. She smiled. She cast sidelong looks from beneath half-lowered lashes. She arched her long swan's throat and swayed her hips.

Her hair, tinted henna-red, piled high and pinned, let a few loose-coiled locks dangle to her bare arms. A fine linen chiton, held at one shoulder by a bronze and coral brooch, fell in drapes and folds that caressed her body, low-girdled with a cord. She'd dusted her face with white lead powder, and outlined her eyes with ink. Her lips and cheeks were mulberry-stained. So too were her nipples; they pressed against the cloth, sheer enough to offer tantalizing glimpses.

Cleverest of all, however, were her sandals, which had inverted lettering embossed deep into each leather sole. Whenever she gained a likely customer's attention, she made sure to place her steps with deliberate care. In loose dirt, sand, soft soil, or wet clay, the soles left clear impressions.

Follow me, invited the message stamped into the earth by her right footprint.

Lotus Street, directed the message of her left sandal's sole.

And, upon the heel of each print, was marked her name. *Euterpe*.

This meant that many of her customers would be literate, therefore more learned… and therefore, usually, wealthier, and better able to afford her services. They could follow her close-on if the trail was recent enough, before blown dust or the passage of others obscured her steps. If not, they would know where to find her, or ask after her by name, when they had time for a moment's diversion.

So, she walked, leaving her line of stamped footprints, her message repeated over and over. *Follow me*.

The agora filled more and more with voices—haggling, laughter, shouting; poetry and speeches—and activity. Scraps of news and rumor flew about like dry leaves, growing greater as they went. Sickness on Mud Street became a plague scare, beggars dropping like flies and the whole city in danger. The mention of a Peloponnesian ship turned into the imminent threat of invasion and war. Yet *more* tragic cradle-deaths couldn't be mere coincidence, but *had* to be proof of a murderous mother-cult. Rain was likely… no, a spell of bad weather… a storm… a flood that would wash waves to the very steps of the Acropolis.

Three ragged children, working as a team, stole eggs one after another from the baskets of a woman who chased them angrily back and forth. A bearded old man in a loincloth stood on a woven mat, waving his scrawny brown arms, raving that a curse was upon them, the *strixoi* were coming, and the end times was near. The dispute between a dung-cart's driver and that of a hay-cart came to blows, prompting spectators to gather and wager and cheer.

Just another day at the agora. People of Piraeus, people from great Athens, travelers from around the Aegean and across the Mediterranean, from Egypt and Phoenicia, from Byzantium and Gaul... people of all kinds and colors made the crowds grow steadily thicker.

Euterpe and the other prostitutes, in their distinctive cosmetics—garish, one poet had mocked, probably after finding himself too poor to afford or too impotent to enjoy their services—drew considerable attention.

Some glanced, some gazed approvingly, some glared with approbation as the women passed. Most of the glares came from other women, free but poor, plain but hardworking. They were the wives or servants of merchants and fishermen, farmers and potters. Those who stole surreptitious glances were, more often than not, those selfsame women's husbands.

Many of those good wives and daughters of Athens might have switched places with her in a heartbeat, though few of them would admit it.

While they tended their stalls, she strolled at her seeming leisure among the columns, fountains and mosaics. While they did their household shopping, she sipped sweetened juice in the shade and smiled at handsome men. Beckoning them. Tempting them.

Follow me.

To enjoy such freedom? To answer to no husband, to live under the roof and auspices of no father or brother? To lounge in her bed as late as she pleased, rise when she wanted, go wherever she wished?

Her figure was firm and shapely, unspoiled by years of motherhood and marriage. Her hands were smooth. She wore fine linen, hair ornaments, and jewelry.

Oh, yes, they envied her, and with good reason.

Sometimes, to her amusement, she even saw dour-faced wives tramping along prostitute-trodden paths, scuffing, kicking dirt, and obliterating the marks.

"They are coming!" shrieked the old madman from his mat. "Beware the gods' wrath! Beware the fiends of Tartarus! They are coming, the sun will bleed, the skies will blacken! Babies dead in their cradles! Grandmothers in their beds! The *strixoi*—"

A boy threw a stone, striking the old man in the ribs. He squawked and sat down hard. Those nearby laughed.

The day warmed. The sun, unbleeding, climbed higher in the unblackened skies.

Euterpe earned a quick drachma from a lawyer's clerk on an errand, then wended her way past more arrays of goods for sale—olive oil, vegetables, perfume, grain, pottery, fish, spices, slaves, figs, beads, tools, honey. She bantered and flirted with merchants she knew, did some more business, bought a wedge of flatbread smeared with a paste of crushed fruit, and lingered to examine a display of brass lamps.

When she saw other prostitutes, they exchanged acknowledging nods or a word or two of greeting, or paused to chat if they were on friendlier terms.

Theirs was a strange sisterhood, one of competition and community. They held themselves far above the *pornai*, who lived wretched lives in brothels under the control of a procurer, but knew their own status to be well below that of the elite *hetaerae*, whose elegant and educated company was much sought-after by the wealthiest and most influential of men.

Some, Euterpe among them, more pitied than despised the *pornai*. After all, age, misfortune, disfigurement, or hard times could reduce any of them to that level at any time. Others of their sisterhood had already come from such a history, having managed to save up enough of their meager earnings to buy their liberty.

An Athenian youth, healthy-looking and more than presentable, paused in his labors. Noticing her tracks and their message, he followed them with his eyes, then favored Euterpe with a long, admiring grin. She tipped her head and raised her plucked, painted eyebrows in a beckoning gesture.

Temptation twisted his features. He was with an older man—his father or uncle, she judged—who stood nearby, arguing with one of the city's tax collectors. As of yet, this stern figure had not noticed the youth's distraction.

Euterpe shifted from one foot to the other with an undulating roll of her hips, trailing a hand down the front of her chiton and inhaling.

The youth looked stricken. He indicated crates of goods yet to be unloaded, and spread his hands in a helpless shrug. She exaggerated a sigh of disappointment, then shrugged herself and tapped the toe of her sandal at her tracks. *Follow me... Lotus Street.*

She moved on. She did more business.

"They slice their own breasts and nurse their young upon blood!" howled the madman, and a basket-weaver drove him away from her shop, swearing, striking at him with a bundle of reeds.

Later that afternoon, another prostitute fell in beside her in the colonnade. Melanthia was dark-haired and pretty, short of stature but rounded of curve, and she brimmed with the latest bits of gossip from their circle of acquaintances.

Phylia was pregnant again, Melanthia reported, and thinking that she might keep this one this time, marry a potter, settle down. Iolanthe continued to drink too much; getting on in years, and not as popular as she'd once been, she was desperately afraid of becoming one of the *pornai* yet hastened her way toward it with each jug of cheap wine. Niobe had seen her orphaned nephew in the company of a brothel owner known for providing pretty boys to men with a taste for cruelty. Glyke's husband, long since believed lost at sea, had returned and been furious to learn how she'd been supporting herself in his absence.

"He dragged her into the street by the hair," Melanthia said, "and was hitting her with a strap when Althea came by. Remember how we always suspected those two shared more than affection? Althea snatched that strap out of his hand and beat him bloody with it."

"What happened to her?" asked Euterpe, both shocked and impressed by Althea's audacity. Free or not, for a woman to raise her hand to any man was a serious offense. No matter how vile the man or his actions were. Then again, Althea was a big woman, strong-jawed and claiming descent from the line of Hippolyta and Antiope.

"She and Glyke ran off together. They haven't been found yet. I hope that they aren't." The wistful pursing of Melanthia's mulberry-stained mouth said that she knew better than to put much faith in that hope. She shook her head briskly, causing black ringlets to bounce, and changed the subject. "How are your sandals holding up?"

"Quite well." Euterpe looked at her friend's tracks in the dust, and saw that her stamped letters were faint, almost illegible.

ollow m... lanthi read one footprint; *olphin Str... lanthia* read the other.

"Yours look faded," Euterpe added. "The soles are wearing thin."

"I know," groaned Melanthia. "I've been trying to save up for those silver bracelets set with blue stones Didos has at his stall, they'd go so well with my peplos of dyed-indigo wool... but, if my customers cannot find me, I'm not earning, and if I'm not earning, I'm not saving, am I?"

"So it is," Euterpe agreed. Seeing that the old madman had relocated his mat to this side of the agora, and was about to begin another insane oration of how the dark *strixoi* would pierce their hearts and kill them in their beds, she said, "We're not far from Gaius' shop. I might like new laces for mine. Did you see the ones Nereia has?"

"With the braided strips of kidskin to the ankles, and the little bronze bells over the toes? Aphrodite herself would want those!"

They went on at a brisker pace, discussing fashion, until they reached a side street that took them to a much smaller courtyard dominated by a fountain depicting the nine Muses with their instruments and implements of their various arts.

Euterpe, as she always did, stopped to honor them, particularly her namesake, with an offering of a coin and murmured praises.

Melanthia, less deferential, smothered a giggle. "And how many flutes have you played of late, oh giver of delights?"

"Hush," chided Euterpe. "Follow me."

The shop of Gaius, the sandal-maker, was tucked away in a corner, almost hidden from view. He lived there as well, sleeping on a cot in the back room, and did not go out much.

Some likened him to Daedalus for clever invention, or cunning Odysseus for craftiness and wit. Skilled though he was, the respectable women of Piraeus and the good Athenian wives snubbed his business. But, as he'd told Euterpe, he wasn't bothered by it.

"Oh, yes, I lose their drab custom," he'd said, "because I have beauties like you coming into my shop... letting me hold, touch, wash, caress, anoint with oil and adorn with my humble sandals their most lovely, delicate, nymph-like feet… and then *you* pay *me*? Tfah!"

Gaius was a former slave, or that at least had been the intention of the raiders who'd seized him from his village when he was just a boy. He'd been, he cheerfully explained, a terrible slave, willful and disobedient, more trouble than he was worth.

It showed. The marks of a dozen different masters were inked upon his body, black and crimson and blue, from all the times he'd been sold or traded. Brands and the scars of so many beatings meant he hardly had an unblemished patch of skin left. His nose and both ears had been docked as punishments. After repeated attempts to escape, both his feet had been severed, the stumps cauterized.

This, the prostitutes who frequented his shop speculated, was why he had such a lavishing fondness for theirs. They all agreed that no one took more care and evident joy in fitting a sandal to a shapely foot than did Gaius. He'd rub them with his skilled hands, massage them with his thumbs. Sometimes, he'd use a horsehair brush to apply a thin layer of colorful dye to each toenail.

If he enjoyed this practice as much or more than their other customers enjoyed fondling other parts of their bodies, the prostitutes hardly objected. Besides, it went no further than that; Gaius was, among his other maimings and misfortunes, a eunuch.

He got around his shop well enough on his knees, or made use of crutches and a wheeled plank when he needed to go out into the streets. Most of the time, he simply hired a neighbor lad to run errands for him.

Melanthia giggled some more as she perched on a stool and extended her legs to let Gaius slip off each of her sandals in turn. He tutted as he saw the worn-down soles, then tutted again when he found the beginnings of a callus. Taking up a rounded piece of grey ash-stone, he began gently scouring at it.

"Is it true," he said as he worked, "that Zetis is leaving us?"

"It's that young man she's sweet on," said Euterpe, bending over a tray of lacings that ranged from coarse twine to lengths of golden wire. "The soldier, the one with the curls. She thinks that if she leaves the profession, he'll marry her."

"That *was* it, yes," Melanthia said. "But he's already promised to someone else. Now she's planning to become a—eeh! that tickles!—soothsayer."

Gaius exhaled a sorrowful gust of breath. "Those exquisite toes, what a shame."

"Slopping around in a goat's liver, looking for omens?" Euterpe grimaced. "How does she expect to make a living doing that? She'll change her mind."

"We can hope," said Gaius, wrapping Melanthia's feet in a cloth that had been soaked in scented oils.

"Maybe not," she said, and propped her heels on a cushioned footrest. "I dined with her last night. She wants to travel to Delphi and consult the Oracle there about dreams she's been having. She says that a darkness descends over Piraeus."

Euterpe, holding up a ribbon-lace dyed Tyrian purple, scoffed. "There's a madman in the marketplace who'll tell you the same for nothing, whether you want to hear it or not."

"The old stick-thin one with the beard?" Gaius asked. He knelt on a low bench by his worktable, cutting leather to measure for Melanthia's new sandals. Nearby rested the set of brass stamps, block, and mallet with which he'd impress the lettering into the soles. They had to be made backward, inverted, that was the trick, so that the messages would be legible once pressed into the dirt. "The one who's been going on about how the *strixoi* are coming?"

"That would be him, yes."

"Tfah! He's been out there for ages. Last month, it was that we were all being poisoned by our own wells and fountains. Now it's the *strixoi* on their flapping black wings."

"I thought *strixoi* were spirits," Melanthia said. "Seductive women who lure and prey upon men."

"Then there are two in my shop even now," Gaius said, and they all laughed.

"Those are sirens, and *lamiae*," Euterpe said when they finished. "In the stories I know, the *strixoi* are birds. Not the bronze-taloned flesh-eaters that Heracles fought, but small birds with red eyes and long needle-sharp beaks."

Melanthia shrugged. "Well, you would know."

"Ah, yes," said Gaius. "Your father."

Her father. The scholar, the philosopher, the fool. Not a madman like the one at the agora, but an eccentric. And, most damaging of all, a bad speaker. It didn't matter how well-read, well-learned, well-educated or well-meaning a man was; if he couldn't hold his own in the arguments and debates, he was lost.

They'd been poor, poorer still after her mother had died, but she didn't begrudge him. He'd tried his best. He'd even taught a girl-child to read, taught her about history, and architecture. He'd taken her exploring in the catacombs beneath the city, and the secret tunnels that ran the lengths of the Long Walls.

"One day, my little Muse," he'd often told her, "perhaps you'll even follow in my footsteps."

Instead, as he grew older, as the palsy and forgetfulness set in, she'd had to become what she was just to keep bread and salt on the table.

Now, men followed in *her* footsteps.

Gaius turned the leather sole of Melanthia's new sandal upside down over the block. He positioned the larger of the brass embossing tools against it, and struck the blunt chisel-end with the mallet. He held it up for their inspection, the lettering backward but clear. Then he pushed it into a shallow pan of sand so they could see it as it would appear on the street.

Follow me, read the message.

The craftsman continued with the more difficult work of stamping the rest of it—*Dolphin Street* on the other, for that was where Melanthia had her rooms, and her name on both sandal-soles.

The neighbor lad who ran errands for Gaius came in when the sandals were close to being finished. Gaius scolded him good-naturedly for tardiness; it was well past the time he usually arrived. The lad said it was because his mother had been called away to sit with a grief-stricken friend.

"Her baby died," he told them, blinking with youthful enthusiasm at Euterpe's breasts. "They're saying she killed it, stabbed it with a brooch pin."

"If she didn't want the baby," Melanthia said, swiveling her ankles to inspect the fit, "why didn't she leave it up on the hillside, like everyone else?"

"She's out of her head." The lad's gaze shifted to Melanthia's legs, for she'd needlessly drawn the hem of her chiton up past her dimpled knees. "Says a bird did it in the night, flew in by a window and poked the baby to death with its beak."

At that, Euterpe and Gaius shared a disconcerted look.

"Weren't you just saying… ?" asked the sandal-maker.

"The mother must have heard some of that madman's ravings, that's all."

"A lot of babies have died lately, haven't they?" said Melanthia, still admiring her sandals. "Do you think there's a new sickness in town? Someone said nineteen beggars and slaves have been found dead too, these past few days, down by Mud Street."

"There's always sickness of some kind or another down by Mud Street," Gaius said. He gave the boy a handful of small coins. "Sardines and some bread, today. A quail egg or two, if you can find them. Perhaps a pomegranate. And wine."

"What kind?"

"An amphora of whatever's cheapest; I'm not feeling choosy. There's a good lad. Off you go."

And, off he went, after a final long look and a grin.

"You'll have a new customer in a year or so." Gaius also grinned as the boy left. He turned to Euterpe, who'd lifted her feet from immersion in a basin of water sprinkled with hyacinth petals. "Chosen which laces you'd like?"

"These," she said. "The red wool cords, with the glass beads."

"Ooh!" Melanthia peered at them. "See how intricately they're knotted! What a pity so few of the men will notice, but then, they don't often look at your shoes."

"I've never understood that about Athenian men," said Gaius. He deftly removed the old laces from Euterpe's sandals, laced in the red ones, and slipped them onto her dried and oiled feet. "Too snug?"

"Perfect," she said.

"Tighten them as needed; they'll loosen as you walk." He traced the crossing lace-pattern with a fingertip. "And how well the color complements your skin. If you like, I'll tint your toenails to match."

"Next time," she said. "I should do some more business before the day's through."

"So should I, if I hope to ever get those bracelets," said Melanthia with a sigh. "Didos just *would* have to be devoted to his wife."

They paid Gaius—as always, he joked that *he* should pay *them* for the privilege of fondling their lovely feet—and left his shop. A fine haze of high clouds had begun to drift in from the west, turning the sunlight to diffuse gold. The scent of boiling lentils, onions, and garlic hung in the air.

Their search for business did not take long; customers approached them before they'd returned from the side street to the main colonnade. Melanthia went off with a hearty, round-faced man in a stonemason's smock, while Euterpe negotiated with a pair of students who seemed more interested in each other than her, but had appearances to uphold.

"Follow me," she bade them once they'd agreed on a price, and led them toward Lotus Street.

On the way back to the marketplace, cosmetics refreshed, she saw the old madman again. He was no longer on his mat uttering his prophecies and proclamations. He huddled on it instead, rocking on his haunches with his eyes tightly shut and his arms wrapped around his bony shins. By the presence of fresh bumps, scrapes and bruises, he must've been pelted with more stones, and maybe with rotting vegetables as well.

"...coming," he mumbled into his stringy grey beard. "They're coming... the *strixoi*... they're coming... you'll see... too late, too late... the sky look to the sky look to the sky they're coming..."

Despite herself, Euterpe looked to the sky. She saw it still hazed, bronzed now rather than gold, but that hardly seemed unusual at this time of day.

Struck with a sudden pity for the madman, Euterpe fished a few coins from her purse and tossed them onto the mat. They landed with a faint clinking. His eyes popped open at the sound, the wild intensity in them so startling that she took a step back.

"There were only a few, at first," he said, staring at her. "Like bees, like ants. Scouts! Sent from the hives, the hives in dark Tartarus. Sent to find weakness and filth, pride, the arrogance of man!"

She took another step back, already regretting having pitied him.

"And they found it!" His bunched, twiglike fingers rose, splayed and shaking, beside his head. "Great Athens, the learned city, city of art and law, philosophy, science! Statesmen! Lawyers! Painted pandering whores! We sneer at the gods in our folly and they will smite us down! Smite us for our greed and decadence!"

Euterpe, quickly, began walking away. Other passers-by paused, and the nearest merchants in their stalls turned to look, some with weary resignation, others with annoyance or accusation because he'd finally quieted and she'd stirred him up again.

He scrabbled after her on hands and scabby knees, clutching at her chiton's draped folds. "Already the *strixoi* come! They have sampled us, sampled the sweet nectar of our hubris! They have tasted of the young and the old, and deemed it *good*!"

She twitched the cloth from his grasp and walked faster. Not running, not quite, but very much at a hurry.

"Now they come for the rest of us!" The madman sprang to his feet. "Humble yourself before the gods! Wash that whore's mask from your face and repent!"

He lunged toward her, and only then did Euterpe throw dignity to the winds. She ran, his crazed laugh close on her heels. Hairpins went astray, spilling her henna-tinted locks. The soles of her sandals slapped the—

Follow me, she thought, and flinched, wondering for the first time if the sandals had been such a clever idea after all.

Even if she outpaced or eluded him, she was leaving a trail. What if the madman could read? Her every stride stamped its message into the dirt, the message with her name and street. What if he continued his persistent pursuit? What if he *did* follow her? Follow her home to her rooms?

Had the laces been looser, she could have kicked them off while running and barely missed a step. But, she'd done as Gaius recommended and tightened them before leaving her rooms again, so they were nicely snug.

She ran on, dodging through late-day marketplace crowds. The hazy bronze afternoon had given way to a smoky, coppery glow. The sun, a bloated ball of red fire, roiled and fumed. The sea stretched glassy and vermillion.

A shrill and terrible wail tore from the old madman's throat. "The sun! The sun bleeds! The sky blackens!"

Euterpe risked a glance back to see how far away he was, and witnessed him hurl himself full-length on the ground. He thrashed there, still wailing, amid a dust storm of his own making. People moved back from him, clearing a wide space where he rolled and writhed.

She stopped, bent double to catch her breath, disarrayed hair tumbling around her face.

Then the day dimmed strangely, not the dimming of dusk or of clouds but something else, some sudden and rising wave of shadow. A faint but growing sound filled the air, a distant whisper that became a rustle that became a thunderous whirr.

A woman gasped and pointed. Others joined her, women and men alike.

Lifting her head, looking westward again, Euterpe gasped as well.

The bleeding sun had vanished behind a blackened sky, as a turbulent cresting darkness loomed over the port-city. The whirr it made was that of wings, a multitude of wings beating.

Birds.

Not a flock but a swarm, a hundred swarms, a plague of birds so as to blot out the sun and cast Piraeus into premature night. Thousands of them. Millions. Like locusts. Like flies.

People stared in wonder and amazement. A few cried out in alarm, or fear.

Then panic engulfed the marketplace as the birds descended with ear-splitting cries, the whirring thunder of wind-whipping wings deafening.

They swept down, scattering, diving, darting amid the columns and buildings. Wet brown-streaked white droppings pattered in a messy rain. The acrid stink mixed with the sour, musty odor of feathers… and then with the hot tang of terror and blood.

Long, thin, needle-sharp beaks plunged and pierced. They hooked onto skin or clothing with tiny, thorny talons and clung like burrs no matter how their victims flailed and battered at them.

"*Strixoi*," Euterpe heard herself say, hardly believing it.

But there could be no denying, not when the proof was all around her. The birds, small and black-plumed, with reddish breasts and bright crimson oil-drop eyes, seemed to not be so much spilling the blood as… as drinking it… swelling fat the way ticks did when they fed.

The madman's ranting… Zetis and her dreams… the cradle-deaths and Mud Street sickness…

It was true.

A man staggered blindly past, his screams were muffled by feathers, his hands trying to pry out the beaks embedded deep in his eyes. A woman ran, hunched over a howling child she held in one arm while she waved her other arm wildly over her head. Two youths stood back-to-back, trying to fend off the attacks with hay-rakes. A little girl dumped cabbages from a large basket, upended it, crawled under, and hid inside.

Braziers got tipped over, spilling coals that ignited hangings and straw. Fires began spreading, adding to the panic. Euterpe rushed with a jostling crowd along the colonnade, almost more carried along than running on her own.

She recognized Melanthia's voice in the screaming cacophony, and saw her friend swatting at a *strix* tangled in her hair. Its beak jabbed again and again at Melanthia's head, digging gashes in her scalp that sent blood trickling down her powdered brow. Euterpe fought against the tide to reach her.

A body—male or female, Euterpe couldn't discern, it was so covered in flapping, feasting *strixoi*—sprawled in her path, a red puddle leaking around it. Her sandals slid and squelched, then left her message stamped in a gruesome trail.

The *strix*, when she grabbed it, ripping its talons from Melanthia's hair, snapped its head around and struck. Sharp pain stung Euterpe's wrist. Far worse was the immediate draining sensation, both burning and hideously cold. She squeezed the feathery body, tried to twist it, to wring its neck or crush its bones, but the hand attached to the impaled wrist already felt weak, going numb. It was all she could do to hold on.

Melanthia, more resembling a theatrical harridan than a prostitute, with her hair in gorgon's snarls and cosmetics smeared, snatched up an urn from an abandoned potter's stall and swung it at the *strix*. The urn smashed to pieces, nearly breaking Euterpe's fingers and sending pottery shards flying, but the *strix* burst like an overripe fig.

Its needle-beak remained lodged in Euterpe's wrist, a hollow tube from which her blood dribbled. Revolted, she pinched it and pulled. It slid out, leaving a puncture in her flesh. She pressed her other hand over the hole, shuddering.

True night was falling over Piraeus now, lit by many more fires burning out of control. The city rang with screams, and the ravenous screeching of the *strixoi*. All around them, people fled and fell and died. There was no escape.

They sank together to their knees, arms around each other, sobs of hopeless horror wracking them both as they waited for their deaths to find them.

Euterpe thought of their sister prostitutes, their customers, their other friends like Gaius. Was this it? Had the old madman been right? Were these the end times, the doom of them all?

She could only be glad she had no family to worry about, that she'd never married, had no children, that neither her mother nor well-meaning, eccentric father had lived to see this…

Her father… her well-meaning, eccentric father who'd joked that she might one day follow in his footsteps…

Who'd taught her to read, taught her about history and architecture… who'd taken her exploring… in the catacombs and secret tunnels below the city…

She rose from her knees. Melanthia looked up, bewildered, as Euterpe drew her to her feet.

"What are you doing—?"

"Hush," said Euterpe. "Follow me."

Only Darkness

by Paul Witcover

One hot Friday night in late July, with the streets of Greenwich Village simmering around her in a stew of rock, hip-hop, and salsa spiced with the sweetness of pot smoke, the wailing of car horns and sirens, and strings of leftover firecrackers going off like popcorn as people laughed and shouted and argued about everything and nothing, Fay looked up from her sketchpad to see a sleek young man standing before the drawings she'd put on display to drum up business. He was fastidiously dressed despite the heat and grime in an expensive-looking dark suit, an unwrinkled shirt of palest mauvette buttoned up to the collar, and a rakish black fedora. Her own twinned reflection gazed at her in miniature from the ovals of mirrored sunglasses. The rest of his delicately boned face was white as Warhol's. A small ruby glittered in his left earlobe like a pinprick of blood. *What have we here?* she thought. *Another vampire wannabe?* The Village was crawling with them. *Or even worse, a mime.*

"May I?"

His voice went well with his shirt. But he'd spoken, at least. *Not a mime, thank God.* Nothing drove away customers like mimes, the natural enemies of sidewalk artists everywhere. He could, Fay supposed, be an off-duty mime... though she found it difficult to imagine mimes were ever off-duty. She stubbed out the cigarette she'd been smoking and inclined her head toward the camp stool she provided for customers. The young man seated himself and crossed his legs with a casual scissoring motion that made her want to draw him as all sharp blades and angles.

She clicked on the lamp affixed to the top of her easel, left off between jobs to save batteries. In the sudden splash of light, the young man's features leapt into stark relief as though chiseled in stone. Fay gasped despite herself, only to realize in the next second that he was wearing theatrical makeup, his face as pale and unlined as the top page of her sketchpad. She felt like the victim of an obscure joke.

"I've been watching you," he said, which didn't exactly set her mind at ease, either. He spoke in a normal tone of voice; they might have been in a quiet studio somewhere, just the two of them. His thin lips barely moved, as if the makeup he was wearing had baked into an inflexible ceramic mask, its smoothness concealing… what?

Suddenly she knew. Her perceptions shifted, realigning as in the instant when a *trompe l'oeil* is pierced, the illusion still present but no longer substantial, floating translucent upon the surface of the real. *Why, he's old.* There was nothing obvious even now, but she knew it nonetheless.

"Your drawings are different from these others," he continued, one eyebrow rising marginally above the mirror shades to both indicate and dismiss her fellow sidewalk artists. "For one thing, you don't use any color, just charcoal and pencil. Why is that?"

Fay shrugged. The question seemed anything but idle. She wondered if he was a wealthy gallery owner or private collector on the prowl. She'd heard of such things. Legendary sidewalk encounters that brought some lucky stiff enough to live on for months or, as with Mapplethorpe, sparked a successful career… albeit with certain strings attached. But Fay was a big girl and could take care of herself. "I don't want to be one of those painters who can't draw, you know?"

"Go on."

"Color can be a crutch. It's easy to rely on it too much, hide behind it."

"I thought that kind of approach had gone out of style with Van Gogh." A name the man pronounced, to her vast annoyance, as *Van Gock*. "Actually, it was out of style even then, but poor Vincent was too *passé de mode* himself to notice."

Passé de merde, Fay thought. "Look, mister, this is a sidewalk, okay?

Not the fucking Met. I'm just trying to earn a living. If you want me to draw you, fine. If not, make room for a paying customer." Not that there were exactly crowds of that elusive breed clamoring for her attention.

To her surprise, the man smiled. Or, rather, she thought, *"smiled"*—all that makeup had the peculiar effect of placing quotation marks around his facial expressions.

"You misunderstand," he said. "I admire your work. It's why I've chosen you." His words, like his expressions, seemed charged with a secret irony. He removed his hat as he spoke, carefully placing it upside down on his lap, then took off his glasses and dropped them inside as though about to perform some feat of prestidigitation guaranteed to astonish and amuse. "I have no intention of wasting your time."

Jesus Fucking Christ, Fay thought, scarcely listening. *Well, that explains a lot.* Like his skin, the man's hair was Warhol white. He wore it slicked back, each perfect furrow so sharply engraved it looked almost too real, like a high-res image. His eyes had the pale, pink translucence characteristic of albinism, a condition Fay had seen in rabbits but never before in a human being.

"I've been looking for you, or someone like you, for a long time," the man said. "An artist immune to the seductions of color. Perhaps you can succeed in capturing my likeness where so many others have failed. If that's so, I may have a commission for you, one that will pay very well indeed."

"A sketch is twenty bucks… in advance." She normally charged fifteen but had heard enough to gamble on the extra five. Sure enough, he dipped his hand without hesitation into the bowl of his upturned hat and brought it out with a folded bill tucked between two well-manicured fingers. "Nice trick." She half-expected his skin to be like ice, or stone, but apart from a certain dryness, she felt nothing unusual as her fingers brushed his in taking the bill. She pushed it into the front pocket of her cut-offs. "Say, I hope you're not keeping all your money up there. Someone'll steal it. The hat, I mean."

"It's quite safe, I assure you," he said with a "smile." "Shall we begin?"

"Sure. That's not a bad pose right now. Do you think you can hold that?"

His answer was to become as still as a statue.

"Jesus, mister," she said. "You don't have to stop breathing, you know."

"I have all the air I require," he said, and this time she couldn't see his lips move at all, as if he were a ventriloquist. *Or a ventriloquist's dummy*, she thought.

"Doesn't the heat bother you at all? I mean, you're not even sweating."

"I don't, I'm afraid. A peculiarity of my condition."

Fay blushed. *Put my foot in it again.* "Sorry. Didn't mean to pry. None of my fucking business anyway."

"That's quite all right, my dear. One gets used to it."

Fay selected a piece of charcoal and began to study his face, searching for an entry point into his soul. Usually, it was the eyes. But his weak, pink eyes reminded her too much of rabbits, and whatever else this man was, he was no rabbit. *A hunter of rabbits, more like.* The chill, fey beauty of his features enthralled her. Their hyper-real perfection like some porcelain figure by Koons. Just as, moments ago, she'd seen past the cosmetic mask of youth to the truth of age it concealed, so now did her senses pierce the underlying flesh as though it, too, were but a mask. What lay beneath was something neither old nor young, a timeless, ageless purity at the very heart of him, a dense, dark egg that glowed with the absence of light like a black hole. It was then that Fay became afraid, for never in all the hundreds of men and women she'd sketched had she seen anything remotely similar.

"You're..." she began, flustered. "You're not..."

"Calm yourself," he said. "And draw."

Fay knew at once that she lacked the skill to do justice to what her talent was showing her. Still, her heart beat with excitement at the challenge. She picked up a stick of charcoal and began to draw. And in the mere attempt to copy what she saw, she felt a power stir to wakefulness in her unlike anything she'd experienced before. She'd believed for as long as she could remember that there was a potential greatness in her, had nursed the belief amid the mundane surroundings of North Carolina like some fairytale secret whose magic could harm as well as help her, but not until now had she realized just how rich her gift truly was… or, rather, could be. Like a breath of air expanding endlessly inside her, for the first time she had a sense of all she might accomplish. All she was capable of. She felt as if her whole life had been a prelude to this moment, a moment that would change her in ways she couldn't begin to predict. Was already changing her. Afraid it would never come to her in North Carolina, she'd gone to New York in search of it. And now, by some miracle, she'd found it… in the last place she ever would have thought to look. Or it had found her. It was exhilarating, dizzying, and frightening at once, a lover as likely to ravage as embrace.

Fay lost track of time, of place. She no longer felt the heat, no longer registered the perpetual Village Mardi Gras going on around her. All that existed in the world was she herself, the man sitting across from her in frozen silence, and the image being born on the rough page between them.

At last she was finished. Exhausted, she looked dumbly at what she'd drawn. It was by no means the most technically accomplished sketch she'd ever produced. Far from it. Yet imperfect though the likeness was, it had something of perfection in it. Something missing until now from even the best of her work. She felt proud, even a little awed. She presented the sketch to the man as if daring his criticism.

He studied the portrait for a moment. Then he began to cry. It was the first thing he'd done so far that hadn't struck Fay as entirely artificial.

"Oh," she breathed. "Your *tears*…"

They were pink, tinged with blood. They left trails down his cheeks like the marks of claws. The man drew a silky burgundy-colored handkerchief from the sleeve of his jacket and dabbed at his face. "Please don't be alarmed." His voice matter-of-fact as a doctor's. "A peculiarity of my condition, nothing more."

In New York, one learns quickly not to pry into the peculiarities of other people's conditions. Still, even in the North Carolina hill country the days when blood meant simply blood were long past. Fay drew back, putting a buffer of extra space between them.

The man tucked the handkerchief back into his sleeve, looking into her eyes all the while. "I wasn't sure this man existed anymore. Or, if he did, whether anyone could find him. But now you've given me a glimpse of him.

Thank you for that."

Fay nodded speechlessly. There was something almost unbearably sad in the regard of his rabbity eyes. She found herself pitying him terribly without knowing exactly why. But she did know it was more than just the obvious fact of his "condition," whatever that might be.

Meanwhile, without another word, the man slid on his mirrored glasses, set the fedora on his head at its former rakish angle, and rose smoothly to his feet.

"Wait!" Fay had to stop herself from reaching out to physically restrain him. More than anything, she wanted to sketch him again. Really do it, just the two of them alone somewhere, with no distractions, no hurry, nothing to interfere with an experience whose memory was already fading like the petals of a flower closing with the setting of the sun. "You mentioned a commission," she said hurriedly to her twin reflections.

His face gave nothing away. The makeup was intact, unsmeared, as if he hadn't shed a single tear.

"Please," she was surprised and embarrassed to hear herself say, for all the world like a street person begging for change.

At that the man produced what looked like a white business card from the same jacket sleeve that housed the handkerchief (and, Fay was beginning to suspect, a plethora of other items). She reached for it eagerly, but at the last second he gave his wrist a flick that sent the card flitting through her fingers like a falling leaf. It landed on the sidewalk at her feet.

He might as well have slapped her across the face. Fay's cheeks burned with mortification and anger. She felt as if she'd ceased to be an artist in his eyes and become something else, something lowly and contemptible and deserving of meanness. She didn't understand what had happened. Despite his tears, she was sure the sketch had pleased him. Had he sensed her pity and taken offense? But then why give her the card at all? And why did it matter so much to her *what* he thought?

But it did. Although part of Fay wanted to ignore the card, let it be scuffed and trampled out of existence by ten thousand pairs of careless feet, she couldn't do it. She wanted another chance at him too badly. All the same, the act of retrieving it cost her something substantial, as if, instead of simply reaching down and picking up the card as she might any other dropped object, she was kneeling to him, abasing herself in acknowledgment of his authority over her. She sat up quickly, determined to disabuse him (and herself) of the notion. But it was too late. The man had gone, taking the sketch with him.

Fay sprang to her feet, craning her neck to catch a glimpse of him amid the masses of people streaming by. For a second she thought she saw the sleek dark wedge of his hat rise above the surface like a shark's fin, but it disappeared before she could be sure. The Friday night bustle and noise crashed over her like a breaking wave. It was, Fay thought, as if the city had gone away for a while, or she had, the man standing between them like a sea wall, his very presence enough to keep them separated… just as his absence had brought them rushing violently back together.

Feeling queasy, she sat down. After a moment, when the sidewalk had stopped lurching about like the deck of a ship in choppy seas, Fay remembered the card. She held it up to the light. Raised black letters spelled out the name A.E. Talag and an address on Cedar Street in lower Manhattan. The name sounded vaguely Indian, but beyond that didn't ring any bells. On the back of the card, 9:00 p.m. had been written with elegance and flair in ink the color of henna. It was like receiving an invitation from the nineteenth century. It occurred to Fay that she'd forgotten to ask, and he to tell, anything about the nature of the commission she'd apparently just been given. There was no telephone number on the card, and she kind of doubted she'd find one in the phone book, either.

Just then a gaggle of giggling Emo girls her own age or slightly older with assorted piercings of the face and body descended upon Fay to have their portraits darkly and starkly done. Talag, it seemed, had brought her luck. And more than luck. Drawing him had left her drained, but now the embers of what his presence had ignited in her blazed up again, and in that fierce, pure, unadulterated light her subjects opened to her like flowers. She saw into them as never before, her eye sharpened to an acuity that went far beyond the superficial guessing games she was used to playing as she worked. In the pasty faces and kohl-rimmed eyes of these purple-haired-and-lipsticked girls alike as clones, Fay saw the fears and yearnings, the memories and secrets they kept hidden—sometimes consciously, sometimes not—from each other and from themselves.

Not that she could have expressed any of it in words. Not even silently, to herself, could Fay have said, for example, "Here is a girl teased and tormented by one loopy, drunken, not-quite-sisterly kiss between roommates that hasn't been repeated or even mentioned since it happened weeks ago yet which she dreams of incessantly with all the considerable guilt, anxiety and longing available to a nineteen-year-old, nominally ex-Catholic, upper-middle-class college student coming face to face for the first time with the mess that is real life." Or, "Here is a girl who sleeps in a bed that was thrown out more than ten years ago, lies there each and every night snug as a bug in a rug and listens with an intensity born of terror, in a lassitude born of experience, for muffled footfalls on the stairs of the dumb, dark house that inhabits her like a haunting." But Fay didn't need words. Her sketches spoke in their own quiet and direct voices of all these things and more.

The giggling girls grew silent as they watched her work. They didn't consciously know, any more than Fay did, what made the portraits so compelling. Why they mattered so much. They only knew they were seeing parts of themselves and of each other that no mirror or photo or video had ever shown them before. Beautiful parts… and ugly parts, too. The longer they looked, the less important or even possible it seemed to differentiate between the two, to celebrate and embrace the one while rejecting the other.

For the sitters, unable to see their own portraits taking shape, the experience was stranger still, as though each mark Fay made upon the page, every line and smudge and shading, was simultaneously being set down inside them by obscure arts of magic that were changing them in ways and on levels they couldn't begin to define, as if the sketch, or the act of sketching, was more real than they were. By the time they held the finished product in their hands, they couldn't judge any longer whether the portrait resembled them or they the portrait… a confusion similar to Fay's earlier sense that she and the world had somehow slipped or been pushed out of alignment.

But a second later it was as if there had never been anything remotely odd or disquieting. It wasn't that things were *back* to normal; they'd never left in the first place. This sort of thing happens more frequently than people imagine. And not only on the streets of New York.

By around two in the morning, Fay's hand had stiffened into a claw and was starting to cramp. She'd lost track of how many sketches she'd done. A few people were still waiting for a turn, but she was too worn out to continue. She felt used up. She packed her things and hailed a cab. An extravagance to be sure, but (she told herself) well worth the expense considering how easy it would be to conk out on the subway. She could see herself sleeping through her stop and waking at some empty tomb of a station to find all her stuff had been stolen. She saw it so clearly it might have been a vision.

Riding uptown, Fay counted her earnings by headlight and streetlight. Then counted them again. There was no mistake. This night, which had begun so unpromisingly, had ended as her most profitable ever. But there was still another surprise in store. When she reached into her pocket to pay the cabbie with the twenty that Talag had given her, Fay found herself gazing into the hundred-dollar eyes of Ulysses S. Grant.

That night, as had happened a handful of times since her arrival in the city, Fay returned to North Carolina in her dreams. Or, rather, to some fogenshrouded hill country of her unconscious mind that insisted on calling itself by that name, for going home can be just as difficult and unsatisfying in dreams as it is in the waking world (which in Fay's opinion was totally unfair). But never before had she come up against a barrier beyond which she couldn't go, no matter how often she flung herself against it.

The barrier was different in each successive dream of that night, but it always began in the familiar and innocuous and ended with her catapulted into wakefulness by a surge of terror that left her heart racing. Her mother's worry-lined face, for example, would smile at the sight of her and then slowly begin to morph into that of the second-shift manager at Popeye's, piggy

Mr. Peery, whose nickname of Greaseman had been as richly deserved as his reputation for what he guffawingly referred to as "sex-you-all hair-*ass*-ment." More than a year of laughing off his smirking innuendos because it was the best-paying job she could find and she needed the money too badly to tell him to go fuck himself had been nightmare enough, surely. Or so Fay would have thought. But apparently not. And there were dreams even stranger and more troubling, such as one in which her mother (why always her mother?) cracked open Fay's bedroom door to announce that her long-lost dad had shown up at last and was waiting outside to say hello, the door meanwhile swinging slowly wider to let light from the hallway come streaming in along with a figure who—surprise!—turned out to be the same man she'd selected years before to play the part of Humbert to her Lolita… except back then his skin hadn't been as white as alabaster. Is it any wonder that Fay got up the next morning feeling more exhausted than when she'd gone to bed?

Fortunately, at the age of eighteen there's very little a quick shower can't cure. That and half a dozen cups of coffee. Fay had the former, then pulled on her cut-offs and a fresh T-shirt and went out in search of the latter. At the local Starbucks, she took out her cell phone and did some searching for Talag's number, based on the address he'd given her. As she'd expected, no listing turned up. She briefly considered paying him a visit now, but she was pretty sure he wouldn't take kindly to it, and she didn't want to jeopardize her commission. He could still change his mind and refuse to sit for her. So she forced herself to wait. She was good at waiting. She'd been doing it her whole life.

The address turned out to be an old brownstone incongruously nestled between two warehouses. Cedar Street was empty of people, its cobblestones littered with the day's refuse. What cars there were did not seem parked so much as abandoned. Night was filling in the spaces around the streetlights. She climbed the steps then hesitated, looking for a bell. But there was only an ornate brass knocker in the shape of a fleur-du-lis. Fay lifted it slightly and let it fall. The resulting sound was louder than she'd expected, and she involuntarily retreated a step just as the door swung open.

She'd half-expected a butler or servant of some sort, but it was Mr. A. E. Talag himself who stood there. He wore a silk dressing gown whose deep russet tones merged into the shadows of the hallway behind him. His slippers looked like something Fay imagined a Renaissance Pope might have worn. His pale skin seemed to shine with a light of its own.

"Nice to see you again, Mr. Talag," she said.

"Right on time." His smile was a consummate performance. "I am very glad to see you as well, my dear. Very glad indeed. Please come in."

Fay stepped across the threshold. Mr. Talag fascinated her more than ever. Without the theatrical makeup he had employed the previous night, his features seemed even more exotic and youthful. Or, rather, ageless. Without a wrinkle or blemish. In combination with his snow-white hair and antique mannerisms, the effect was uncanny. All at once she realized that he had worn the makeup to *lessen* the strangeness of his appearance, not, as she'd assumed, to heighten it. Far from wanting to draw attention to himself, Mr. Talag had been trying to stand out as little as possible in the freak parade that was Greenwich Village on a Friday night. Fay didn't know what to think.

Mr. Talag seemed aware of her confusion and, if anything, amused by it. He stood almost unbearably close as he ushered her down the hall, which was lit with flickering gaslight, and spoke in a whisper that she had to draw closer still to hear. "I'm so pleased you decided to come, my dear. Times being what they are, it's not every young woman who would accept an invitation like mine."

"I had to sketch you again," Fay heard herself saying without having intended to confess it. She felt drugged by his presence.

"Of course you did," he agreed smoothly. "I present something of a challenge. A mystery. Do you find me attractive? Please be honest."

"Yes." She was unable to lie. "And repellent."

"Such is the nature of art, is it not?"

Mr. Talag led her to a room that seemed to have been preserved unchanged from the mid-nineteenth century. Gas lamps flickered on the walls, which were painted an off-white, like faded parchment. There was a marble fireplace like a vast grotto, in front of which, and to either side, were low divans whose plush upholstery hinted at reds and golds. The ceiling was so high it reminded Fay of the rooms at the Art Students League. Strangely, there didn't seem to be any windows.

Upon the walls were portraits of her host. Oils, water colors, sketches in charcoal or pen and ink. Fay examined them in a daze. Mr. Talag appeared in costumes ranging from the early nineteenth century to the present, and each portrait was executed in a style appropriate to the period whose dress he affected. She realized that she was looking at a virtual timeline of modern art history: Romanticism, Impressionism, Cubism, Surrealism, Post-Impressionism… The works bore the signatures of Géricault, Delacroix, Renoir, Sisley, Whistler, Picasso, de Kooning, Warhol, Basquiat, and other names she knew and didn't know. A portrait in swirling lines and colors was signed, simply, Vincent. The only constant from portrait to portrait was the subject, who seemed to be the same age in all of them. They were the most perfect forgeries imaginable.

"I think you'll agree I have ample cause to be proud of my little collection," said Mr. Talag.

Fay turned to him. "How… ?"

"They are all genuine, I assure you. As you can see, many artists who subsequently achieved a certain renown assayed my portrait over the years. Yet until last night, not a single one of them succeeded to the extent of making me weep. That was a gift, my dear. A true gift. And a sign. For when my kind weep, it means we have lived too long."

"Your kind?" Fay wondered if she was about to faint. She let herself sink heavily into one of the divans. "What… what are you?"

A look of "sadness" settled over Mr. Talag's perfect features. "An old man sick to death of a life without joy or meaning. Neither beauty nor ugliness exists for me anymore. Neither good nor evil. Everything has been equally debased by this culture of mindless irreverence and vulgarity. To exist in such a tasteless and insipid age pains me more than I can say. It is an affront to everything I believe in. I've been looking for you, or someone like you, for a very long time."

"Please don't kill me," Fay said, fighting in vain against the strange listlessness that had possessed her.

"Put that thought from your mind. Would it calm you to sketch me?"

Fay fumbled for her sketchpad. "I… I can't stop shaking."

"Please try."

She couldn't help but obey. As she worked, Fay began to lose herself in the sketch as she had the night before. Her perceptions of her subject were keener now, sharpened by the terror she felt, and by the helplessness, too, as if her only escape lay on the rough paper, in the portrait taking shape there line by line. When it was finished, she fell back in the chair, exhausted. Somewhere a million miles away a needle was pricking her. She felt as if she had been drawing upon her own skin, the stick of charcoal in her hand as sharp as a razor, as cold as an icicle.

"Not yet," Mr. Talag said.

Fay forced her eyes open. He was standing in front of her, examining the sketch; she hadn't even felt him take it.

"Exquisite," he said. "You have a rare talent for capturing the soul of your subject, my dear. Now you must come with me. Don't be afraid."

"I can't help it," she said.

"All of this will soon be over," he replied soothingly.

Fay rose to her feet and followed him into another room. An artist's studio, also gaslit. All around her were paintings and sketches such as she had never imagined a human being could create. Everywhere she looked she saw something wholly new and undreamed of. Her fear was overwhelmed, extinguished. "Are these yours?"

Mr. Talag "smiled." "A hobby of mine."

The paintings and sketches exposed her own work as crude and sentimental, utterly bereft of talent. The work of other artists fared no better by the comparison. Talag's compositions were daring yet finely controlled, so flawless in conception and execution as to be utterly impossible. "They're *perfect*," she said, almost crying. "The work of a great artist."

"Do you think so? I find them, on the whole, disappointing. But perhaps we always judge our own work too harshly. Or perhaps your eyes, my dear, are simply dazzled by a light to which they have not yet grown accustomed."

There were no self-portraits among the many works in the studio. This struck Fay as rather odd. She asked Mr. Talag why, with all his talent, he relied on other, lesser artists to render his portrait.

"You've touched the very heart of the matter," he said.

In the center of the studio stood a large oblong object covered by a paint-bespattered cloth. Mr. Talag yanked away the cloth, unveiling a full-length mirror. He stepped up to it. His dressing gown and slippers were reflected in the glass. But not the body within. Not his head, not his hands. "You see that my condition precludes certain modes of expression. I can, so to speak, hold a mirror up to nature, but not, alas, to myself. I want you to sketch my portrait here, on the face of the mirror."

Fay felt the blood in her veins turn to ice. "I don't understand."

"I think you do," he said. "You'll be giving me a rare gift. Something I parted with a long time ago, never dreaming I would miss it." He struck a pose. "If you're ready, my dear… ?"

Crayons were laid out on a table beside the mirror. Fay picked up a black stick and began to draw. It came easier now, as if her brief exposure to Mr. Talag's influence had improved her talent somehow. Her concentration was so intense that she lost sight of her own reflection in the glass. It seemed to Fay that she was not so much sketching his features upon the surface of the mirror as calling them up from its depths. She lost all track of time. All that existed was the portrait taking shape. When it was done at last, her strength deserted her, as if she'd poured her life's blood into the drawing. She collapsed to the floor.

Mr. Talag was suddenly beside her. He bent as if to kiss her, but she drew back weakly with a despairing moan.

"I simply wish to give you a gift in return for the gift you've given me," he explained.

"I don't want it!"

"You may regret refusing it."

"Please, no…"

"I won't force you." Ignoring her now, he shrugged out of his robe and stepped up to the mirror as if to kiss the face she had sketched there. His body was as white and perfect as a Greek statue. Wisps of fog began to fill the outline of her sketch upon the glass. Fay tried to move, to get away, but her limbs were heavy as stone.

The fog thickened, seemed almost to harden. It spilled down from the neck where she had stopped drawing, overspilling the lines like milky blood, then coalescing into the shape of a man. The body was blurry and unfocused, but the features of that face were preternaturally sharp. It was not Mr. Talag's portrait but instead his reflection that was captured there. Or even more than that somehow, for it seemed realer to her than his own face did. She saw that he was weeping again. Pink tears furrowed his cheeks. He leaned forward with a strange, choking cry that did not seem a perfect imitation of anything.

There was an explosion of light as his lips touched the glass. Then only darkness.

When Fay awoke, she got to her feet and staggered to the mirror, afraid of what she wouldn't see. But there she was, her features superimposed on the sketch of Mr. Talag. It took her a moment to realize that the sketch was no longer a bare outline; the image of Mr. Talag filled it now, like a photograph. She touched it with trembling fingers, disbelieving her eyes. Her reflection gave back a twitchy smile over his pale face, the mouth open in an endless scream, whether of pain or triumph she didn't know and didn't want to know. Pausing only to gather her drawing materials, Fay fled the house.

Outside, it was daylight. Fay wished she had some shades, but it wasn't long before the brightness stopped hurting and she felt more like herself again. When she got home, she slept until the next morning. Then, still exhausted, she dragged herself to a life-drawing class at the Art Students League.

The charcoal felt clumsy in her hand. Try as she might, she couldn't get the figures to come out right. It was as if the lines of communication from her eyes to her hand had been severed. Each flat and lifeless line she drew was like a razor drawn across her soul. Yet she couldn't stop. The other students noticed that something was wrong, and put their own sketches aside to watch. Finally, the instructor asked if she was all right.

Fay had forgotten where she was. Shaking her head, she stuffed her materials into her bag and ran from the room. On the street she hailed a cab and gave Mr. Talag's address, drawn not by hope but by its utter absence.

The townhouse was boarded up, as though no one had lived there for years. No one answered as Fay pounded and kicked at the door. After a while, she turned away. Cedar Street was busy and colorful, with trucks loading and unloading at the warehouses and noisy crowds of buyers jostling each other. She felt like she hadn't seen it, really seen it, until now. There was an instant when the light fell in a certain way, and she reached for her bag, thinking automatically of how she would sketch it. But, again, her hand would not obey. She saw the finished drawing in her mind but could no longer understand how to translate it to paper. Weeping, Fay sank onto the steps.

No one gave her a second look. In New York, every block has its weeping women. Finally, though, a boy crept up beside her and, with the delicacy and daring of an artist, snatched her bag and vanished into the crowd.

Flies in the Ink
by Megan Lee Beals

Henry Nevins drained the bottle of whisky into his burning throat and slammed the empty vessel down onto the table with more force than his feelings should have allowed. In the weeks since his daughter never arrived in Virginia he'd used up all the sorrow he had for this life, and Detective Palmer's news that the search had to be given up for more pressing matters hardly affected him. The kerosene lamp shuddered and he watched it closely through dirty glasses, daring it to fall and light him and the whole damn tattoo shop like a bonfire, but the flame settled before the oil could earnestly slosh. He blew over the top of it, grinning madly at the idea that the fumes of his breath could light those lacey white curtains on fire. They were the last touch remaining of his wife in the dim tattooist parlor, a scant bit of elegance rarely found among the rough Westernly types that sauntered bowlegged into the shop and asked for cowgirls on their forearms or rattlesnakes wrapped around their biceps. These young men knew as much of the Old West as Henry; their daddies worked the shipyard or the rails. A few that came in from the outskirts were loggers. All of them Tacoma boys, Northwesterners, but The War made all of them patriots, and ain't nobody going to mistake a rattlesnake for a Limey's mark. Let no one forget it was the doughboys had to pull those European asses out of the fire.

He scoffed at the little soldier boy he imagined in the appropriated barber's chair across the parlor. He couldn't care for wars. Not since his daughter vanished from a train and no one would do him the decency of telling him how she died. Stories of the Railway Skinner ranked near as high on the front page of *The Tribune* as the invasion of Belgium, but the moniker was noticeably absent from all of Detective Palmer's reports. So Henry tatted up the soldier boys and sent them off to fight a world away, and drank away the evenings until he could sleep again. Tonight's bottle was empty. Sleep would come soon. But his waiting was interrupted by frantic fists pounding on the door.

The shop had been closed for hours. It was far too dark for company, and he was too far in the cellar. But the fists kept pounding and a small girlish voice whimpered, "Please, sir, please let me in!"

Henry's feet found the ground. He drifted toward the door mumbling, "By the hairs of his chinny chin" and fumbled with the latch until the door opened as far as the chain would allow. His girl was there, holding a carpet bag. His little girl Jane with her straw-blond hair, and she was crying.

"I'm so sorry to bother you, sir, but I saw a light on and my husband was meant to meet me at the train station and it's so cold outside and I don't know where to go…"

No, this wasn't Janey. Damned whisky had clouded his eyes again. This girl's eyes were too wide and her teeth were long. She was still talking. Henry shook his head to clear the fumes.

"Please, mister! I just need a place to wait until the tram comes by. It's so cold outside. I won't keep you long." She smiled, pleading, and Henry stared again at those teeth. Teeth shouldn't be that sharp. He peered around the door to get a closer squint-eyed view. The girl wasn't wearing any shoes. No shoes! What kind of girl takes a train without shoes? The liquor took hold of his heart and he damn near cried looking at her poor little frozen feet. He was not so lost a lamb that he couldn't see a girl in need. Henry nodded *yes, yes* and took the chain off the door and opened his heart to her. She stood there, toes touching the threshold.

"I can come in?" she asked at the wide-flung door.

"Yeah, you can come in. Come in. You need some socks, girl," said Henry.

She bull-rushed past him and ran for the other end of his parlor, far from the door and the outside.

He closed the door and held up a hand. "You wait here, girl. I got extra socks in the back. No shoes that'll fit you." The shoes were in his daughter's room under the stairs, all of it untouched since she left on the train. When he got news of her disappearance, he closed the door, denied anyone access, and kept it shrined to her.

The girl cocked her head like a small dog and watched him stumble out of the room. Her snarling face was frozen, confused, and slowly her curled lip lowered over the fangs as she listened to him creak up the stairs into the kitchen. She was hungry, she was always hungry, but the man was a curiosity. The whole place smelled heavy and sharp with liquor. She sat in the large leather barber's chair and waited for her meal to walk back in the room. This prey was too drunk to fight, and just this once, her curiosity could stand to win against her stomach. She wrinkled her nose. There were different smells under the whisky: chemicals, iodine, and soap. She breathed in deeply just as Henry walked back into the room. Under all the smells, she found dried blood.

"What is this place?" she asked harshly, the girlish lilt gone from her voice.

"Tattoo shop," said Henry from around an unlit cigarette. "Here, girly. They'll be big, but they're clean and warm." He pressed a pair of good wool socks into her hands. "What's your name?"

"Betty," she said. The name was two years old. She had acquired it shortly after peeling herself out of a putrid black pool of violent death to find herself surrounded by the pieces of an older man and woman with torn out throats. Her first memory was the feel of her cold hand over her own smooth neck and the noticeable lack of a pulse. The name might once have been hers. The people, too, might have been important, but she had no memory of either. "Betty" belonged more to a letter pinned on the frame of a mirror in that death-soiled house written from "your beloved cousin" in Nashville. No one had ever asked her name.

"Name's Henry. Henry Nevins." He pointed vaguely to the backwards letters on the window above the name of his shop. She wasn't putting on the socks. He took them from her and unfolded them, then bent to help her put them on. The invasive effects of the liquor were waning now with someone to protect, but the whisky still toyed with his eyes. "Where'd your shadow get to, Betty?" He laughed as he said it under his breath.

Betty pulled her feet up onto the chair and bristled. "You're talking crazy, Mr. Nevins."

Henry tossed the socks onto her lap. "You can do it yourself, then."

Betty was staring at the board of tattoos on the wall. Most were the ones you could get anywhere. Eagles. Snakes. But her eyes were on the top left corner, where Henry kept his own designs sketched from the stories he and Jane used to read together. He read to her until she learned the letters, and for years after she'd follow him around the house and read her favorite passages and ask him to draw the characters. Henry held his forehead to avoid looking at the wall. He couldn't remember the last time Jane read to him.

"Why does this place smell like blood?" asked Betty.

Henry sniffed at the room. His head was hurting, and this girl was odd.

"Did you draw all those?" she asked, eyes trained on the wall.

"Not all of them."

"That bat." She pointed at the drawing of the woman, half-naked with a long red scarf wrapped tight around her throat. A large bat held her in its wings. It was a gruesome drawing, one his daughter insisted upon, and one he left on the wall in tribute to her. Henry had read *Dracula* to his daughter twice when she was little. She must have read it three times at least after that.

Henry and Jane were alone with each other. His wife died in childbirth, the rest of the family lived in Virginia, and in secret defiance of his wife's meddlesome family, he tattooed his daughter one week before she left. Janey begged him for the drawing of Dracula, and he obligingly depicted it between her shoulder blades, but he covered the woman in a modest negligee. "It's beautiful, Mr. Nevins. But the wings are a little off. They don't bend like that."

He looked up at the drawing, barely visible in the gloom. The girl was staring at it, unblinking, and her mouth was parted just enough to show the points of her fangs. The mirror he used for his clients hung over her shoulder and reflected an empty chair. His fingers buzzed, but the liquor was too long ago to be to blame.

"This isn't real. You're a vampire."

She nodded slowly and settled into the barber's chair. "Yes. I was going to drink your blood. Do you have a tattoo? On your skin? I love tattoos. I once met an illustrated man on the train going from Nebraska."

Henry looked around the room for a weapon, or a cross. His hand rested on a little vial of blue ink. "What do you mean 'was'?"

"I mean that I'm not going to drink your blood, Mr. Nevins. I'm an artist, too. Us artists have got to stick together, right? If I draw something for your wall can you put it on someone's skin?"

"Only if they'll ask for it. I don't choose for people."

She smiled brightly, showing the long fangs. "They'll ask for it. I'm a great artist."

Henry chuckled, at her enthusiasm, at death, at the long impossible night he'd been having.

"What are you laughing at," asked Betty, her eyes narrowed to evil, reddened slits.

"That's real kind of you, Betty. Real lady-like. Thank you for not drinking my blood." He laughed harder and bowed to the scruffy little barefoot girl in his barber's chair. She straightened in it like a queen, then flung herself from the chair to thrust a long finger at Henry's chest.

"Don't think you're off the hook, mister. See, you've invited me into your house, and now I can come and go as I please. A girl's got needs other than a full belly, and as I said, I'm new in town…"

Henry shrunk under the vampire's finger and held up his hands in protest. "Look, kid, you are way too young."

"A place to stay, Mr. Nevins!" She huffed at him. "You're lucky I'm an artist, too, or I'd never forgive your wicked temperament."

Henry blinked, hard, and shook his head to drive away the dream. When he looked up again, he saw Betty's eyes staring into his own. Her face was softer, and her voice was light, so like his Jane when she was little, begging another hour to read before bedtime.

"It's late, Mr. Nevins. You're going to go to sleep, and I'm going to take that room off the parlor." She turned her head to indicate the closed door to Jane's room, and Henry weakly shook his head, unable to protest any further than that. "The door will be locked in the morning, and you won't open it up for anything. Goodnight, Mr. Nevins. Sweet dreams." She kissed him on his forehead, and he slumped over, asleep in her waiting arms. She lifted him into the barber's chair and pulled up his shirt sleeves to check the wrists. Betty clucked her tongue at the bare arms, then opened his shirt to check above the heart. Her first guess was wrist, but with those smudgy glasses he looked like he could be a heart man. There, fuzzy from fine blond chest hair was a bright blue swallow with a golden heart in its beak. She buttoned up his shirt and left him on the chair.

❦

Henry awoke to the bright winter sun streaming in through the window. He was on his barber's chair, his watch was unwound, and a muffled voice yelled to him through the glass. Henry rubbed his face and got up, went to the door, and met Charlie Kane, his twelve-thirty appointment.

"Should I reschedule?" Charlie glanced sideways at the tattooist's red eyes, the stubble on his chin. Henry gulped down a glass of water and got reacquainted with sobriety.

"No, no. Couldn't do that to a fella just before he ships out. It was an eagle?"

Charlie nodded and pointed up at the flash wall. He settled on an eagle gripping a knife in its talon. Henry grabbed the card off the wall, but his eye was caught by an askew card. It was his woman held by a bat, carefully redrawn and hung over the original drawing. She'd corrected the wing, and lowered the eyes of the woman, making her more demure and satisfied with the horror inflicted by his Dracula. Henry glanced to the door leading to the small room under the stairs. She was in there. The vampire. His cheeks flushed and he placed Betty's card back on the wall, then started up the machine. Charlie flinched as Henry swabbed his back with alcohol, and

Henry settled into a normal day.

He tried, in between appointments, and after washing his face, and late in the day when he closed up shop and made a tasteless dinner of tinned sardines and old bread, to open the door to his daughter's room. Each time he walked past, his hand would almost reach to press against the door, but a cold pit of dread would open up in his stomach and he'd go back to the kitchen and pace. A vampire was haunting his daughter's room, violating her memory.

Among the discarded daily contrivances littering the alley behind his shop, he found a broken chair, and spent his evening sharpening one leg to a wooden stake. He might have bought garlic, had he thought of it before the grocers closed for the evening.

Henry stowed his weapon in the little end table next to his tattooist's chair. He took everything out of it, cleaned his tools, and placed them back in around the stake, as if it were another instrument used to mark the skin. With the table organized, he moved to the rest of the parlor. His evening was consumed with cleaning and he was almost able to forget the reason he started until the whole shop gleamed deep orange and red from the sunset. When he heard a flutter behind the door to his daughter's room, he set the rag down and stood at attention. The sun dipped behind the mountains. The Puget Sound turned black. Jane's door opened, and Betty smiled winningly at him with her arms stretched over her head.

"Did you see?" she asked. "I fixed your bat." She yawned and clipped over to him in a pair of new brown shoes that Henry never could have afforded. He disliked them, they were flashy, but he was relieved she did not wear his daughter's things.

Betty took the card off the wall and handed it to him, leaning in too close to his arm. Her hair was glued to her head in grimy clumps, and her face was still sooty from the train.

"You found some shoes?"

She laughed. "That's not all I found! Some high-society lady was cavorting outside the Rialto last night with a boy half her age. The boy got away, but that lady was a bleeder. More than enough to quiet my rumbly stomach."

Henry paled. "You killed her?"

Betty cocked her head. "What do you care? You know anyone with tickets to the Rialto last night?"

"That's not the point, Betty. You can't go round killing people if you're staying in my house."

She grinned and nodded. "Of course, of course. Did you tattoo the improved picture on anyone while I slept?"

He shook his head. She pouted. "Poo. It's all right, though. Your design was nice, but I've got some real knock-out ideas."

Henry looked past her shoulder to his daughter's darkened room. The door was closed. He willed himself to run to it, and lock the vampire out, but his feet would not obey. Betty tugged on Henry's shirtsleeves.

"Aren't you curious, Mr. Nevins? You do want to try something new, right?"

Henry sighed and sat down hard on the stool next to the barber's chair. "This whole situation is new, Betty." He kept glancing at the mirror to affirm her lack of reflection. "I just don't think I really need an artist in residence, you know?"

Betty pursed her lips over the fangs and raised one eyebrow high. "You have it all wrong, Henry. You are working for me. I can still kill you at any time."

"Right. Because you're a vampire." Saying it aloud made it no less ridiculous. Betty didn't see the joke.

"You caught on pretty quick, Mr. Nevins. Most people don't call me that until I've got my teeth in their neck."

His eyes swept over to the door to Jane's room, then snapped down to the floor. "I've read *Dracula* more than a few times." He smiled, in spite of himself. "I recognized the signs."

"Dracula?" asked Betty.

Henry's smile faltered, and he sighed at the vampire sitting in his parlor. "There are a lot of books in that room you stole from me, Betty. You ought to read a few."

She sneered at him. "No need to make personal remarks. Fetch me some of those little paper cards and a pen. Your art board wants refreshing."

Henry resisted the urge to bow before turning to dig out some old cardstock from the supply cupboards. He glanced in Betty's direction, but didn't take the cards to her. He tested the freedom further by hesitating at Jane's door, but that was still off limits. He carried his rebellion into the kitchen and tossed the cards onto the table. Henry was free of all obligation save that regarding his daughter's door. He heard Betty get up from the chair in the parlor, and reveled in the ability to ignore her by busying himself with the coffee pot. She sat down at the table and began to sketch. With the pot on to boil, and the vampire lost in her drawings, Henry left to stand at the threshold of his daughter's room. He couldn't raise his hand to open the door. Betty coughed; a forced and unnecessary sound, and called to him from the table.

"You can't go in there, Henry. That's my room, now."

Henry clenched his fists. "When's the last time you touched a bar of soap, Betty?" The scribbling in the kitchen stopped. Chair legs scrapped across the floor.

"I hadn't much a chance to wash on the train, you lout. There's no call for cruelty about it."

He walked back into the kitchen to find her standing over the sink. She was shifting about the mugs and plates stacked there; life without Jane left Henry with excess, and little remembrance for doing his own dishes. She spun on him as he approached her. "You aren't making it easy on me, hiding the damn soap. And if I bothered you so much, you only had to say something."

Henry leaned down and got a bar of soap from under the sink. He handed it to her, and adjusted the water so it wasn't so hot it would burn her hands. "I can get you some towels," he said in apology.

"Yes, thank you. This whole business doesn't have to be unpleasant, you know. I can be a very kind employer." She took the towels from him and scrubbed her face.

He took the coffee off the stove and sat down with a cup. "Why do you want to run my tattoo shop, kid?"

She started on her hair. "I'm not running the shop, that's still on you. But I want to see my drawings on somebody's skin. You need to do that for me, Henry. I love tattoos. I just can't imagine anything lovelier than someone wearing around my ideas." She paused to run the towel over her head and wrap up her sopping hair. "When somebody asks for my drawing, you have to make the appointment for night so I can see you put down the ink."

Henry sipped his coffee and leaned across the table to take a look at her cards. As he picked up the top card, she spun around and snatched it from his hand. Water dripped down from her hands and hair and spread to the card, bleeding the ink. "Oh now look what you did. No peeking until I'm done. You should know better, as an artist."

Henry's shoulders slumped and he shook his head at the impetuous dripping thing in his kitchen. "Some rules. You just demanded to watch my work start to finish."

She smiled at him and patted his head. "That's because I'm the boss. Now, you should get some sleep while I finish up. Tomorrow night you'll be tattooing late. And I get to watch!"

He fought back a yawn and tried to finish his cup, but it had been a long day, and last night's sleep was in a cramped barber's chair. Henry pushed his chair back from the table and went upstairs to bed. He drifted to sleep smiling, as the girl worked contentedly in the kitchen below.

His kitchen table was clean when he woke, with ten carefully stacked cards set in the middle next to a note decorated with tiny flowers. The dishes were done, minus one broken plate left in a puddle of water on the counter, and the towels were folded and wet. He hung the towels on the back of the chairs to dry properly and read through Betty's note.

> *Your kitchen was in a deplorable state. I cleaned it to improve my own productivity. Here are ten new designs. I've already thrown out the ten worst ones on your wall, and I am well on my way to improving the*

rest of them. See you when the sun goes down.
Yours sincerely,
Betty

The note ended with a carefully etched black heart that dripped dry ink down the page. Henry combed his fingers through his hair as he leafed through the new cards. The designs were beautiful, but far too intricate. She sketched insects for him, bees and hornets and flies, with lines in their wings so fine they were more felt than seen. And flies? What maniac would stain his skin with flies? He went to the parlor to fit her new cards on the wall. She had removed most of the eagles, and a few of the uglier roses. The wall was spotty, and she left the unworthy cards piled together on the floor. None of his own designs were discarded, and he hung her new cards next to his in unconscious pride. Henry picked the cards up from the floor and slipped them into his back pocket, then left for the diner down the block.

He had coffee and eggs. Later he bought sardines, potatoes, a fresh loaf of bread, and in a moment of whimsy, three carrots. The greengrocer had garlic. He decided against buying garlic. Henry Nevins had no appointments that day, and he did not open his business for walk-ins. He went to bed early, excited to wake when the sun went down.

Betty knocked at the threshold of the open room upstairs where Henry once slept with his wife. Henry rolled out of bed fully dressed, his mouth tasting old and stale, and he found his smudged glasses with the palm of his hand.

"We have an appointment, Mr. Nevins."

Henry pushed his glasses up his nose and squinted at the smiling girl at his door. "You're up already?"

"It's nearly midnight. I can't find the keys, so you need to unlock the door for him."

He did, and let in a haggard old man who smelled of soured wine and sourer clothes. Henry's lip curled and he looked past the man at Betty, grinning with all her teeth as she took the man by hand and led him to the barber's chair.

"Betty, the shop's not open this late. Sir, I'm sorry, this is all a mistake."

The man coughed and reached into his crusty coat to pull out a fat wad of bills that he waved in the air. "S'no problem of money. I got money."

"He has an appointment, Mr. Nevins. Didn't you check the datebook today?" She clucked her tongue and put on airs of disapproval. "You had the whole day in the bright sunshine and didn't even think to check that datebook. Well, no matter." Betty turned back to the man in the chair. "You just sit tight there, Jack. Mr. Nevins is truly a knock-out tattooist, even if he can't remember his dates. But that's what he has me for!"

Jack nodded sleepily and smiled at Henry. "Great girl you got here."

"Sure..." muttered Henry as he ran his finger across the datebook to find "Jack" written down for twelve o' clock midnight. The handwriting matched Betty's note from the morning. He called her over and motioned for her to follow into the kitchen, where he grasped her little shoulders and shoved her down into a chair. She sat without argument and folded her hands in her lap.

"You're angry with me."

Henry dragged a chair close to her and sat down. "You're messing about my business, Betty. Where'd that old bum get the dough he flashed at me?"

She shrugged. "He had the cash when he made the appointment last night. I was just taking a little walk outside and he found me and said 'Hey aren't you that girl from the tattoo shop?' and I said 'Yes, certainly, I keep house for the tattooist' because you know I did those dishes, and then he wanted a tattoo and I figured if he was awake so late one night he won't mind the next so I made the appointment for late. I just want to see you do it, Henry. I want to see how it's done."

He narrowed his eyes and stared at her until she blinked and turned away. "Are you stealing from me, Betty?"

"No!" She looked him true, with eyes wide and wet at the idea of being called a thief. Henry did not buckle, and her face grew feral. "You don't got that kind of money in this house, anyway," she said, baring her teeth.

Henry knew she was right. Jack coughed up a lung in the parlor. Betty jerked her head at the kitchen door, her face back to its girlish pout. "You got a customer waiting."

Henry grabbed a basin from under the sink and filled it with water.

"You want to watch, you got to help me clean him up first."

Betty took the soap from the sink and skipped out of the room. Henry just sighed.

Jack chose Betty's fly. He wanted it on his chest, crawling down from the right collar bone. Betty washed his skin with care, and stood at attention with a damp cloth that was both unneeded and unasked for. She watched until the blood started to well and mingle with the ink, then her eyes glazed and she leaned in so close she nearly hit Henry's hand. Henry lifted up for a moment and growled from around his cigarette. "Take a walk, kiddo."

"Yes, sir," she said, and walked out of the parlor in a trance. Henry didn't see her split apart into a hundred bats and fly off into the sky. Jack was too drunk to care.

Henry had a habit of staying up late to watch Betty work. As the sun began to set he'd put a pot of coffee on the stove and set out the pens on the table. Henry placed his favorite nearest the stack of paper. The nib was gold, a birthday present from Jane and far too fancy for him. But he liked it, and she, the girl locked away in his daughter's room, delighted in the bright, fine things that eventually fell into humble city homes.

"You're not rich, but you sure got class, Henry," she told him one Sunday night with the end of the pen notched in her fangs.

Henry had been retracing some of her less macabre designs onto paper to train his muscles in her lines. The task was mindless and cheerful and he could watch her sketch her nasty insects from across the table, but at the word "class" he set down his pen and eyed the woman over the sparkling clean lenses of his glasses.

"I got class," he repeated, sullenly, and she laughed out loud. "What makes you think I got any class?"

She shrugged and set his favorite pen down on top of a loose sketch of a blackbird rending apart the flesh upon which it would be inked. "You do. You got airs about you that I'd never have. Can't have airs when you come from a hole in the dirt."

Henry furrowed his eyebrows. "You mean like Dracula?" She had been reading the book, and they had discussed their mutual admiration of Mina Harker, but about her own vampirism she remained coy. He only knew that she drank blood and couldn't stand the sun.

"No, not like Dracula. You don't think I got a damn crypt hidden away in that little room, do you? The place I woke up in, as a vampire I mean, wasn't more than just a little hole carved into a hillside in the middle of nowhere. It had two beds, a stove, and one window peering out across a dead scabby land with a dead scabby garden that couldn't feed a mouse. I don't know who I was before I was this, but I know she didn't have any airs about her."

Henry reached across the table to take her hands, but she pulled them back and reached up to her throat.

"I don't know how I got made like this. But I know I haven't made anyone else like me. So I may not be good, but I'm not evil."

"You killed that woman at the Rialto."

Her hands dropped into her lap. "I had to eat someone, Henry. I didn't want it to be you."

"You don't have to kill them, though. Doctors can give blood and they can take it. A man can lose a little blood and still get by."

A smile briefly flashed across her face and she gripped her arms tight to steady herself. "You're right, Henry. Just a little blood won't kill."

She couldn't stop at just a little blood. The hunger took her as the first drop hit the tongue. The hunger replaced Betty. There was no Betty, only the bats—flocking and frantic at the smell of blood. They cannot stop until a body falls dead on the floor, eyes milky and skin completely pale. It ends before she can think to pull away. The hunger eats until sated, and leaves poor Betty alone to deal with the bodies.

Two years was not enough time to get used to the bodies. But it was time enough for practice. She took to the rails when the death of the illustrated man caused a manhunt in Nebraska. Betty roosted in the boxcars with the luggage and animals that screamed and thrashed at her unnatural smell. At night she walked up and down the passenger cars in borrowed clothes until she found a lonely person who wouldn't be missed. The hunger let Betty choose her victims, and it led them out onto the deck where the engine would mask their screams. When the feeding ended Betty rolled the bodies off the end of the cars to be found months later with her several states away. A decent way to see the country, but by the time the rails ended in Tacoma, Betty was ready to settle down.

"Betty?" asked Henry.

She looked down to see her fingernails had pierced the flesh, and bored down into the muscle.

"Betty, darling, you're hurting yourself," said Henry, and he got up from the table to help her. She loosed her fingers and rubbed away the sludge-black blood that seeped out of the quickly closing wounds. Henry wet a washcloth, but the marks faded from her skin before he could hand it to her. She took it anyway and held it tightly in her lap.

"It's all right, Betty. It doesn't matter where you come from. You're living with me, now."

Her head snapped upwards, and she met his eyes with a glare. "I'm not living. Not really."

Henry shook his head. "You're living enough to make a mess of my kitchen every night and beg me for ink. That's living if you ask me. And you're not going to kill anymore, because you've got a place to stay, all right?"

Betty nodded and placed a hand over her stomach. It was always tight, always hungry. Soon it would be impossible to ignore. But Henry was so sweet to her. He wanted so badly to make the monster into a good little girl that he gave her everything she asked for. And he let her design the tattoos. So she smiled with lips closed over the fangs and hugged him tightly as the rushing blood in his heart drowned away every word but the ones he wanted to hear.

"I won't kill anymore, Henry. Just a little blood. I'll be good. I'll be good."

The first body found in Tacoma was lying on the beach, skinned and drained of blood. It washed ashore a month and a half after Betty came to stay in Henry's daughter's room on the opposite side of the port from Union Station, but the papers quickly attributed it to the Railway Skinner. Henry ignored the papers while he shopped for new pens, and he paid for penny candies at the counter before remembering that Betty had no use for them. His shop had become a night operation in the weeks since Betty came to stay, and more of his clients chose insects and bats off his wall. Betty was by his side while he worked. Her stomach had grown stronger at the sight of the little blood that would break through the skin when the needle traced her art, and she could stay the hunger until the work was finished.

Business picked up when Henry moved to odd hours. His was the last shop before the train station, and news of his macabre designs spread among the dock workers and loggers who wanted a token of home before going off to war. Most were happy to oblige his late hours, but it was Betty who charmed them at the door with a close-lipped smile and convinced them a tattoo made at midnight had more power.

Once, Betty tried to take the needle. She begged Henry to let her, on a handsome young man named Teddy Keene who asked in the same earnest voice as hers. Both of them insisted that ink on skin couldn't be so different than ink on paper, and Henry was by now so taken with the girl that he let her try. She stuck it too deep, right away, and the blood welled up bright and red.

Betty bit the boy. She unhinged her jaw and set her jagged teeth into his shoulder and drank until he passed out from fear or from pain. Henry flung the small table aside and wrenched her up from the boy's shoulder, his hand grasping at the drawer for the wooden stake. But there were tears in Betty's eyes, and her hands covered her mouth in shame.

"I'm so sorry, Mr. Nevins. I'll never… I'll never…"

Henry held her and kissed her head. He sent her to her room, and cleaned the boy's wound. He shoved a fiver in Teddy's pocket and carried him two blocks to the bar, woke him enough to get some whisky down his gullet as he comforted the kid about that dog bite on his shoulder. Poor Teddy; a bite like that would need at least a month to heal, and he didn't protest when Henry made the appointment for noon.

※

Teddy's body was found under the Eleventh Street Bridge a week later by a longshoreman and his dog. The skin was removed from his left shoulder, and not an ounce of blood remained in his veins. The newspapers got to the scene before the police, and *The Tribune* ran a picture of Teddy's face under the headline "Railway Skinner: Last Stop, Tacoma." Henry didn't see that paper, but news of the boy's death was brought directly to his door.

Detective Palmer pounded his fist on the door of Henry's shop late that evening, breaking Henry from his trance as he set up the inks for his first appointment of the night. Henry unlocked the door and opened it as wide as the chain allowed. His mouth parted slightly at the sight of the detective, and he opened the door wordlessly, afraid to even mention her name. Palmer shook his head.

"It isn't Jane, Henry. I'm sorry."

Henry nodded, sullen, and went back to his inks.

"I'm not interrupting anything, am I?"

Henry glanced over to where Betty slept behind his daughter's door. "Just laying out my first appointment, detective. What are you here for?"

The detective cleared his throat. "Do you remember a fella by the name Teddy Keene?"

Henry stayed his messing with the inks and stood straight. "Yeah. He was in just last week. He wanted a cockroach on his shoulder in blue ink." Henry placed himself between Palmer and the door to Jane's room.

"A cockroach?" asked Palmer.

Henry forced a laugh. "Got quite a call for insects lately," he said, and pointed up to the flash wall where Betty's cards were hung. Palmer shuddered.

"Can't imagine why anyone would want a cockroach. Did Teddy act funny at all while he was here?"

Henry shrugged. "Don't know him well enough to say if he seemed off."

"Anything odd happen that night?"

Henry leaned back against his barber's chair and crossed his arms to keep the detective from seeing his heart race. "Yeah," said Henry as he pictured Betty's teeth clamp down before she could finish the line work. "He got cold feet after the first few pricks. He wasn't sure if his mother would approve of her boy getting inked. I told him not to worry about it, patched him up, and said we could finish another time. Or change the picture. Then I walked him down to the bar, we had a few drinks and parted ways."

"You didn't see anyone follow him?"

"What's this about, detective?"

"Some fella in the port found Teddy's body this morning. He was missing the skin off that shoulder."

Henry doubled over his stomach. "Jesus, Palmer!"

"We can't get a single lead on this, Henry. The papers think it's the Railway Skinner, but it doesn't fit. The Bureau has been on that case for over a year, and the bodies are littered all across the country. There've been four like this in Tacoma over the last month, but the Skinner never stays in the same place for this long. Damn papers have been reporting the Skinner's every move. My money says we've got a fan of his work trying to duplicate it closer to home."

Henry shook his head, hand over his mouth.

"You were my last hope for this kid, Henry. You might have been the last one to see him alive."

Henry collected himself for a moment. "Sorry, detective. I don't remember seeing anyone else that night. Maybe check at the bar."

Detective Palmer stared at him for a moment then held out his hand to shake. "I'll give that a shot. Thanks' Henry. If you think of anything else, just give me a call."

It was thirty minutes past sunset when Detective Palmer left the tattoo shop. Henry drew the curtains and turned his sign to read "closed." From the other side of the door, Betty quietly tapped the wall.

"Betty? Did you kill that boy?"

The tapping stopped. "I'm so sorry, Henry."

He stood silent next to the door, unable to touch the wood to break it down.

"Henry? Are you mad at me?"

Henry leaned against the wall next to the door.

"I can't help it, Henry. It just happens."

"You know it's wrong, Betty."

"It is wrong. I know. But I treat them so well." She opened up the door and stood fast in the entrance. "I want to show you something." Her cold frail fingers held onto his hand and she led him into his daughter's room. "Look, I don't forget about them like some old piece of meat. I love them."

Henry stood back in the room and let his eyes adjust to the gloom. The weak light from the parlor hit the walls and illuminated the skins tacked onto the plaster. Rawhide; cleanly cut from the flesh, but preserved by an inexpert hand. Most were small, hardly bigger than the cards she drew on, showing common flash pieces of sparrows and hearts. Her centerpiece, lit up by the doorway, was big enough for Henry to imagine the man who once wore it. It was carved from the shoulders and neck, around both sides, and down even to the buttocks, every inch inked with fish and mermaids and full sail ships. The knife she'd used had cut across some of the pictures. The whole man must have been tattooed head to toe.

"This one is my favorite," she whispered as she took down a large piece from the frame of the mirror and passed it to him. It was the fly Henry tattooed across that old man's chest two months ago. The ink was seated well into the flesh, the scarring from the needle had healed seamlessly. She must have waited weeks after that night before she killed him.

"You did beautiful work of my drawing, Henry. I couldn't just let that walk away," she said as he set down the fly.

"Why'd you do this, Betty?"

"They're just so pretty, Henry. I couldn't let them go to waste."

"They're calling you the Railway Skinner," he said as he rounded the room. Over the doorjamb was a meager scrap of skin stretched out against the wall. It was wet and chalky. Torn where the needle tried to ink the skin. Teddy Keene. She'd stuck the knife into the marks made by her teeth and skinned him just hours after he left the bar. To the left of the door, over the little desk where his daughter used to illustrate all the stories they once read together, was a larger patch of skin. It depicted a young woman with a long red scarf collapsed into the wings of an enormous bat. Jane.

His blood drained. His stomach lurched, and Henry could not tear his eyes away from the remains of his daughter. The Railway Skinner stood next to him, and all he could think was how that idiot detective didn't pin his daughter's case to the biggest serial killer in the country. He turned, slowly, and faced the small woman who smiled at him with parted lips just barely showing the tips of her fangs.

"Do you want a tattoo, Betty?" he asked. His face was hard as stone and he prayed she could not hear his heart beating against his chest.

She laughed. "I got so many."

"These ain't yours," he said, and his body was again under his control. He walked out of the room, slamming the door behind him and nearly caught her heels as she tried to follow.

"Henry, please, I thought you'd understand."

"I understand that you got a thing for tattoos, Betty. And I'm offering to give you one." He forced a smile for her and pulled the chain to turn on all the lights around the barber's chair. Betty flinched away. Henry took his inks out of the drawer and began to mix them. He glanced up at the clock and calculated the time till sunrise.

"Henry, I can't get a tattoo. You've seen my skin—it just closes up so fast."

She was shivering in the middle of the room.

"I know you want this, Betty. So where do you want it?"

She walked to him, and turned to let him unbutton her dress.

"I might hurt you," she said over her shoulder. "Sometimes I just hurt things when they scare me. So I might hurt you."

He unfastened her dress down to the small of her back and motioned for her to lie on the reclined chair. She sat.

"All across my back. I want that fly. Exactly as I drew it. No variation. Center the wings on my shoulder blades, and the head points down." She craned her neck to look at him in the eye. "I might kill you if this hurts."

He nodded without meeting her gaze. "It's going to hurt." He flicked the switch on the machine to start the needle vibrating and began to freehand the fly onto her skin, digging the needle deep.

She flinched under his hand, and a thin black line appeared on the small of her back. Her skin came apart at the line and fluttered upward. She whimpered and gripped the edge of the seat, and the skin grew back together. He worked calmly, etching away the minutes till sunrise, taking care with every tiny line in the fly's wings. The lines he carved into her skin with the needle closed almost too quickly for the ink to seep in. He ran over his work twice for every line, and kept a steady pace as the clock wound down. At ten minutes to six, he pressed down hard through the skin and broke into the muscle.

"Stop, Henry!" She growled, and the skin peeled up from under the needle in three leathery black wings. He started backwards, nearly dropping the needle as she spun to face him. Her eyes were all black, and faint patterns of wings crossed her face. "You're hurting me on purpose!"

Henry straightened on the stool and stared down at her, unafraid. "You can't go under the needle without a little pain, Betty."

Betty set her jaw as she realized her mistake. She shouldn't have shown him the skins. He wasn't ready. But they belonged to her, the skin and the blood and the lives she took to go on living, they were gifts from that endless hunger. And the girl with Dracula tattooed between her shoulder blades, Betty brought her back to him, in the blood that lingered in her veins. But Henry could never understand the service she'd done him, and she snarled, baring her fangs. "You don't have any right to be mad at me! I never lied about what I am."

Henry set down the needle and turned off the machine. "You killed my daughter," he said, and the fury finally surfaced in white hot rage. His hand closed around the wooden chair leg he'd sharpened to a stake. "You killed my Janey and you knew it all this time." His voice broke over the words, and he choked back the tears. He stood, and Betty backed away as the skin on her face began to peel. "I'm never going to let you kill again," he said, and he lunged for her heart with the stake.

"You don't have a choice!" she screamed at him with the last of her face as her skin tore into wings and swarmed into a hundred bats. The swarm descended upon him, taking small bites from his skin. He ducked his head and stumbled back toward the window, swatting away at her when he could dare to leave his neck unguarded. His hands were nicked and bleeding; bats clung to his arms, and the sun rose up over the city and Henry tore the lace curtains down. The bats screamed and Betty flocked up from him and flew in a swirling mass into his daughter's room. She slammed the door as soon as she had hands, and he heard the click of the lock.

"Don't you dare open this door, Henry Nevins! I'll kill you if you open this door!"

He ignored her screaming and began to pack his inks and needles into a small crate. He took his cards off the wall and set them in with the rest of his equipment. Henry collected the cards she drew, then pushed the lot under the door. He grinned without joy as he heard her feet scamper back toward the bed.

"I never wanted to hurt you, Henry. You pushed me! You hurt me first!" Her voice was frantic and strained, and he heard flapping. "I didn't know she was yours."

He left her alone to stare at the door in her room full of decorated skins as the stairs creaked over her head. Something large hit the floor above her, and he dragged it down the stairs, thudding on every step. He glanced over to the door as he packed his life into the large black chest, and saw Betty's smoking fingertips scoot his daughter's skin under the door. The fingers drew back and she whimpered behind the door. "I'm sorry, Henry." Her voice was tired and thin. "I'm so sorry."

Henry draped a dishcloth over the remains of his daughter and gingerly packed it into his chest, unwilling to touch the sacred thing with his bare hands should his fingers burn away.

"I'm sorry, too, Betty," he said as he emptied a bottle of kerosene on the door.

"No!" she barked as he struck a match. He held it to the door until the flames caught on strong, then left the house with his chest and walked down to the train station. He was on the train to California before he heard the sirens wail and barrel up the hill. The firemen saw a room full of skins burn away as they searched for survivors, but when the flames were extinguished nothing was left of Henry's shop but cinders and ash.

The Hungry Living Dead
by Nancy Kilpatrick

At last I have died the true death and am in Hell, Réjean thought. He paused on the sidewalk, assaulted by the discordant sounds escaping through the cracks in the red brick wall. This club, like many others he had been to, was located in a run-down area of the city, in a structure built more than one hundred years ago. Not a particularly creative period architecturally, he thought, but at least it holds a flavor that the modern slabs of concrete and steel piercing the sky lack.

He sighed. They were all alike, these places. Follow the steps down into the chilled earth. Over the worn door with a peephole hangs the inevitable, nearly invisible sign, this one with the word *Sanctuary* burned into a black plastic chevron. Knock and, provided you look the part, they open unto you.

Inside, the air was dense and stale, pungent with the odors of sweat, tobacco, and a variety of intoxicants. His nostrils stung; his aesthetics were offended. A cacophony of instruments and voices careened off the black walls, impaling all in their path. A tomb for the living, he thought. Dank. Filthy. Hidden. Crawling with repugnant life forms. At least it was dark.

He had come here out of desperation. They possessed blood. The ruby river of life would be tainted with impurities, but he needed it to survive. It was abundant here. And, more importantly, they gave it willingly.

Réjean moved to a gloomy corner. He felt dozens of voracious eyes staking his back. His costume fit the purpose: a greatcoat and pants of velvet, and a silk ascot, all ebony, of course. His shirt glittered knife-blade silver. The high calfskin boots were a color light could not penetrate; his heels clicked smartly against the painted concrete floor, but only he could distinguish the sound amidst the cacophony. A layered cape rested on his broad shoulders, the type he had once worn in daylight, when he had walked as one of the living.

These youths loved theatrics, and the outfit, the most flamboyant in the room, attracted them, which was why he wore it. He swung the cape back over one shoulder dramatically, laid the cane with the silver wolf's head tip on top of the small round table, and then sat. He removed the gloves slowly, for effect, scanning the room with disdain. Even before he draped the leather gloves across the cane, a female stumbled toward him.

Young, barely twenty, emaciated, as most of them were. Dressed in black, from her fashionable Doc Martins, tights, miniskirt and Gothic lace blouse, to the leather jacket she wore, the front studded with safety pins and stainless steel grommets. The back, he knew, would display a grisly picture of a skull, or a fanged version of Murnau's *Nosferatu*. Her shaved scalp made her eyes appear large and liquid. As she neared, he noticed a spider tattooed on one side of her bare head.

Silently he gestured for her to sit. She nearly lost her balance but finally perched on the edge of the chair opposite him. She stared at him and tugged at the dozens of earrings and clips along her left outer ear. He knew the game perfectly; withholding would force her out. Eventually, she sucked in her generous lower lip, painted mold green, took a drag from a nearly finished cigarette, then blurted, "You look just like Lestat!"

He'd heard this before, of course. Many times. The look was intentional and he had often silently thanked Mrs. Rice for painting such a clear portrait that resembled him. He laid his head back against the wall, lowered his eyelids and stared down his nose at this *fille* in what he knew would convey a taste of the danger she craved. She had seen such looks in vampire movies. She knew how to respond.

The girl moved her chair closer. As she did so, *Interview with the Vampire* fell from her jacket pocket. They both reached down to pick up the worn paperback. Their fingers touched.

"You're ice!" she said, shocked. Intrigued. Her breath stank of beer and cigarettes. The dross of other substances seeped from her pores.

"You can melt me," he assured her, his voice floating along the air.

"How?" She took an agitated drag, but only the filter was left. Her eyes glittered.

"I think you know." He heard her heartbeat quicken and felt the vibration as strongly as if he held that organ in his palm.

She glanced across the room and gestured wildly to a male sitting at the table she had vacated. He joined them immediately. Tall, painfully lean, holes in the requisite spots in his black denim pants and tight tank top. A ferret hung over the back of his neck, under his tied-back jet hair. The rat-like animal, sensing danger, scurried beneath the motorcycle jacket.

The male noisily dragged over a chair and sat with them. Réjean inhaled the odor of tart sweat wafting from his body, tinged with an undercurrent of sweet sex. The young man's lashes were stained and lined in black, creating an androgynous look. His glassy eyes shone intensely, but he was not as intoxicated as the girl.

"Jason, man." The boy held a palm up to be grabbed in the modern ritual of greeting.

"I am Réjean." He grasped the warm hand and held it; Jason, too, felt the chill. The expression of disbelief on the young face faded to excitement.

"Man, like are you really the undead?"

"Of course." There was no need to hide the truth. So many people drank blood now, every newspaper and magazine, every TV talk show featured stories of *real* vampires, that Réjean knew he could safely disguise himself as one of these deviants. Whatever these two before him believed was irrelevant. "For the blood is the life," he said knowingly, stating clearly his true purpose for being here.

"You got it, man!"

"Hey," the girl pipped up, "tell us about, like, how it was, you know, when you were human and everything. And how you got to be a vampire."

"Yeah, let's hear some stories. You must have been like a prince or something." The young man pulled a plastic box from his jacket, opened it and took out three capsules, which he swallowed. The girl helped herself. The box was offered to Réjean.

He stared at them blankly. They were famished infants, squalling to be fed. And yet even if he could feed them, which he could not, they would never be full. "Perhaps later. After refreshment."

Jason's leg jerked frantically for a few seconds, out of sync with the music. Suddenly he stood, but the girl hesitated. Réjean looked into her starved blue eyes, eyes that had seen so much and yet understood so little. There was nothing there worth capturing. She lived for the night, for death, and normal life was as alien to her as it had become to Réjean. Her hesitation did not stem from fear but *ennui*.

"Like, let's hit the back room," Jason said. "Get up!" He grabbed the girl's arm and she stood, a zombie obeying a command. When they disappeared behind a beaded curtain, Réjean sighed. He picked up his cane and gloves and followed.

The narrow corridor he entered reeked of urine and mildew. It was long and dark, but he used the stray light as a cat would. He passed the only washroom; the door had been torn from its hinges. A girl sat on a toilet seat injecting a powerful substance into her arm while another female knelt between her legs, noisily consuming her juices. The seated girl stared at Réjean as he passed, her sunken eyes brimming with lust and hatred. He could tell from her odors that before morning she would be dead in the truest sense of the word.

Jason was framed by a doorway at the end of the corridor. "In here, man. Nobody'll bother us."

The small, windowless room was empty, except for the paper and broken bottles littering the hardwood floor. Réjean closed the door and slid the bolt. A yellow bulb on a cord dangled from the ceiling, enough light for all of them to see by. The girl shivered; no heat reached this desolate vault.

Jason used his boot to scrap clear a space. He began to undress the girl.

Her small breasts were round and full, the nipples firm from the chill.

"There is no need for that," Réjean said.

"Whatever, man."

Jason sat on the floor and pulled the half-naked girl down. Réjean stood staring at them, the true children of the night, dead before they had been born, disenfranchised from their rightful inheritance. And yet he envied them. Life was within their grasp, if only they would seize it.

"So, like, where you take it from?" Jason asked.

"Where would you like me to take it from?"

"My cock." The young man grinned lasciviously.

"There is a vein in your neck that will do."

Jason snickered but pulled off his jacket. The ferret leapt into the air, hit the floor, raced into a corner and hid beneath a wadded up sheet of newspaper.

Réjean squatted before them. They both stared at him with the innocence of those jaded to pain. For some reason he felt an urge to nurture them and yet he knew they could not receive what little he had to offer. They needed him to be harsh; it was the only love they understood. And he needed their blood.

A crust of dirt coated the young man's skin, but Réjean had long ago learned to ignore the unpleasant. He pulled Jason to him. The vein, weak, had been overused, but adrenalin pumping through the slim body helped it plump in a way that provided easy enough access to the coppery treasure it conveyed.

Réjean closed his eyes and his teeth instinctively found the entrance way to hot bliss. Blood coated his mouth and the moment the thick substance slid down his parched throat he moaned and pulled hard on the ragged wound.

A face flashed before his eyes. The face of someone dear. *Étienne, ten years younger, who so resembled him, laughing, sunlight glinting off his fair hair.*

The boy groaned and Réjean clutched him close. *Étienne embraced him.* "Mon frère! Mon ami!" An arm slipped around his neck. *Étienne kissed him on both cheeks.* Jason kissed his jaw.

Réjean struggled to take only half of what he needed. To stop now was excruciating, but there was still the girl.

Gently he pushed Jason back until the young man lay on the floor, his eyes closed, his legs apart. His diaphragm contracted and expanded rapidly. A hand moved to his crotch, unzipped his pants, took hold of the erection. Réjean had a vague memory of the sensations that must be coursing through the boy. But his own lifeless body could no longer appreciate such delights, and the memory was as cold and dense as the walls of the tomb in which he spent the daylight hours.

The girl proved submissive and he decided on second thought to undress her completely. She helped him strip her skirt and tights away. Her slim body, pale as a Death Lily, seemed on the verge of something—opening, closing—he could not be certain. He held her firmly with one arm and ran a hand over her breasts, forcing the nipples to firm from more than the cold. He roved the swells of buttocks, squeezing and pinching until she twitched in a semblance of life in his arms. He slid down her hairy mons and slipped a finger between her legs. The flesh inside felt dry and cool. He stroked her until she heated and moisture flowed over his hand and she moaned softly.

The vein he chose was in her breast, near her heart, at the center of a tattoo of a Black Widow spider. As he bit, her nipples hardened and thrust at him. Her head fell back. She pressed her groin against him in a grinding motion, and he felt or imagined himself stir.

Hot blood swelled within him and another memory crystallized. *Amulette, on a sultry midsummer's day, the blue lake behind her, waist-length hair lush across her full breasts, his hand gently pushing the hair aside. His lips tasting her warm salty flesh, the bud eager to firm to the worship he offered. She moaned and shivered beneath him. His groin felt heavy and hot. The scent of her fiery sex wafted up to tease his nostrils.*

He sucked harder, clutching the girl to him, struggling to bring life to the memory. As his body fed, for precious moments the past revived, igniting a ray of hope in his dark existence. *Amulette cried his name over and over. He thrust one last time, impaling her impossibly deep, until their bodies seemed to merge.*

The girl slumped against him at the same moment he could hold no more. Reluctantly he stopped. The memory evaporated.

The girl's face looked soft, dreamy. Her full baby lips had parted as though at last she was ready to receive something from a withholding world. Blood snaked along her breast from the wound, painting her pink bud scarlet.

Looking at the two of them was torturous. They could not appreciate what they had. No matter how bleak their existence, their access to memories, both good and ill, allowed them everything. He was full of their life's blood, yet hollow within, unable to seize even his own past. Being with them left him impoverished.

To have what they have, what they take for granted… Bitterness cut through him. He had been cheated. He needed to leave before he did them real damage.

He headed toward the door.

"Hey, man, that's some rush. Lemme take yours." Jason struggled to his feet, his body weaving.

"I do not share my blood," Réjean said coldly.

"You do me, I do you. That's the gig."

"You said you'd tell us stories," the girl slurred, her voice whiny. Already her body, ripened by his hands, was losing its fullness, retreating to the familiar, the insensate.

"You do not appreciate what you have and yet you want what is mine?" Réjean felt astonished by such greediness.

"Man, don't upload this shit. It's my turn. Get over here!"

The girl crawled across the floor. She grabbed the hem of Réjean's cape and tugged it. "Come on! You promised you'd tell us about your life and stuff."

He felt repelled by them. It was as though they were intent on consuming everything he possessed, which was so little. They wanted his blood. His memories. His life, if they could get it. Like leeches, they would take from him until what little he had was theirs and he was left with nothing.

"Man, I want some of yours, and I want it fast and hard!" Jason jumped on him, tearing his shirt from his body. The girl yanked the cape from his shoulders. They would drain him if they could and toss away the shell. He did not have much but what he had he must protect.

He lashed out. Jason flew across the room. The boy hit the back wall with a thud. Réjean kicked at the girl. She rolled over and over screaming; he heard glass crunch beneath her body. He raced from the club and into the black night, fleeing through the dark streets, seeing nothing, terror clinging to him like a nightmare. The cemetery was miles away but he returned hours before sunrise.

His ancient coffin offered a peculiar kind of comfort and the cool stone walls of the crypt kept the world at bay. He lay trembling. Memories had surfaced yet he could no longer recall what they were, or their significance to him, but the longing embedded within those recollections lingered. A longing that he knew he could never satisfy.

He clutched himself, but his hands were cold dead things, the flesh of a corpse. Any assurance they could provide grew stark: he was alone. He would be alone always.

Except in the world of the night, a world populated by hordes of the ravenous living dead.

Josephine the Tattoo Queen
by Joshua Gage

DRISCOLL, TEXAS

Right this way, gentlemen, right this way. Step right up with no delay to see the living wonder of our day. From her ears to her ankles, wrist to wrist, her ice cream scoops to her cherry twist, not one inch of skin is left unkissed by ink and needle. And for one dime, that's right gentlemen, the one-tenth part of a dollar, you will receive an intimate tour and connoisseur's edification of this gallery in the flesh. Gentlemen, step into the tent to meet Josephine the Tattoo Queen, lady of one hundred tattoos.

THE DANCE

The stage was lit by a hanging string of naked bulbs, which caught the dust inside the tent in a lambent halo. Ruben Admison found himself in a press of men who shuffled in the grass, converging towards the stage until he was practically leaning on its rough boards. The air thickened on the moans of Mae West, who sang from a worn 78 about a guy who takes his time, its clicks and pops echoing the soft crickets outside. A slow foot parted the curtain, softly turning in time with the music, until it became a calf, and a whole leg. The barker outside had not lied. To Ruben, it was as though a painting was wearing dusty socks, as every inch of ample flesh that came through the curtain was decorated. Here there was a vine of crimson roses, there a flock of sparrows with ribbons in their beaks.

As Josephine slipped through the curtain, wearing nothing but a silky half-slip tied at her hip, Ruben seemed to lose himself in the designs on her body. It was as though the music, the tobacco smoke and whiskey breaths of the other men, even the stage and Josephine herself, faded into one sinusoidal tempest of primal pictures. Ruben felt as though he were standing not on the grass beneath a tent at a carnival, but on a wide beach beneath a giant blossom of moonlight. Boats crashed offshore into giant octopi, their sailors caressed beneath the foam by lascivious mermaids. A giant eagle, talons splayed like forks of lightning, wrestled in the sky against a snarling panther, saliva dripping from its eager fangs.

Abruptly, the music stopped, and Ruben was thrown back into himself. Then from the other side of a stage, another record began, this time the strong *bajo sexto* of a driving *norteño*. With one shake of her hips and quick movement of her fingers, Josephine undid the half-slip and sent it fluttering to the grass. There, undulating in all the ample glory God gave her, was Josephine. Ruben found himself enthralled, his heart racing in time with each curvaceous ripple marked in ink. He felt the music bore through him, the rolling r's of the singer's Spanish trilling his skin into goose bumps as Josephine gyrated before him. He stared, wistfully, as she shimmied around the stage, then squeezed herself between the curtains as the music slowly faded and stopped. Amidst the ululations and applause of the drunks around him that scratched at his ears like rusty nails on sheet metal, he wrapped his arms around himself, squeezing his ribs as if to hold them together, as if they, and the heart beneath, would burst open without the support.

THE SUMMONS

The bamboo slapped Ruben in the chest like thunder in a clear desert sky. He had been leaving the tent with the rest of the shuffling crowd, when the barker caught him with his cane, almost knocking him off balance. "Slow down there, son. Let me talk to you for a bit," the barker said, hooking Ruben's arm and pulling him closer. "You look like a curious young ace. Let me ask you this. Did you enjoy the show?" He grinned conspiratorially, a chuckle whistling through the gaps in his teeth. Ruben pulled back, but nodded. "I'm sure you did. I'm sure you did. Now, son, let me offer up a proposition to you." With this he leaned closer and dropped his voice to a whisper. "How would you like the privilege of a private performance by Josephine? No stage, none of these other cake-eaters hassling you, just you and her in an all-night exclusive that you'll never see by the light of day."

Ruben's heart leapt. "Sure," he said, and smiled. "Sounds great."

"I thought you might like the sound of that, son. Now, let us negotiate on a pecuniary level. I can arrange such a tête-à-tête, for, let's say, a five-spot."

"Five dollars? That's almost half a week's salary. No deal."

Ruben turned quickly to walk away, but the barker caught him with the crook of his cane and pulled him back. "Come, now, son. I'm not trying to bleed you dry. You ain't got that kind of green. Fine. Let's be honest. Who does in these days of want and woe? Work with me, son, work with me. How about I knock a checker off the call? Four dollars, son. Josephine has a map of these here forty-eight United States tattooed on the inside of her thighs. Four dollars, and I promise you a moonlit geography lesson you ain't never gonna forget."

Ruben knew he could scratch together an extra few bucks over the next week, especially if he worked overtime at the restaurant. It would stretch him thin, but he kept thinking about the dance, the way Josephine's thighs shuddered against each other on stage to the rhythm of the music, and imagined being able to reach out and touch the lines that marked her body. Almost as if by its own volition, he felt his hand reach into the pocket of his trousers, and pull out four wrinkled bills.

"'Atta boy! Follow me, son, follow me." The barker scurried to the back of the tent, around the stage and out into the cool night. Ruben followed the barker as he wove behind the show. Ruben's young body began to tremble with anticipation as they snaked in and out of the tent shadows to the very edge of the carnival and up the dimmed stairs of a trailer. His eager heart seemed to mimic the delicate rhythm the barker tapped out on the door with the crook of his cane. The man silently opened the door with a ceremonious bow to Ruben, who stepped inside.

A simple lamp blushed the back end of the trailer through its red shade. Ruben stumbled towards the light, tripping over boxes hidden in the shadows until he arrived at an empty bed with a small nightstand beside it. He quickly spun around, ready to chase down the barker and demand his money back.

Suddenly, in the penumbra of the lamp glow, a place where Ruben would have sworn had only been dust and shadow earlier, stood Josephine, cigarette tucked between her lips. Her hand rubbed her naked hip as she exhaled a silvery smoke ring and said, "So, you're my date tonight."

AFTERGLOW

Josephine struck a match off the wall of her trailer and lit another cigarette. She inhaled a deep drag, then nuzzled into Ruben's chest, breathing the smoke out across his naked skin. She slowly curled a finger in his chest hair, the ashes from her cigarette falling like dust across him.

"So," she said, "first time?"

Ruben stammered, but Josephine smiled and placed a finger on his lips. "Don't worry. I already knew. A girl always knows."

"Was I… ? Was it… ?" Ruben found himself struggling for words.

"Oh, you did fine, sugar. Don't worry. You'll be a big hit with the girls when you get back home."

Ruben looked around the trailer, eager to find something, anything, to shift the conversation. A worn copy of *Green Light* by Lloyd C. Douglas rested on the bedside table. "You like to read?" asked Ruben, immediately regretting it.

"Sometimes. It helps me get from town to town."

"What's that book about, then?"

"A doctor. Mistakes. Life." Josephine said, pulling another drag off her cigarette. "It's sort of preachy, though. Evelyn, who does the snake charming act, gave it to me to read. Did you see her show?"

Ruben shook his head. "No, just yours."

"What a gentleman," Josephine smiled, then rolled back onto the pillow. Stretched out beneath the lamp light and up close, Ruben could see that, despite what he saw on the stage, Josephine wasn't completely covered with tattoos. Thin seas of bare skin rolled between the continents of ink on her body. With one finger, he traced the lines of a butterfly on her shoulder.

"Where did you get all your tattoos?"

"Oh, here and there," she said, sitting up on her side.

"Seriously, why did you get all of them?"

"My, you are inquisitive, aren't you? Did you know that the word gargoyle has to do with the sound the water makes as it pours through them? Well, what if I told you my body is a cathedral, and these are the gargoyles, keeping me safe. You should hear me dance when it rains," she said with a wink. "The way I see it, we pay for our sins in this life so we're clean for the next. Each one of these is for some sin I committed, to let God know, to make sure we're even. This here," she said, pointing to a small star behind her ear, "is when I threw a rock at my brother when we were kids and hit him on the head. He had to have five stiches, and still complains about the scar when it rains. And this flower here," she said, pointing to a rose on her ankle, "is for the first boy that ever loved me. Each petal is a tear that he cried when I broke his heart."

Ruben felt completely baffled by this shift to talk of gargoyles and sin, and wondered if he shouldn't have asked more about the book. "Your body is a cathedral?" he asked, trying desperately to catch up with a conversation that had clearly left him behind.

"Indeed," she said, then kissed his neck. "You know, you paid four dollars, which means you have me all night. I think we should say our prayers before bed."

As she continued to kiss his neck, Ruben thought about how making love was nothing like he had expected. He had always imagined working his way to New Orleans, and bedding a soft-spoken Frenchie on satin sheets with lace, surrounded by rich oil paintings, perhaps waking to a glass of brandy or heady cigar. He knew, more likely, that it would have been to some farm girl in a hayloft somewhere where he was working the summer as a hand to make ends meet.

There were particular sensations he had never imagined, in any of his wildest fantasies. He never expected the taste of cigarettes when he first kissed a naked woman. He never expected the stench of elephant dung and motor oil creeping through the window, vaguely masked by the smell of cheap rosewater on her skin. He never expected a woman to look so odd naked, all the seamless curves caught up behind girdle and brassiere unfolding when left unsupported, rolling into shapeless mounds of flesh.

He never expected so many teeth.

COTULLA, TEXAS

Right this way, gentlemen, right this way. Step right up with no delay to see the living wonder of our day. From her ears to her ankles, wrist to wrist, her ice cream scoops to her cherry twist, not one inch of skin is left unkissed by ink and needle. And for one dime, that's right gentlemen, the one-tenth part of a dollar, you will receive an intimate tour and connoisseur's edification of this gallery in the flesh. Gentlemen, step into the tent to meet Josephine the Tattoo Queen, lady of one hundred and one tattoos.

Stabilization

by Daniels Parseliti

> *What kind of beings are these anyway,*
> *Who in the end have to be scared away with poison?*
> —*Rilke*

There are coloring books for children. Elephants in tall grass. Giraffes eating tree leaves with their young. There are boxes of crayons. There are perhaps eight of us, all dressed in blue paper scrubs and hospital socks. There are walls made of cinder block. A gaunt, silent, blonde woman has drawn a pretty girl's face in red crayon on recycled paper. In the picture, the girl's nose is impossibly thin for a crayon drawing, like the woman sharpened the wax tip with her fingernail. The blonde woman is so pretty, she looks like she belongs on television. But she wraps herself in an old blanket and barely moves. I wonder if the picture is supposed to be her. The thought of drawing with crayon makes me sick to my stomach.

My left shoulder hurts from last night's injection of Ativan. It didn't stop my raging, so my right shoulder hurts from last night's injection of Haldol. I have blood spots on my arms from all of the needles. I pull the Band-Aid off the crux of my elbow and see three large purple bruises from where the nurse in the ER drew so much blood. Today I take my Ativan. When I'm sober the Ativan works. I didn't want to take it, but I did. Today I am Japanese steel. Pounded hard, thin, and brittle. I have to meet with the doctor and I want to be sharp, but not as sharp as I am. I have to act normal.

I have to act normal. German steel, not Japanese.

I return to my bed to sleep because I can't stand thinking about being here, here, where the only thing to write or draw with is a crayon. The bed is slippery, covered in plastic. So is the pillow. How many people have pissed and shit in this bed? I'm sliding off. My head slides off the pillow. My body doesn't fit on the bed. When I lie flat my feet hang off the end, propped on a slab of wood. I have to curl like a fiddlehead. I desperately want to sleep. But I can't. A saw-toothed voice fills the ward. I cannot close my bedroom door to stop the voice, because bedroom doors here must remain open at all times. This fact is posted on every bedroom door. This fact terrifies me. The voice will not stop talking about how it is feeling better. About how it tried to kill its mother and that her back and hips are sore from when it dragged her down to the floor and bit her neck, and that the stitches in her neck are healing. But it doesn't have those thoughts anymore. It feels better now, it isn't angry. Because it doesn't have those thoughts right now. *There was so much blood when I bit into her neck*, it says. It has been so angry its entire life. It didn't realize it could feel anything else. I need more Ativan. Please, I say, more Ativan, or Haldol, I don't care. I'm falling off my bed. I have one thin grey blanket that falls off me. Everything is round and I need to sleep. I slide onto the floor and do push-ups until I can't. I get back in bed, then slide off again and do more push-ups. Where is my ex-wife, I wonder. She should be coming to pick me up. I will call her when I can, when I feel better, when I can talk to her and not sound insane.

A nurse tells me that it is lunchtime. Something that looks like ground beef between two doughy white buns. I shuffle to the table and sit down. Everyone shuffles. A man stands in the middle of the room and asks if he is in a movie. He throws his arms back and says that he is an actor. His teeth twinkle and his body arcs. I take a bite, chew twice, and spit out my food. I eat three chunks of canned pineapple and throw the rest away. A tall black man in scrubs with cornrows says, "You didn't like your Sloppy Joe, Mr. P?"

"Not hungry," I say.

I hear the saw-tooth voice and then he is in front of me. Saw-tooth looks to have teeth that shape the sound of his words. They are small and jagged and jutting. There are spaces between them large enough to fit cigarettes. Several look to be broken and sharp, like shattered pottery. The teeth are fixed in a purple mouth, the mouth fixed in a head the shape of an inverted strawberry. The head is disproportionately large for the size of his body. The boy is perhaps 4' 11" and 90 pounds. His eyes are giant, surrounded by bruise-blue coffee cup rings. He does not blink, he does not sit, he does not stop talking. He is so slight and so sharp. *I just kept thinking, bite her neck, bite her neck, bite her neck, and I did, I just did, and I sucked on it, as hard as I could, and I dragged her down, so I could keep sucking because I wanted her to die, I wanted to suck the life out of her. I don't think like that anymore, I'm getting better, don't you think I'm better? And I jumped on her back and dragged her down to the ground, by pulling her head back, by pulling on her hair, and biting into her neck, it was bad, it was really bad, and she is still hurting from it. But I get so angry, I can't control it, I have no control over it, but I'm getting better, I never knew, all my life, that I could be better. Do you know that I am twenty-six? I know I don't look it.* He looks like he is thirteen. He does not blink. He goes from table to table telling people this story, the same energy and earnest enthusiasm at each. He tells the blonde girl, who sits at a table covered in coloring books. She does not look up at the boy and this seems to make him angry, twitchy. He pauses in front of her, a literal unblinking pause, his arms flexing, thin metal tubes, little popping blue veins, kinks for elbows. He stares, his lips pulled back, his bottom jaw jutting, his teeth exposed.

"Mr. P, please come this way, the doctor will see you now."

"*You get to see the doctor now?*" says saw-tooth, in front of me again. "I suppose," I say. "*When can I see the doctor?*" he asks the nurse. "You are on the list," she tells him. "*I want to see the doctor!*" he yells. "You will," she says. He sticks out his bottom jaw, baring his teeth.

The trip to see the doctor is a tremendous cruelty. To get to her I have to walk down a hall, at the end of which is the locked exit/entry door. Behind the door is an elevator that operates by key. It is the only way out. The thought of the door makes my heart pound and my fingers tingle. It makes me sweat. It makes me dizzy. All of me wants to run to the door and to pry it open. I will jump down the elevator shaft. There must be other floors from which I can escape. I don't belong here. I have to seem normal. The doctor's office is just before the exit.

The doctor's head is surrounded by a mane of flame. She is half woman, half beast. I think of Rilke's "Archaic Torso of Apollo." Her face is bronze, and through the bronze shows two pure white and blue eyes, a set of straight white teeth, glowing. She has large fake breasts that rest, immobile, on levers of flesh. She wears Capri pants and high heels.

"Please have a seat," she says. I sit on a rounded plastic chair, gripping the sides. She sits across the empty room, writing on a pad on her lap, her presence burning up the atmosphere. A nurse sits off to my right, watching us. We make an uninterrupted triangle.

"So, Mr. P. Can you please tell me how you are feeling?"

"I'm fine. I don't like being here."

"Are you thinking of killing yourself right now?"

"No."

"Could you please show me the cuts on your forearms?" she says, crossing her legs and tapping on her pad. The linoleum floor is cold through my socks.

"Look, is there any way that I can get out of here today? That kid is scaring me."

"Can you tell me why you think you are here?"

"Yes. Sure. I reacted badly to a bad situation."

"Okay... Can you be more specific?"

"I have a hard time dealing with my ex-wife."

"Okay."

"Look, I thought everything was going to be fine. I felt fine. I had felt fine for weeks. My ex-wife stopped by to drop a lamp off at my apartment. She said she just wanted me to have it back, that she knew how much I liked it and felt bad about keeping if for so long. I know that. It wasn't her fault." I stare at the floor and tap my foot.

"All right, can you keep going?"

"I thought everything was going to be fine. But she showed up and had a new tattoo on her wrist. This bright black thing that looked like a bunch of grapes. It was shining. I was already kind of drunk. I don't know. I didn't want to see her to begin with, but it was my favorite lamp and I figured what the hell. But then there she is with this new, glistening, tattoo, on her wrist. So I asked her about it, and she just refused to tell me anything. I wanted to know where she got it and what it meant. She told me she wanted me to have the lamp and that everything else was no big deal. I should have told her thank you, and asked her to leave it on the steps. She should have worn long sleeves."

"The tattoo made you very upset. Does she have others?"

"Yes, but those are old. From before she met me. She never got a tattoo when we were together. But now, I don't know, she's reliving her youth or something, having someone draw on her. She had to know that it would make me upset to see it. I was just trying to get her to leave. I didn't want anything bad to happen. I was trying to feel better. To get away."

"By cutting your wrists?"

"I don't know."

I remember screaming at a doctor in the emergency room. He kept asking me to calm down. Once my blood alcohol count was low enough to let me out of emergency, they brought me here. They strapped me to a stretcher, bound my arms, drove me here in an ambulance. Some guy rode with me the whole way. I kept apologizing to him, that he had to do this, that he had to be with me between hospitals. I miss my ex-wife so much, I thought on the ride over. I miss her so much. I just want to talk to my ex-wife. I always miss her when I am sober, even though I am afraid. I just want to talk to my ex-wife.

"They'll figure out something when you get to the hospital, sir," said my chaperone.

"Can I please just get an arm free so I can talk to my ex-wife on my cell phone? Where are my things? Can I please see my things? Where are my things?" I was covered in so many blankets. My arms hurt.

※

The floor has grown colder under my feet. "That kid is really scaring me. He seems like he might kill someone. I've never seen anyone like that."

"Jeffrey is fine. He is well medicated."

※

Jeffrey is not fine. Jeffrey will kill me if he doesn't receive enough attention. He will suck the blood from my neck.

"Can I please leave today?"

"I don't think today is a good idea. Here is what we are going to do. I'm going to prescribe you 400 mg of Tegretol twice a day, 6 mg of Risperidone once a day, and 4 mg of Ativan three times a day. Let's see where that gets you over the next couple of days. It will help you calm down. You seem very agitated."

"In the next couple of days…" I am trapped here. Breathe, I think to myself, try not to seem insane, seeming sane is the only way to escape.

"Look, I had this girlfriend once. A girl that broke my arm, actually. She was a real bitch. We'd moved into a new apartment, and the night we'd moved, in the bedroom, there were like a hundred moths, flying around. We didn't know where they were coming from. Just one hundred shitty, regular moths. Finally, we figured out that the top of one of the windows wasn't fully shut. We shut it, and we vacuumed up all the moths. About an hour later, I was watching TV in the living room and I heard her screaming. 'There's a moth in my ear, there's a moth in my ear!' She was just screaming and screaming. So I go into the room and I look in her ear and there is no moth. But she keeps going at it, for fifteen minutes. 'I can hear its wings beating!' she says. I try blowing in her ear. Nothing. I stick tweezers in there. Nothing. The whole time I'm thinking to myself, 'This is it, she's finally lost her fucking mind. I'm going to have to bring her to the mental hospital.' Then I had one last idea. I took a cap full of vodka, bent her head over the sink, and poured it in her ear canal. After about five seconds, guess what came floating up? A moth. So, it's like, I can seem crazy, but really, there is a natural reason for it. A reason outside of me."

"Can you tell me more about the cuts on your arms?"

"These? They aren't even deep. I mean, if I really had wanted to, I would have."

"Can you please unwrap the bandages for me? The nurse here will rewrap them for you. The wounds need to be cleaned, anyway."

"These are just scrapes."

"You wouldn't have needed stitches if they were just scrapes."

"I was drunk."

And then the lion holds up a document in her jeweled paw that says that a doctor has "committed" me. It is, the lion explains, a signed affidavit attesting that I was a threat to myself and to others. The document, at least visually, is hilarious. It has been written in a looping, junior high school kind of script, the kind of writing that girls used in letters passed behind the teacher's back in class.

"It looks like a fucking clown wrote that note. A fucking clown wrote that, and it's going to kill me."

I feel my body tightening, my hands losing their grip on my chair, and I am sliding forward, my head leading.

"Can't you see? A thirteen-year-old wrote that. Where did you get it? Is it dosed with perfume from fucking Walgreens? Is there a Chapstick kiss somewhere on the document serving as a watermark? Is your brain a fucking hash of jelly and shit?"

Four hands on each arm, four arms on each leg, a hard hit of Haldol in my shoulder and a hard board with cuffs for my hands and feet and men carrying me into a room to strain against the cuffs, a bit in my mouth to bite on until the light turns pure white and red and blossoms. Losing consciousness, I turn my head to the door and see saw-tooth staring at me through a small window, mouth open, gnawing on the glass. His teeth make little ticking sounds as he gnaws. Help, I try to say, *help*, but the Haldol is digging in and all that comes out is slurred and through a gag. *I'm going to die if he gets in the room,* the thought is clear, *He's going to rip my neck open and I'm going to bleed out on this table...* Somewhere in the Haldol, going down, coming out, I don't know, I realize that saw-tooth's mouth is not his own, not his own purple opening, but the mouth of some kind of vampiric parasite that has eaten its way into his giant strawberry of a head, some kind of hungry, needlish, parasite that feeds on blood. It has sucked him near dry, kept him small by absorbing his nutrients as it grew.

♥

Dinner time. "Mr. P. You want to eat dinner?"

I am sick of being by myself. Trying to move, my body feels made of ice, ready to crack. I slide off the bed. It takes several moments to get my balance. I shuffle to the dining room, which is also the social room. I sit by myself. A grilled cheese. "Cheese bread, Mr. P," says the man with cornrows. He gets to leave, I think.

On one of the walls a man is drawing with his finger. It looks like he is trying to draw a door. He traces the outline, over and over.

Those who eat, eat slowly. It is a confused operation. A very tall, thin man with bare feet lifts his sandwich to his mouth and holds it there, opening his jaws with monumental deliberation. It seems like minutes. Without taking a bite he drops his sandwich onto his tray and pushes his fingers into is, spreading it apart. He then stands up, looks from side to side, and sits down again. I pull my sandwich apart as well. White cheese and white bread. I cannot eat. They have generic ketchup here. I return to my room and urinate. Half way through I can feel urine running over my testicles. It soaks my paper pants. I return to bed.

♥

I'm in the TV room with the blonde. "Do you find me attractive?" she asks. She does not look at me. She stares at the TV. Her voice is lower than I had expected.

"Yes."

"So would you fuck me right now?" I'm not sure I heard her correctly.

"The guards would stop us," I say.

"Jerk off under your blanket. Then maybe I'll eat your cum." She looks at me and runs her thumb and forefinger down from the corners of her mouth, until they meet in the middle of her bottom lip. She drops her hand and lets out a little smile.

"Will that stop him?" I say.

"What?"

She must know something that I don't about the saw-tooth vampire. I've never seen her eat. She must be starving herself so she will not appear to be food. Looking at her now, she seems near dead, lethargic and desiccated. "Can you eat semen, will eating semen stop the vampire? Will it stop saw-tooth?"

"I don't know what you're talking about," she says, and she looks down and pushes on a thick purple vein that runs along the bones on the top of her hand.

"But you think so?"

"I don't know, maybe."

"I don't think I can cum."

"Just do it. Under your blanket, in your hand. I'll eat it. Please, I'll eat it."

"The drugs keep me from getting hard."

"I want you to try. Do it to my picture." And she places the red crayon drawing in front of me.

My penis is like a dead mouse. Saw-tooth appears at the door.

"What are you guys watching?"

"A movie," I say, and I look at the blonde, who is now fully wrapped in her blanket and staring at the picture of herself.

"Did I tell you that I might get out this week?"

"Yes."

"What are you guys doing?"

"Just sitting here, that's all." And then the blonde says, "We need time alone."

She has bird bones. Hollow. Easy to snap. You could pick her up with one hand. Because her bones are hollow, her bones can be filled. You could fill the hollows of her facial bones with lead, and she would never be able to lift her head. She would crawl across the earth grinding her face into whatever it passed over. Then she would be no flesh, just bone, then bone opened to the hollow, for all the lead to leak out, then she could lift her head again. But her face would be gone, just open bone.

Saw-tooth looks confused. *"You don't want me in the room with you? Why not? Why don't you want me here with you?"* He starts to shake. At first it is barely perceptible. *"What's wrong? What did I do?"* He covers his ears with both hands. His arm hair is standing on end and his veins are bulging blue. His neck throbs and his face has turned bright red.

"Nothing," says the blonde, and she folds her picture and slips it back into her blanket. "Never mind, just come in."

"What's wrong? What did I do?" he says again. Saw-tooth extends both arms in a juvenile, questioning gesture. His eyes are open as wide as possible. His mouth seems to chew his tongue and the vibration of his body fills the room, passing through the air and to the walls and the plastic of the chairs, and then it penetrates me. The hairs on my arms start to shake. I can feel the organs in my body.

"Just come in," says the blonde.

"I wanna know," he says to the blonde, his eyes fixed on her, his voice the steady volume of polite conversation, *"what I did."*

"It wasn't about you, Jeffrey," she says, "it was about us."

Everything in the room seems covered in a cold dust. It makes me itch, makes my skull tingle. Jeffrey stands there, staring at her. I try to speak and all that comes out is the warm air left in my lungs. Nothing in the room changes. The dust seems to be eating into my skin, boring into my muscles. I want to squirm but cannot. Somehow, I get a few words out. "You didn't do anything," I say. "Come in and sit down."

Saw-tooth looks at me, looks past me. It feels like several minutes.

He rocks on his heels. *"Okay, fine,"* he says.

"Thank you," I say.

The blonde does not speak. She gets up to leave. Saw-tooth sits down in her chair before she can exit the room. He is sweating. I am cold.

"I can try harder next time," I say to her as she walks out the door. "What if I eat it myself, will that stop, you know?" She turns and looks at me angrily.

"You can't eat it, it's for *me!*" she says, her lips pulled back. Her teeth look blue.

◊

I am afraid to sleep. At night I walk up and down the hallway. I can see everyone lying in their beds. I cannot hear saw-tooth, but I expect to, soon. The loop I walk does not change. The rubber hash marks on my socks do not change. Everything here is curved, blunted. My sink. The central station where the nurses sit. The chairs are all injection molded plastic, rounded. The tables in the social and dining room are round. The social room is also the central room, and it itself is circular. Only two wings break the circles, the male wing on one side, the female wing on the other. I walk loops down and up the male wing. I am thirsty to talk to my ex-wife. The TV room is oval. There is a sign that demands that the patients do not move the chairs. I walk loops up and down the male wing. I don't know what will happen when I am sleeping, or when I wake up. I continuously imagine saw-tooth, on me in my bed like a giant white spider, so much stronger than he looks, his jaws going for a clench of muscle and bone and sinew on my neck, sucking the life from me. I am afraid to sleep.

◊

I open my eyes as I lie in bed and saw-tooth is standing in my doorway staring at me. I feel cold. I cannot move. I have been lying naked in the snow. I very much wish I could close my door.

"*You sleeping?*"

"No." My ability to speak surprises me. When he wants, saw-tooth takes my voice.

"*You looked like you were sleeping.*"

"I can't sleep."

"*I can't sleep either. I don't remember when I slept last. I'm tired but I don't sleep.*"

"How long has that thing been in you?" I ask.

"*Always.*"

"How do you get it out?"

"*It doesn't come out, you can't get it out. You can only make it quieter. You don't want to try to get it out. That is what my mom did. It's quieter now. I'm better.*"

"Were you hungry for her? Did you feel hungry for her?"

"*She made it come out. She did it. I can't control it.*"

"Where did it come from?"

"*My dad. He gave it to me. He's dead.*"

The blonde, saw-tooth, and I are in the television room. I cannot get warm. Out in the common room, a man in scrubs is singing/screaming "Bohemian Rhapsody." I don't know how he is staying warm. I haven't seen the "actor" all day, and it is bothering me. Last night, lying in bed, every time I shut my eyes I could see saw-tooth. Where was he when he was not speaking to me? I could see him, gnawing on the actor's spine. I could see him filling his stomach with the actor's blood. I am so cold I cannot move my arms or legs.

Saw-tooth is talking. "*I'm better now, I think, the doctor said they might be able to let me out in the next few days. Do you think I'm better? Do you think they will let me out tomorrow?*"

"I don't know," I say. I don't know what day it is. My head is mud. The blonde does not talk.

"*Why are you in here?*" says the saw-tooth to the blonde.

"I don't want to talk about it," says the blonde.

"*You don't?*"

"No, I don't."

"Oh, Okay," says saw-tooth. Even feeling like I do, I wonder if this refusal is going to set him off. His entire body is a compressed coil. He twitches, and with every *no* a great unwinding takes one more step towards reality. His breastbone protrudes like the air has been sucked from him and he wiggles his fingers. I would be too weak to stop him.

"When you get it, in your room," says the blonde to me, "keep it in your hand and come find me. Then you can watch me eat it. Keep it warm."

"Okay, I'll try harder."

"I need it," she says.

Saw-tooth smiles, like he can read our minds.

◆

I need to call my ex-wife. What time is it? I'm not sure that she will pick up a call from an unknown number. I plan to leave a message asking her to pick up the next time I call. She has an out of town number, so I need to have one of the nurses behind the counter place the call. I think they like me well enough, but I feel like doing this is an imposition. The chairs by the phone are difficult to sit in. The cord for the receiver is only a foot long. Maybe eighteen inches. The length makes it very hard to talk on the phone. I realize I do not have her number memorized. I do not have my things. I cannot call. Please come and get me, I say, crying, please, please. I'm not as crazy as the people in here.

◆

"How did you get here?" asks the blonde.

"I was trying to get away from my ex-wife. I wasn't feeling well, and when I'm not feeling well, I have a hard time around her. Bad things happen when we get together. Things that I don't want to happen. She brings things out of me."

"How long were you married?"

"Three years."

"And she left you?"

"Yes. I'd changed. I wasn't the same person. It was good that she left."

I open my eyes. I am in bed and saw-tooth is standing in my doorway. He is rocking his upper body. When he is in my doorway the bed does not feel as slippery. I feel stuck in it.

"Are you awake?"

"I don't know."

"Do you think I am better?"

"I don't know. What are you going to do when you get out of here?"

"Eat."

"Are you a vampire?"

"My mother said that to me. Said I was a vampire. She said it a couple of times. I don't know because my father is dead. Do you need me to drink your blood? I'm not supposed to."

I think for a moment. "Please don't drink my blood."

Saw-tooth laughs a ripping laugh. *"I like you… I wouldn't do that!"*

"Would you do it if I asked you to?"

"I'm not supposed to do things like that. I'm not supposed to let it out."

"I just want to know what you want. So I can help. Do you ever do what other people want?"

"No. But I have a hard time controlling what I want… It makes me feel so much better to do what I want."

"Do you want to watch me sleep?"

"I don't know. Maybe."

"I deserve you."

"It's hard to sleep."

"It is."

"The blonde lady told me that you and me and her are all the same."

"I don't know, I don't know what that could mean."

"She said you would know what it meant. Said she was sure of it."

❦

There is a window at the end of the hallway on the men's wing. The window is not literally seamless, but it is seamless. On the wall of the wing, someone is tracing a door that they will never walk through. Jeffrey is a vampire. I am sure of it. "Jeffrey is a vampire," I say to the doctor. "A heavily medicated vampire. He even confessed it to me. How many of us in here are? We aren't going to make it out." She increases my antipsychotics.

❦

I can see Jeffrey, I can see the top of his strawberry head and one of his dried apricot ears as he bites into my neck. I can feel his jagged teeth ripping my artery and a hot flow of blood and his hot little tongue, his tongue stabbing me. I feel myself getting colder and colder, I need more blankets. All the blankets slide off of me.

❦

"What can I do to help you, Jeffrey?"
"Just don't help it come out."
"I won't, I promise."
"But I think it might come out soon."
"Why?"
"You know what it feels like to get mad. Like you've got this terrible itch, and if you scratch it, it will just get worse. Once there was a woman who couldn't stop scratching her itch and scratched through to her brain!"
"When I get mad it feels like all of me is on fire. And I can put the fire out, I can pour water on it, and the more water I pour, the better it feels. But later I realize that the fire was really water, and the water was really fire. And that is where the terror comes from. Do you understand?"

Saw-tooth looks almost gleeful. *"A doctor once told me that burning and itching were the same thing,"* he says.

I will not let myself sleep. I keep my pills under my tongue and spit them out when I can get back to my room. To get them down the sink I have to let the water run for a long time. I realize I can spit them into the toilet.

The nurses do nothing here. I lie in bed and saw-tooth stares at me for hours, terrorizing me. I tell the doctor, I tell the nurses, but they do nothing. Absolutely nothing.

"Jeffrey can't hurt you," they say.

"He's going to kill me. I'm sure of it. He puts visions of it in my mind. Of how he is going to do it."

"Just be nice to him," they all say.

"I have no choice," I say.

I have no choice. I am locked with him in a concrete sarcophagus.

The blonde tells me that she has seen me eat pineapple and that it will make my semen taste good. "We need another way to get rid of the vampire," I say. "What has he been eating? The actor is gone. The man who was tracing lines on the wall is gone. I didn't see him leave, but they were mopping the floor the morning I noticed he was gone. When will he get hungry again? He must be getting stronger."

The only coffee we get in here is decaf. It tastes like acid and iron. It tastes so good I drink cup after cup. "You really like that coffee, Mr. P," says the staff. The coffee tastes like outside, I say. I cannot contact my ex-wife. I have no parents. I don't know what I have left outside of here, but I need to get back there. There I can have coffee that is not decaf. There I can get food that does not make me want to vomit.

"How did you get here?" asks the blonde.

"I think I was trying to get away from my ex-wife and realized I never would."

"You got in here the same way Jeffrey and I got here."

"I don't know. Am I like Jeffrey and you? How would anyone know? I've never drunk anyone's blood. Have you?" The blonde turns away.

"Would you rather kill yourself than your ex-wife?"

"Jeffrey, he is a different kind of *being*. A different kind of *thing*."

"You don't sleep. Jeffrey doesn't sleep. I don't sleep."

"Look at him. Listen to him."

"You'd totally rather kill yourself than your ex-wife. You're just like us." And the blonde laughs.

I cannot sleep. I am walking loops in the hall. Saw-tooth is making yipping sounds in the common room. The blonde is curled in her blanket watching television. Why won't they let me out of here? I don't understand. I am not a vampire. I am not a vampire. My ex-wife is still alive. I did not kill her.

"How did I get here?" I ask the doctor.

"I thought you knew how. You told me how"

"I'm not sure that was correct. I thought it was correct, but I'm starting to doubt those memories."

"Why?"

I'm not sure what to tell her. I want to get better, but I also want to get out. It's no good if I don't get better, but I'm not as bad as anyone in here. And I really want to get out. I am normal when I am out. I am not normal when I am in here. Locking me up does not make me normal. The space is so small. The drugs do nothing. I cannot sleep. I am trapped here with a vampire who wants me as his friend. But it might be better for both of us if he just killed me. The blonde thinks that I am a vampire too. I do not know why. I can't tell if she is screwing with me. I don't know if she has the capacity. But I have not been able to cum for her, and she is angry. I don't know what kind of thing she is.

"Did my ex-wife put me in here?" I ask. "I keep trying to remember exactly what happened, but I can't. She should have put me here. But I can't remember if she did or if I did."

"The doctor put you here."

"Bohemian Rhapsody is gone," I tell the doctor. She sits there, gleaming.

"He was released."

"How?"

"He is better."

"How? He sang Guns N' Roses' 'Sweet Child o' Mine' the day before he left."

"He liked to sing."

"Did Jeffrey kill him?"

"No," she says, laughing.

I am wearing thin, blue, paper scrubs, like the first day I was admitted. Everything is linoleum, plastic, or painted cinder block. I live in a concrete sarcophagus. I begin to rip my shirt off. I begin screaming.

"I hate these fucking clothes. I want a T-shirt. Can't you please get me a T-shirt?"

"Security!" calls the nurse.

"Where am I going to go?" I ask, still ripping. "I'm wearing a piece of fucking paper! My pants are always falling off. I am not human! I am not human! What do I need to do? I just want a fucking T-shirt!"

I am surrounded by large men. I can feel a great heat through my body, swelling, the first heat I can remember in days, maybe weeks. I would like to kill them all. They drag me naked through the ward, but this is nothing new. Everyone can always see everything here. Some people look at me. Some don't.

⟁

I open my eyes. I feel absolutely flat, dimensionless. Saw-tooth is not gnashing at my window. I was hoping he would be there.

⟁

Saw-tooth and the blonde are in the TV room when I enter. Saw-tooth is sitting at the blonde's feet. She is stroking his hair. It gives me a feeling of comfort.

"What are you two doing?" I ask.

"We're the only three left here," says the blonde. "No one else has come in. It's just us left."

"Left for what?" I say.

"I'm still gonna get out," says saw-tooth, and then, *"Where are we?"*

"Maybe we'll be here for a long time," says the blonde.

"This is where they keep vampires, Jeffrey," I say.

"Are you both vampires too?"

"Yes, Jeffrey," says the blonde.

"Yes, Jeffrey," I say. I feel my teeth with my finger for a change, for something jagged. "This is where they keep vampires, Jeffrey, this is where they keep vampires until they aren't vampires anymore."

"Will we get better? The doctors tell me I'm getting better."

"Will we get better?" asks the blonde.

A Virgin Hand Disarm'd

by Mary A. Turzillo

Modesty was not the custom on this clove-scented island, Will knew. The beautiful dark girl, Mawar, wore no more raiment than a cat, except for the ornate markings on her face, body, hands, and feet. That and the luxuriant veil of her black, silky hair. She had taken off her sarong and invited him to swim. How could a woman with so few adornments command such respect with a glance of her black eyes?

Mawar had caught his heart like one of the golden fish, the gohu her tribesmen caught for the elders to dine upon.

"Mawar, though I am but a poor seaman, the least and youngest on my captain's ship, I beg you to stoop to my low station. Mawar, please, marry me."

"But how could I lie with you?" she mused. "You have no embellishments upon your hands. How will you pass through life's seasons with such bare fingers?"

Will looked down. His father was a glove-maker, but his hands were bare on this epic journey. One of his gloves had been lost, or stolen perhaps, in Nova Albion, along with his boots.

Her own hands were covered with finely-drawn patterns—eyes, and flames, tiny deer, the moon, sun-wheels.

"But still, you are the finest man I have seen in all my life. Your babes will be fine, too; tall and with that bit of sunlight in your hair. And with skin so pink and light. And your eyes are the color of clouds. So, come, let us lie here on this warm sand."

Dishonor her? His wits had fled. He was so roused that he thought to take her after simply drawing aside his codpiece, but she puzzled at his pins and buttons and soon had him raw as a boiled egg.

And then she laughed, in surprise, not ridicule.

"It's true what my kinswomen say, then," she said. "These Englishmen do not subject themselves to the tooth. So how may they properly confront the world?"

Will was still engorged with passion, but her laughter somewhat wilted him. He said, "I have sailed for three years. I have seen parts of the world your chieftain and your silly gossip mothers will never see."

She mock-gaped at him. "And perhaps the sun burned off your markings?"

Then she threw herself back on the sand and rolled away from him, stopping to prop herself on one elbow.

"Without the marks upon your hands, you may pass many seas, but you will not pass the River of Death. Maligang will not allow it."

"Who is this Maligang? I have heard of it, but—"

She sighed. "Maligang guards the afterlife. Surely your people have heard of him."

"Sooth, but we call the river Styx, and the goddess who owns it has the same name." Most of his sense had flown to his engorged cod, but he thought to add, "There is a ferryman, named Charon. But a coin pays his toll, no images upon the skin."

"What ignorant fools your men are. Are your women equally benighted?"

She sprang up and deftly wrapped her sarong around her.

"Must I be marked with pictures, like you, before I am accounted a true man?" He was having trouble stuffing himself back into his clothing. When he'd left England, this whole affair of love-making had seemed somewhat less urgent. Oh, he was mad for love, but too shy to approach even the loosest of maids. But he was sixteen now, an age when tumbling a maid was enough to drive a man to do anything.

"Oh, I've seen you're a true man, and a fine one. Eager as a puppy. But it would disgrace me to have such a lover, all undecorated as you are."

He made a quick decision. He'd forgone the needle and dyes before, though many of Drake's crewmen had pictures from several islands, all over their bodies and even their faces. "I'll be decorated then. Take me to your surgeon, or whoever does this frightful work."

She softened, and her black eyes showed pity. "Really, sweetling, if you hope to cheat death at the end of your life, you must be clad in dye."

She strode off, leaving only her flower scent to compete with the spice that hung over everything on the island.

He had seen many of his crew-mates drowned or pierced by arrows or lead, but he wasn't planning to die soon. Dye, die. He'd promise anything.

Mawar's body rivaled that of a goddess. Of course, what did he have for comparison? What maid had he seen naked, back on the banks of the Avon?

He'd fallen into conversation with her so easily, after just a few days while Drake's other men were foraging for necessities on this Island of Diamond, as they called it. Though he let his fellow sailors believe that he had trouble with the Latin and Greek they had taught him at school, he learned languages easily. And so did Mawar. Were she come to the English court, she would be accounted a wit.

What the court would think of her painted sleeves, he could only imagine.

So they traded wit and flirtation back and forth, she teaching him her tongue and he teaching her English, while Drake traded and cajoled and extorted what he needed to sail back to Plymouth.

Now Mawar was asking him to take on the body-paintings. He would do so. By the Cross, he would marry her if she would have him, no matter how many drawings he must have on his pale, if sunburned, flesh.

And so he went with Mawar to her granddame, who advised his decorations should start with his hand. Would Mawar marry him? Of course! She had promised. And yet, he noticed several handsome men on this island with whom she exchanged admiring looks.

The artist who was to decorate him turned out to be a venerable and richly decorated old dame. She was called the *tufunga*, if his ears did not betray him. Mawar had counseled him to give her a gift. Fortunately he still had one of his father's second-best gloves. Only the left one, but she seemed quite happy with it, though it was too big for her clever hand.

Also to his surprise, Mawar's relative had provided a feast, with song, dance, and a dish called *papeda kuah ikan*, with a rich yellow fish soup, and snake fruit.

This was perhaps to soothe him for the pain to come. The tufunga offered him no anodyne. *Tuak*, fermented palm wine, was forbidden to initiates, and he had no access to Drake's store of rum. He was made to lie on the floor while the tufunga held his skin taut with her feet, and positioned a bone disk with a small hole filled with dye made from a burned nut above his hand. She then took a huge tooth—from a shark, he later learned—and poised it above.

He braced himself, but shrieked like a woman in childbed when the hammer-stone hit the shark's tooth, which then pierced his skin. Ashamed at his lack of manly courage—good God, he had been half-drowned once, and it had been less horrific—he clenched his teeth until he thought they would break.

He was dimly aware that Mawar and her two sisters were singing sweetly as they knelt nearby. He could barely translate the words—something about *I wish I could take this pain instead of you—if I give you a bracelet, it will someday break, but this tattoo is a jewel that you will take to the grave and beyond—*

He would have been touched, but he was too busy stopping himself from howling.

When the pain slacked off, the tufunga wrapped sacred leaves around his hand and arm and tied them with a deft knot.

❖

Will cut the knot and let the leaves fall away from his arm, which still stung like fury. The head of a beast was printed on the base of his thumb, and its body and limbs coiled around his wrist and forearm.

Mawar gazed with admiration. "The tufunga chose well! This is the *naga* of great power. It poisons deer and even men, and then eats them. Your hand will perform great feats, and you will pass the River of Death with ceremony."

He grinned. "So, I am immortal?"

She frowned, but then said, in English, "Yes. That is your word. Immortal."

"So now we may—"

"Not yet! You must have the other arm done, and then wings upon your shoulders, that is, if the tufunga gives you wings. And then—"

"But we—do your people not practice marriage?"

She seemed confused. "Of course. But only after you have taken more of the marks of manhood."

She nestled against him and he felt again the heart pang and the rising of his manly spirit, but he only said, "I do not see this naga picture on any of your tribesman."

"Oh, that is a special one. The tufunga saw great power in you. So she gave you the naga. The komodo naga."

❖

Will went to Sir Francis and told him that he planned not to sail when *The Golden Hind* left Moluca.

"Do you say so, sirrah?" said Sir Francis. "You astonish me. I give you special treatment. While the other men subsisted on sea biscuits, you were allowed jerky from my own store, and an extra ration of water."

"My pardon, your honor. When we reach England, I will get money from my father to repay your kindness."

"I have a hold full of silver, gold, and spices. I doubt your glove-stitching father will give me anything I would value more than one of the sea biscuits you so proudly disdained."

Will had broken his teeth on the sea biscuits as humbly as any of the crew, but he said nothing.

Sir Francis continued, "I need you on this journey. You helped me make speeches to inspire my men. You have an alacrity for the tongues of the Portugee, the Spaniards, and the many dark men of the forests and islands. I cannot let you dwell here while I assault the island nations."

Will felt a cold chill.

"I noticed," said Sir Francis, "That you've taken one of the body-marks the natives here adopt. A dragon, is it? I suspected you were planning to stay. And so—"

Three of the crewmen sprang up from their seats and grabbed Will. He struggled cleverly, but they put leg irons upon him. He was chained to the deck of *The Golden Hind*.

Mawar came to him in the night. Her hair was wet, and her sarong was wrapped around her waist, concealing almost nothing of her lithe, decorated body. In the moonlight, the lineaments of her markings looked like delicate dark lace. The seaman set to guard him paid her no heed, for he knew of Will's misfortune.

She put her wet face to his pictured hand and kissed the naga.

"I am sorry, Mawar," he said, again and again.

She pressed closer to him, then, with the same deft fingers she had used on the beach that day, undid his garments. She threw aside her sarong and lay beside him. She opened herself to him, honey and salt. He knew nothing of the art of love, but his body instructed him as he penetrated her secret places. His pleasure both intensified and overcame his sorrow. They slept, then coupled again, and again.

The sentry woke them as the sun broke over the horizon. Mawar stood without a trace of embarrassment; her beauty, her dignity, and her tattoos were equal to the robes of a queen.

Will stood too, pulling his breeches on, his emotions and heart undone.

"Listen," said Mawar, her lips against his ear. "I know you cannot return. Your country is a world away, and few have come from there to here even once. But I am in my part of the moon where children are made. And I believe I am a fertile one, though I have not yet born a babe. I believe perhaps this night we have made, between us, a child. I will tell the child of his beautiful father with the naga tattoo. And though we are apart, my heart will belong to you until I cross the River of Death."

"No! Come with me. Sir Francis will allow not allow a woman aboard *The Golden Hind*, but you can dress as a boy. I will find clothes to cover you—to cover your —your loveliness—and—"

She pressed two cool fingers against his lips. "I am afraid of the deep sea. I love you, but this is my home. I will not forget you, I promise."

"But I want to marry you!" And then a horrid thought occurred to him. "You've just been toying with me. Your mother has picked a husband for you, and now I'm an exotic pleasure, soon to be forgot."

"No. Part of you stays with me." She pressed her hands against the birds painted upon her belly. "I believe it will be a girl."

◆

When *The Golden Hind* sailed into Plymouth, Will felt his sea-legs under him turn to land-lubber's legs. He gazed with a boy's longing at the gold-green fields of England, nearly at harvest.

Will had his seaman's pay, and this he spent on a new pair of boots, and passage from Plymouth to Milford Haven, then a carriage ride, and a night at an inn, with a meat pie and ale to fuel his drive toward his father, his mother, his home, and the few books he owned.

◈

Will felt embarrassment that he had lost and given away the fine gloves his father made for him —they weren't John's best, of course, since those were made of more costly leather. But when he strode up the path, the first thing he saw was his mother, with a load of wet clothes ready to pin up to dry.

Her eyes grew as wide as coins, and she dropped the laundry, heedless of the dirt. She ran to him and grabbed him tight. "Will, Will, oh my sweet boy, where have you been? We feared you dead, or taken up by authorities for poaching."

He embraced her—she was shorter than he was now, by a whole head. "I've seen such things—"

A woman was standing in the gate to the Shakespeare house, daughter of a neighbor his father had done favors for. Her eyes met his, and she smiled a slow smile. "Young Will has grown to be a man." She sauntered past him and his mother, then turned and winked over her shoulder.

"Anne is a bit backward in company," said his mother, wiping the tears of joy from her eyes with her apron. "I'm sure she is near glad to see you as I am."

In his experience, Anne wasn't all that bashful. "She'll be back," he said.

◈

And she was. Before he was even settled in helping his father to cut and stitch fine leather, this same Anne set to wooing him.

She became tedious in her attentions; a pretty enough girl, and as virtuous as the next, but God's body! Why would she follow him every day and every where?

Will thought of the black eyes and dark, sweet skin of the love he'd left the wide world away, but this woman was here. Her mouth was sweet, and in a field blossoming with aconite and yarrow, she had her way with him.

And soon after, she announced that he was to be a father.

After the hasty wedding and the birth of his little pink-cheeked daughter, he became restless. A few years later, the birth of the twins, Hamnet and Judith was a joy, especially the birth of a son to carry on his name. But he chafed under daily routine at his father's shop. By candle or moonlight, he wrote poetry, most notably the history of Lucrece, a virtuous woman raped by her husband's enemies.

And he thought of Mawar. Perhaps there was another daughter, a half-world away, a toddler now with velvet-dark cheeks and enchanting black eyes. The thought agonized him. He went down to the port once or twice, but had no stomach for a long sea-voyage, nor for abandoning his wife and three children.

And no doubt Mawar was, despite her vows of love in her own language and in English, long since wed to another man, mother to a dark man's children, or even, may God forbid, dead.

The dragon image on his hand seemed to stand out when he was in his father's workshop, a mockery of his leather-cutting skills, or lack thereof. His hand ached, and he found himself cradling it and wanting to stick it in cold water. He was not content to make gloves.

An actor was murdered in a theatrical company traveling near Stratford-on-Avon. On impulse, he went to the troupe's leader and volunteered to stand in for the actor—he had learned the lines after seeing the play but once. But one performance, and Will knew he was meant for the stage. He sought roles in several troupes, finally achieving a part with the Lord Chamberlain's men. London, at last! Stratford-on-Avon was his home, Anne was his wife, and he had three fine children, but he was stage-struck.

He excelled as an actor, but his dragon-tattooed hand itched every day until he made time to write, and write, and write. The tattoo tickled, almost like a kind of lechery, and he could ease the itch only by writing histories and comedies. The ease was short-lived after each work: three plays about Henry VI and the rollicking, romantic *Comedy of Errors*. His tattoo began to torment him as if the dragon was afire. It burned, and he could ease the pain neither by drink nor by plunging his arm into cold water nor by the distractions of the city, but by writing of severed arms, maidens raped, tongues cut out: the bloody tragedy *Titus Andronicus*. He thought of Mawar when he wrote of the vixen Tamora. And was Anne Lavinia? These were but caricatures of the women: perhaps his Mawar was still true to him, at least in her heart, though he had left her on the Island of Diamonds. And Anne—she was certainly no helpless ravished virgin. He sought his place in life. His alacrity with language, discovered by Captain Drake, won him applause from audiences and actors—and enough money for fine things for Anne and his three children.

It was the beginning of a satisfying career, almost enough to make up for the emptiness he felt when he thought of those islands, the sea, the heady perfumes, the red lips, the sharp wit of a woman who learned languages easily, and those black, black eyes.

Ⅳ

He wrote of travelers in love with exotic strangers: the twins Antipholus and Antipholus, shipwrecked and sea-traveling, and of Emilia, the long lost wife and mother. He wrote of lovers torn apart by ill-haps. He wrote of shrewish wives—

And when Anne decided to come to London to see one of her illustrious husband's plays, he learned to regret using her as inspiration. Not that she was really the termagant he so deliciously portrayed in *Taming of the Shrew*, but there were some touches she couldn't avoid recognizing.

"How could you!" she railed, following him back to his lodgings and amazing his mate Thom Kyd with her ravings. "I do not wonder that you never bring your work home to your own dear family. You think I cannot read?"

In fact, Will knew very well that she could read; it was one of the reasons he'd agreed to marry her, aside, of course, from her swelling belly. Some of his fellow dramatists carried desks and materials everywhere they went, but Will kept his in London to speed his journey to Stratford-upon-Avon.

"I cannot carry my work everywhere with me, sweet wife. Please give me back my bonnet and stop beating me with it."

"You hate me!"

"Not at all, honey-love. I model Kate's docile sister Bianca upon your sweet self. And stop that." A loose ribbon slashed his face. "Or you will put out my eye, and then where will you be for a bread-winner?"

Later, he would name a prostitute in one of his plays Bianca, but if Anne noticed that, he would pretend it was but jest.

He always loved a woman with spirit.

And then their son Hamnet was murdered. Will blamed himself a thousand times over, and in his grief had no anodyne. Some two years later he expressed his anger and grief in a play where a son mourned his father and sought his killer, just as Will mourned his son and tried to find who had killed Hamnet.

The play was a huge success: themes of murder, suicide, regicide, despair, madness resonated with the London of his time.

And, acknowledging his own eminence, but sorrowing that his young son was not alive to continue his name, he sat for his likeness to be made.

He'd sat for his portrait before, but this was special; a friend wanted to paint him.

A fine portrait. His company had pooled funds to commission it, and it looked enough like him to suit. But—

"The hand," said Will.

Nicholas looked up from his work, and swabbed his brush on his palette.

"I would you would show my hand from the palm, not the back."

"But then tattoo will not show—the dragon—"

"I do not flaunt my dragon, Nicholas. And dear as it is to me, I think some might think me gone over to the side of savages if the image were seen."

◆

Hamnet's sweet young ghost haunted him, not in the way of a furious spirit, but always there, always the torment of what might have been had the lad grown to adulthood. Will blamed himself for the boy's death: if he had resided in Stratford-upon-Avon, he might have seen the danger.

He thought of lost children, and wondered if Mawar had born him a child. It would be a daughter, she somehow knew. Called—well who know what Mawar would call her? He would call her Miranda, and make her the centerpiece of a play about a distant island, one not so different from the Island of Diamonds he had visited with Sir Francis.

He sat scribbling, his secretary copying sides, until the whole thing was dazzling and done. A shipwreck, for did he not remember the horrors of the raging sea? Traitors, men who dealt in thievery and murderous plots, like the one against his own son. Counselors, lords, treacherous brothers, jesters, sprites. One he would call Ariel, who could command the elements at his master's will. A witch who had imprisoned Ariel. A young man in love, Ferdinand. A scholar and scientist, a master of the elements, deprived of his just position as Duke of Milan. He would call the hero Prospero!

And best of all, the magician's daughter, Miranda. She was the portrait of his daughter, living in that island country, Molluca.

He himself would play Prospero.

And at the end, he would beg the audience to "dwell in this bare island" and free him, who commanded all the charm of the stage, with the clapping of their hands.

◆

His audience adored it. And they adored Prospero, maybe seeing Will and Prospero as the same person, the man who mastered the elements for the short hours of the play. And then, he mostly retired, scribbling only a bit for his own amusement, or to add a touch of fire to some upstart's effort.

〚◈〛

But then the sickness took him. He had lived hard, and loved many women, and lost what was most precious to him: an island wife, and an English son. The true cause of his illness was a broken heart.

After many months he knew this was his end. He had been a sinful man, betrothed to two women, and really, wasn't he truly married to that woman he had loved on the Island of Diamonds? He had lusted, he had written some words that the pious might called wicked. So he was shriven, and if the minister noticed the strange pagan dragon marking on his right hand, he made no obstacle of it.

〚◈〛

After he was shriven, he unclenched his hold on life, as if he were floating in a calm sea in the wake of *The Golden Hind*. And then he washed up on a beach, and walked further. At last, he came to a dark river, guarded by a creature taller than any man, decorated with all the animals Will had ever seen, both real and faerie. He knew this was the spirit of the river, Maligang. And the spirit would not let him pass, though Will took from his mouth the penny his daughters had placed there.

This was the Lake of Blood.

"You are unmarked. No man may approach the Bawang Daha without the mark of passage."

And Will saw thousands of Englishmen and women wandering in the darkness beside the fatal river. But he held up his hand and showed the marking to Maligang/Charon.

"But you have not killed a man in battle," said the Maligang. "Your markings are on but one hand."

Will spied the bodies of warriors underneath the water's surface, and, looking closer, he saw that maggots ate at their flesh.

"With this hand," said Will, "I have slain hundreds. They lie on the stage of the great Globe, and when the people have applauded and left, my dead stand up and live again."

And the Maligang smiled slightly, for after all, a great magician may equivocate with a god. And the spirit took his hand, put him in the barque, and rowed him to immortality.

Summer Night in Durham
by Cat Rambo

(for Ann Kakaliouras)

Some supernaturals have trouble adjusting to the human world.

I keep telling the vampires that tattoos are just a bad idea where they're concerned, but still I get two or three of them in a night, more on the weekends. They want the same clichés the living do: Celtic runes and cartoon devils and names of loved ones mostly, but the daring ones ask me to etch them with religious symbols and then giggle. Tonight, a pleasant evening when the summer heat lingered in the air and everything was sweat and locust-buzz, one vampire told me he'd never seen a lady tattoo artist before.

I said, you haven't seen any since you Turned, or they would have told you what a bad idea this is.

He blinked at me as though he didn't understand what I could possibly be saying. He had this puzzled look on his face under all the stubble and the little bit of eyeliner around his eyes. Most vampires wear jewelry, but this one didn't have anything precious on him other than a gold hoop in one ear and a possible filling or two.

I could tell he expected me to be scared of him. Instead I was just tired. It was almost the end of my shift, and I'd already explained this to three other vampires.

Look, I said. Vampire flesh doesn't tattoo the way human skin does. It keeps bleeding, keeps seeping fluid, and never heals. I don't think that's what you want.

He blinked at me again and seemed about to say something when a sound from the doorway made us both turn our heads. His girlfriend stood there, a human woman with skin like cream and roses, not a tattoo visible on her. Her hair was like spun gold, with a hint of red, as though fire lurked in its heart.

He said somebody should get a tattoo. Glenda, how about you?

She sneered. She said, that's not why you want me. It's because I look unsullied. Virginal.

He shrugged and mumbled something.

What's that, she demanded.

Folks, I interrupted, did you want to get a tattoo or did you want to move along? Because I get paid by the hour, not counting tips. I stressed that last word in case they didn't get the point.

He drew himself up like a movie Dracula, puffed his chest, which would have been more intimidating if he'd been dressed in formal wear rather than jeans and a t-shirt reading "The dead do it all night long."

You don't dictate to the likes of me, Missy, he said. Behind him, his girlfriend rolled her eyes so wildly I thought that they would pitch out of her head.

I'm not dictating, I said. I just think we could all save ourselves valuable time if the vampire community would learn that tattoos are a human practice they may wish to forgo.

I could tell my lack of fear put him off. He sized me up, trying to figure out whether I was predator or just deluded prey. I stared back and let a bit of fire show in my eyes.

Maybe it was that, or maybe it was just that dawn would be coming in a few hours, but he shoved twenty bucks at me with an apologetic shrug and nod and sauntered out the door with girlfriend in tow.

The receptionist put her head in through the doorway. Your next one's here early, she said.

This is a shitty way to earn a living, I told her, and she just looked back at me.

If that leprechaun hadn't taken all my gold, I said louder.

Lucky you had a trade to fall back on. She shrugged.

At least the next one wanted something pretty, koi all up and down her leg. That I could do, so I drew them in blue and green and orange and white, details so fine you'd swear you could see the fins ripple, and in the water between them, coins falling, copper pennies and silver denarii and soft, shiny, delicious doubloons.

When I finally took a break, I went outside to smoke. The vampire was waiting, lingering despite the hints of false dawn sizzling across the parking lot gravel.

They told me I shouldn't fight you, he said. His look was angry but there was question in it. He was smart enough to know that there's always a bigger fish.

You're very new, I said. Or you'd know that there's plenty of non-humans around, hiding in ordinary skins. I smiled and let a hint of tooth show.

It was wrong of me, because I knew he'd take it as a challenge, and he did. He came at me in a rush of fangs.

I would have swallowed him whole, but that would have been wasteful, so I just yawned fire and watched him burn. They go up fast, vampires, and when they're gone, it's just ash and gleanings.

No gold fillings in his teeth, but the remnants of the earring remained. I picked the tiny puddle of melted metal up and held it in my hand. Every little bit helps when a Dragon is rebuilding her hoard.

His Body Scattered by the Plague Winds

by Adam Callaway

Grimshaw's mind was torn through the tunnel connecting dream to reality by the sound of chimes. His eyes fluttered opened as he tried to figure out where the crashing noise came from and where he was. He turned on his side and looked at the framed sketch of a beautiful woman that lay on the pillow next to him. She had blue-white hair the color of glazed porcelain, eyes like inkwells, and a small, smiling mouth.

Naveana, he thought, *I'm in my bed and that chime means someone is at the door.*

Grimshaw got up, smoothed the wrinkles from his black coat and trousers, and walked into the bookshop proper. Someone stood in front of the door, silhouetted against a white blizzard.

He unlocked the door and opened it just a crack, then jammed his foot behind it. Vagrants often tried to push into a warm shop during these storms.

"What do ya want?" Grimshaw asked.

"I got books to sell," the man on the other side said. Only his voice betrayed his gender. All other distinguishing factors were encased in layers of coats, cloaks, and mantles.

Grimshaw stuck a hand through the door. "Gimme."

The man on the other side reached into his mantle and brought out two slim volumes. Grimshaw took the books and paged through them. One was a collection of legends of the Fiend. Interesting, but not popular or in good condition. The other was an anatomy primer with some decent diagrams of plague victims.

"Three chars for the lot," Grimshaw said.

"Worth at least a nova," the man said.

"Four chars is all they're worth."

"One full nova." The man's voice was old, tired, even a bit frantic. Where his eyes weren't bloodshot, they glowed as softly as new snow.

"Look," Grimshaw said, brandishing the books, "these are outdated, late editions, and in poor condition. If you think you can get a better deal at another bookshop at this particular time of the dead of night, be my guest. I will give you five chars for the both of them, and that's only 'cause I'm cold."

The man paused for a moment before sticking out his hand, palm up. Grimshaw reached into his pocket, grabbed five copper coins, and deposited them into the man's outstretched hand.

"Looks mighty warm in there," he said.

"It is. Goodnight," Grimshaw said, then slammed and locked the door. The man tested the knob and left.

Grimshaw tossed the books onto his ebony counter. One stuck, but the other overshot and landed behind the counter. Grimshaw swore and walked to the backroom of the shop.

A bottle of sleep syrup sat empty on the nightstand. Grimshaw picked it up and watched thick, honey-colored liquid roll along the sides of the bottle. Hardly a dewdrop's worth remained. It wouldn't even make him light-headed.

Grimshaw set the container on the table and placed Naveana's picture next to it, and then went to set a kettle to boil. It still had yesterday's tea in it, but it'd do to wake him up a bit.

"Fiend knows I won't get back to sleep without that bitter syrup." A ring of paper circled the little finger on his right hand, and he spun it as he waited for the tea. It was bone white, and felt of soft down.

The kettle whistled. Grimshaw poured himself a mug and went to have a look at what he had bought.

"Where'd you go, you bastard?" he asked the book. Even with a lump of feuerglas glowing like a handful of embers, the space behind the counter was dark and cluttered. Old, forgotten stock sat piled, ready to collapse at the slightest breath.

Grimshaw thrust the fist-sized piece of warm, glowing glass into a tent-like crevice under two massive atlases.

"Ha! Hide from me will you?" Grimshaw said, setting the feuerglas down and reaching for the book. He could just feel the cover under his fingertips. The leather was smooth. Perhaps of a higher quality than he had originally thought.

He slid the book out and stood up. A large lump of feuerglas sat in a dish on the counter, appearing more bonfire than embers, and nearly as hot as an iron stove.

"Let's see what I wasted good copper on today," he said, studying the book. Someone had spent hard money getting it rebound in calf's skin, and the remnants of a brass lock hung from the cover.

"That's different," he said, opening the book. He knew the Church banned books on the Fiend all the time, going so far as to burn entire stores for stocking them, but he had never heard of someone going through the trouble of locking an old book of legends.

"A cautious parent, maybe," Grimshaw said.

He paged through the table of contents. All the usual legends were included: *Torn from a Paper Womb; His Tattooed Body; Mistress of the Fiend; Magic of Dark and Hollow Places; The Final Death of the Inked Man; Skull Born; A Thousand Lives in Fire*. No forbidden lore or signatures or anything to distinguish this copy from ten thousand like it.

He bent the pages into a curve and flipped through them at speed. A scrap of yellow-brown paper, jarred loose by Grimshaw's haste, floated down like a dead leaf.

"What's this?" he asked, catching the scrap in his hand. People left bookmarks in the books they sold to him all the time. In Lacuna, bookmarks were a sign of wealth and respect, separating those who ate with silver from those who ate with their fingers. Grimshaw had found ribbons of gold with woven silver tassels, magnetic clips inlaid with pearl and jet, and even sheets of feuerglas shaved so fine that they could be bent and rolled like leather.

The bookmark that had floated into his hand, though, was disgusting: the color of a diseased limb, puckered like scar tissue, bearing single word written in black.

"Together," Grimshaw muttered, looking up in thought, not noticing that the word now glowed a faint white.

"Why would someone write that on a bookmark?" he looked back down. The paper seemed to have flattened out while he was thinking. Grimshaw reached to flip it over, and clapped his hands.

"What the Fiend?" he said, scratching his hand where the paper had been resting—where the paper was now stuck. When that didn't work, he started to shake his hand back and forth, like it had fallen asleep and he was trying to wake it up.

Oi! You're making me dizzy.

Grimshaw stopped shaking and slowly looked around. Someone was in the shop with him.

That's better. I forgot what a bother senses can be. Hey, what's your name?

He dashed through the stacks, searching, paper-palm forgotten.

"I know you're in here. Show yourself! I have a blade."

Down here buddy, and I don't think you'll take a blade to your own hand.

Grimshaw stood still and opened his hand. The word "Together" had faded to a pale white.

"Hello?"

There ya go. How ya doing? Name's Chernyl.

He looked around one more time, then raised his hand to his face and slowly uncurled his clenched fist. The bit of paper was now marbled with wisp-like arteries. No longer the color of half-tanned leather, the bookmark now had a healthy, peach hue.

"You're that scrap of paper," Grimshaw said as if stating a fact.

Yessir, that'd be me, but it's actually scrap of parchment. Paper's made'a wood.

"You're that scrap of parchment."

We've already established that, or is you some sorta mockingbird?

Grimshaw backed up until he hit a stack and slumped to the floor.

"You used my blood."

Just a bit. For the iron you see. I've been anemic lately.

"I-I'm Grimshaw."

Grimshaw. Good name. Lotta power in a name like Grimshaw.

He ran his finger over the parchment, trying to separate the wrinkles in the parchment from the wrinkles in his hand.

That tickles. We're buddies, but not like that.

"How?" Grimshaw asked.

That's a mighty big question. Why not make it smaller?

"How can you talk?"

Not really talking buddy. Just thinking out loud.

It was then that Grimshaw noticed that he wasn't hearing the paper speak; the deep, scratchy voice was echoing inside his head.

"How can you think? You're just a—"

Scrap of parchment. I know what I be, Grimshaw. I don't know how I be, but I be.

"Any ideas at all?"

There was a silence in his head, but Grimshaw believed he could feel the parchment—Chernyl—thinking.

Prolly has something to do with the Plague.

Grimshaw jumped up, holding his hand at arm's length.

"The Plague? The Fiendborne Parchment Plague? Where you slough off sheets of skin by the ream?"

Calm down. I was fixed in brine, photo-like. Damn near pickled, in fact.

Grimshaw looked at his hand. If Chernyl was Plague-ridden, Grimshaw'd already be cracking and flaking.

"Something to do with the Plague—what? Trapped you? Preserved you?"

That's the kicker: I dunno. When I was tore all up and scattered by the Plague winds, me memories were too.

Grimshaw sighed. "How do I get you off my hand?"

Ah, and I thought we was bonding for real, like.

"Chernyl."

Fine. Seeing as it's a small question, I'll answer it. No Fiend-lovin' idea.

"What do you mean?"

Outside 'a lopping the thing off, I've no idea what you'd do to get rid'a me. Maybe a different scrap would know? For now, just think'a me like a very thin leech. Eat plenty of red meat, too. Don't want ya fainting on me.

Grimshaw paced the room. The sky outside turned gray with the promise of dawn.

"So, you're telling me that I have to find another scrap of demon paper and attach it to my body in the hopes that it's the part of your mind that knows how to get you off me?" Grimshaw stopped pacing and stared at the brown-yellow patch on his hand.

No, Chernyl said, *I'm telling you that we have to find all the scraps.*

Grimshaw sighed.

And don't forget to eat more red meat. They'll be hungry. You know, Grimshaw paused, *for the iron.*

᎘

"How?" Grimshaw asked, buttoning up his third overcoat. The blizzard had quieted down, but it was still cold enough to freeze the blood solid in your veins if you weren't well protected. Ice Rigor, they called it.

There ya go again with those big questions, but I'll tell ya anyway, 'cause we're buddies.

Grimshaw's hand flexed and moved without his effort.

This here hand's mine now, see? I will point you in the right direction. His hand curled into a fist with just the pointer wavering like the needle on a compass.

"But how do you know where to go?"

Instinct.

Grimshaw had reconsidered the blade when Chernyl first had taken control of his hand, but he had wrested control back with a concerted effort of will, which had calmed him a bit. It was still unnerving to see his fingers flex and wave by themselves.

But is this any stranger than a piece of possessed parchment talking in your head? Grimshaw thought.

No, I wouldn't say stranger, Chernyl said.

Grimshaw hung his head.

"You can read my mind?"

I can hear your thoughts. Difference there, buddy.

Grimshaw reached for a scarf, but only one hand found the thick fabric.

"Chernyl, let's make a deal. I get control of both hands until you need to use one, okay?"

Whatever you say, boss.

Grimshaw's other hand shot forward toward the scarf. He wrapped the long length of heavy wool around his head a few times and then secured everything under a stocking cap. Finally, he pulled on two pairs of wool mitten liners and then waterproof leather mittens over the top of them.

"Let's get this over with," Grimshaw said, and stepped out into the cold. The only exposed skin on his entire body was an oval from his eyebrows to his lower lip. Still, the cold penetrated his layers of clothing immediately. He sucked in a breath and felt little ice crystals form in his lungs.

Slowly, through your nose.

Grimshaw knew he couldn't form words through the shivering, so he thought them.

If I close my mouth, my lips will freeze together.

If you don't, your lungs'll get frostbitten.

Grimshaw didn't have the will to argue. Already, snow caked his eyelashes and he felt the tip of his nose freezing solid. He closed his lips. A thin weld of ice formed, and kept them closed.

Where to? Grimshaw asked. The wind picked up and threw his outermost cloak out behind him. It cracked like a bullwhip.

Grimshaw's hand pointed forward.

Down this street two blocks, then a left.

How far is this first scrap?

Two blocks and then a left away.

Grimshaw thanked the Fiend that at least something went his way today.

◊

Grimshaw cursed the Fiend for Chernyl's gift of understatement. The first scrap had been in a poster for Malakai's Premium Invisible Ink, and it had been two blocks and a left away, but that left had stretched until the sun hung high in the east.

He tore the second scrap of Chernyl from the corner of the poster and stuffed it into his pocket.

Why not take off yer glove and give me a little more to work with.

Ha! I'm not going to just give you bits and pieces of my body. We'll collect the rest of you lot and get it done in one fell swoop.

Suit yourself buddy, but jus' warning ya: may take a bit longer than it should if 'n it's only the one scrap'a me. The more scraps, the quicker. For sure like.

You really are a right bastard.

They walked in silence back to the shop. Grimshaw's skin tingled when the warm air hit his face, and then followed the usual cycle of relief, pain, incredible pain, relief, normalization, as his body warmed back up.

Grimshaw stripped out of his winter gear but left a pair of glove liners on. He wanted to be able to handle the second scrap without letting it touch his skin. And he wanted to keep the sickly brown patch of Chernyl out of his sight.

The scrap had "Together" written on it in black, just like the first, along with the torn letters of the poster.

"I think you're lying about leaving my body once we find the rest of you."

Grimshaw, I'm hurt. I thoughts wer was buddies?

"The paper only has 'Together' written on it. Nothing else. No 'Apart' or 'Leave' or 'Remove.' What would happen if I wrote that on you?"

You wouldn't wanna do that, Grimshaw.

"Why?"

'cause it's only me. I wouldn't be able ta control what is "Removed" or what came "Apart." It could just be me leaving your hand, or it could be your hand leaving you.

"Maybe we should try anyway?"

Grimshaw's gloved left hand clamped on his right, pinning it to the arm of the chair he was sitting in. There was more strength in that hand now then there had ever been before.

No. Buddy.

He could feel the bones in his wrist grinding against each other as the grip tightened.

"Okay, okay," he said. "Just trying to rile you up, you know, like—like buddies do."

There was the briefest of pauses, and the hand released, back in Grimshaw's control.

Aye, Grimshaw. Like buddies do.

The blizzard bent back on Lacuna, keeping Grimshaw and Chernyl inside for first a day, then two. Grimshaw passed the time by reading. Chernyl spent the time bothering Grimshaw.

Who's the broad? Chernyl asked, using his hand to grab the picture of Naveana.

Grimshaw snatched the picture back. "None of your damn business," he said, voice low and cold as the winter wind.

Buddies tell each other about their sweethearts.

"Buddies mind their own damn business."

Ah, come on Grimshaw. She's quite a looker.

"How can you see her anyway?"

I see through you, and you've been staring at her for an hour now.

Grimshaw set his book down.

"Promise to keep quiet for the rest of the day if I tell you?"

Cross me heart.

Grimshaw tried to figure out if that meant his heart or Chernyl's, or if a paper man could even have a heart, and gave up.

"Her name is Naveana, and she was my wife."

Was?

"She passed five years ago from the Plague."

Chernyl made a tutting noise. *Poor thing.*

Grimshaw picked his book up again. "Yeah, well, that's that."

No reminiscing or heartfelt stories or nothing? Just that you was married and now yer not?

"You wanted to know who she was and I told you. Now please leave me alone. I don't like to talk about it."

Then don't. Just think about it.

And Grimshaw, tired and frustrated, did.

Naveana held the spoon up to my mouth.

"Open up," she said. The wriggling brown mass on the spoon smelled of burnt wood and turned earth. I shook my head.

"Viritov Grimshaw, you open your mouth this instant."

I patted my belly, indicating I was full up of wriggling brown mass.

"Fine, fine," she said, lowering the spoon. I sighed and found myself biting down on silver.

"Gotcha! Good, right?" To my surprise, it was delicious. Like a combination of lamb jous and briny capers, but with the texture of soft butter. I nodded my head.

Naveana pushed a hair behind her ear and cocked her head to the side. "Why do you ever doubt me?" she asked, smiling.

"Because I'm a right idiot," I said, wrapping my arms around her and kissing the top of her head. Her hair smelled faintly of plum.

"And to think I could have married an alchemist," she muttered.

"Yeah, me too."
We laughed until the maître d' threw us out.

◈

What a lovely lady.
"I'm not done yet."

◈

The physician smeared what look like bacon fat on a thin, transparent piece of parchment and pressed it onto Naveana's swollen belly. We both held our breath as he dropped a spot of ink onto the paper. The ink floated on top of the paper for a moment, and then began to trace the delicate curves of the child.

"It's a girl," the physician said, bending close to the paper. There were tears in Naveana's eyes and a smile that nearly split her face in two, and it was like I was seeing her again for the first time. She was beautiful.

◈

It's okay buddy. I'm good now.
"Shut your mouth."

◈

She wiped a tear as it rolled down my cheek. Our daughter—Felice Kay Grimshaw—lay cold and blue in her crib. The midwife shook her head and pulled a white blanket over the still form of our little girl.

◈

Please stop Grimshaw. I can't—

"Once more around the fen. Right buddy?"

◈

I looked through the silk canopy at Naveana crumbling in our bed. The Plague had taken her in under a month. I hadn't been able to touch her that entire time, under pain of death by Plague or pulping for violating the quarantine. Still, I pushed the silk to its limits to grasp her hand one more time. It crumbled in my grasp.

She coughed and a cloud of flakes shot into her little tent.

"I love you," I whispered. She coughed again and was still. I rolled her in the silk and handed her to a Scribe of the Church, as the law says. I allowed another Scribe to burn our marriage bed, as the law says. I allowed a third Scribe to search the entire shop for any scrap of Plague skin, as the law says. After the devouts left, I pried loose a floorboard and reached underneath for a piece of Naveana, already rendered inert by fixative. Holding that piece of paper, I slumped into a corner and wept.

◈

Grimshaw spun the ring on his finger and wiped his nose on his sleeve.

That'd be her, wouldn't it?

He nodded. "Will we really be able to find the rest of you quicker if I attach this other scrap?"

Yes, buddy.

Grimshaw sighed and took off the gloves. He lined up the torn edge of the scrap with its inverse on Chernyl.

"Together," he muttered. The word glowed white. Grimshaw felt Chernyl smile in his head as the scrap took hold. Red arteries spread through the piece, making Chernyl momentarily lightheaded.

Didn't I tell ya to eat more red meat?

◈

With the help of the second piece, Grimshaw found an entire arm's worth of Chernyl being used as a blanket by a woman sleeping in a box a dozen blocks away.

"Why didn't you meld to her?"

Broad prolly can't read. You gotta read the word.

Back at the shop, Grimshaw wrapped the scrap around his arm.

"Together," he said, nearly fainting. Blood poured form his body into the sheath of parchment. The world became a pinpoint of light as blackness pushed in from his peripheral vision.

Sit down, buddy. Take it easy.

Grimshaw half-collapsed on the floor, breathing heavily. He was thirsty, head pounding with dehydration and anemia.

Now, from wrist to shoulder, his arm was encased in the mottled parchment. His fingertips were still clear of Chernyl, but it was a moot point. He couldn't have wiggled his pointer finger if he had the will of the Fiend.

Grimshaw ran his hand over the sheathed arm. He could almost, but not quite, feel the motion. He brought a fist around and punched his bicep, but it only registered as a dull pressure.

Ow. Buddies shouldn't hit, man.

"If I can hardly feel it as flesh and blood, I doubt as paper you can feel more."

Parchment, man. And it's a spiritual hurt. Like a betrayal, one buddy by another.

"Says the parasitic parchment that took over my hand."

Fine. We's even then.

"Even."

Grimshaw picked up a book and tried to ignore the constant tugging on his shoulder as Chernyl went about his own business. He kept his head turned to the right to avoid looking at the ghost limb.

After the fourth time the stool nearly tipped over due to Chernyl tugging on his body, Grimshaw had to find out what the disembodied arm was doing.

Chernyl had an entire ream of parchment—good, lambskin parchment at that—and was scrawling at speed. Already, a stack of about twenty pages lay covered in tiny black script, as precise as a typewriter.

"What are you doing staining high quality parchment?"

Writing my memoir, of course. What else should I do while you sulk between two covers?

"Could you at least use less expensive paper? I have a cord's worth of rough-cut, fifteen-pound bond in the back."

Would you ask the Timescribe to write on anything but hammered gold?

"Wouldn't dream of it."

Exactly.

He sighed and went back to reading his book.

Grimshaw dreamed he was swimming in the Broken Spine just like when he was a child, splashing his older brother. The bright orange sun hung in the sky like a ripe fruit.

"Throw me again, Verome," Grimshaw said, tugging at his brother's hand. Verome smiled.

"Okay," he said, although his mouth didn't move. Verome grabbed Grimshaw under the arms and lifted him into the air.

Grimshaw giggled with delight as he anticipated the splash. He plunged into the warm water of the Broken Spine and sunk like a poorly thrown skipping stone. He opened his eyes and started to paddle toward the rippling orange ball above him, and felt something cold wrap around his wrist, cutting into his arm. Blood bloomed in the water before spawning bright red jellyfish. He breathed out in alarm and started to swim furiously toward the surface, but the tentacle dragged him deeper and deeper until it was nearly black.

Grimshaw stared at the ceiling above his bed, veins popping from his head as the hand around his neck squeezed harder.

Chernyl. Let go, Chernyl. Let go, buddy, he thought as loud as he could.

He used his free hand to pry at the hand encircling his neck.

Just as Grimshaw was about to black out, the hand released.

Oh Fiend! You okay, buddy? I's having this mighty strange dream. I was one'a them kraken things on the hunt. Just as I snatched a juicy morsel, ya roused me with yer shouting.

"Wasn't. Shouting. Just. Thinking. Loudly," Grimshaw said, panting.

You gonna live, Grimshaw?

A growl escaped Grimshaw's throat.

Then no harm, right, buddy?

Grimshaw rubbed his neck. He could feel the heat where Chernyl's hand had squeezed the life from him. A full bottle of sleep syrup sat on the nightstand next to Naveana's photo, but he was too shaken to go back to sleep. He got up, and set the kettle on the stove.

"You tried to kill me. You were the kraken in my dream," Grimshaw said as the kettle heated.

Ah, Grimmy, you can't take that so seriously. I wasn't trying to kill you. Just having a dream.

"You nearly killed me."

Trust me, buddy, if I wanted to kill you, you wouldn't be here asking me why I tried to do it.

Grimshaw dumped a spoonful of tea leaves into the pot. "I'll never be able to sleep again unless I strap you down for the night."

So be it. Another option would be to go and find the rest of me. Then you wouldn't have to worry about my idle hand.

"We've only found two more fingers in a week of searching. Never find the rest of you at this rate."

Chernyl was quiet for a moment. *Ya know, buddy. There may be a way to expedite the process.*

The kettle whistled. "And that would be?"

I think I know where me head's gone.

"Seriously?" Grimshaw asked, ducking behind a caryatid of the Worldscribe. Dozens of sculptures of the gods of Lacuna ringed the Church: Timescribes scratched the seconds onto sheets of gold; Lifescribes tattooed the names of newborns into books of living skin, and crossed out the names of those who needed to die; Worldscribes hammered history into the sides of mountains, their thousand floating eyes showing them all events. The sculptures held up the coliseum-like Church of the Scribes, encircling the penance area, where a yearly auto-de-fe took place.

They think it be some relic of an old devout given to the Plague. Miracles happen when they scrawl on it, like.

"This is like stealing from the Monarch of Ars."

More like the General of Dem, but it be the only way. I have an idea, though.

"Anything to prolong the inevitable."

You got a quill and ink handy?

"What? No. Why would I?"

Hmm. That'll complicate it, but not matter. Just follow my lead.

Chernyl pointed to a dark archway leading into the Church and Grimshaw followed. Chernyl's arm shot out and grabbed a brick, swinging them into a different hall.

"Pointing will be just fine," Grimshaw said, regaining his balance.

Sorry. Just got excited. Don't know where me head went.

Grimshaw sighed and followed Chernyl's directions, taking a left here, a right there, diving into a prayer alcove to avoid a devout.

"We nearly there? My heart can't take much more."

Yeah, yeah. Hang in there, buddy. It'll be the next alcove on your right.

Grimshaw ducked into the alcove and sat on the stone bench inside.

"Now what? We're lost in the largest Church in the known world, surrounded by armed devout guards, trying to steal their greatest relic."

We need something to write with. You got any qualms about cutting yourself?

"What? Yes. I mean—no. Wait, why?"

You'll find out if you do it.

"Gah, fine." Grimshaw stuck his thumb between his teeth and tore a small hole in his skin.

Write "Open" on my arm somewhere.

Grimshaw wrote it. "Now what?"

Now tear it off, slap it on the brick, and say the word.

"But I worked hard to find that scrap of you. What'll happen after I tear it?"

Just trust me, buddy.

He tore the scrap that read "open" from Chernyl's arm and pressed it to the brick floor underneath them.

"Open," Grimshaw said. The word glowed white, and then Grimshaw was falling.

He awoke in the dark, broken masonry pressing into his back and legs.

"Er," he said, blinking, "You've made me blind or dead or both."

Buddy's being a bit of a baby. We're just in a lower chamber. Thumb's still bleeding?

"Everything's bleeding."

Use everything to write "Fire" on my arm. Then tear it and say it.

Grimshaw did as he was told, and a spark of light illuminated the chamber. Unlit candles stood on ledges running along the chamber's wall. Grimshaw lit one with the scrap of paper.

"Where to now?"

Start walking and I'll tell you when to stop.

"Put your hand on the wall so I don't get lost."

Chernyl pressed his fingertips against the wall. Grimshaw held the candle out in front of him and started walking. The small glow of the candle didn't allow him to see more than five feet in front of him at a time.

There's a left coming up. Take it.

Grimshaw rounded the corner. There were no ledges in this hall. Instead, portraits of past Scribes lined the walls.

Know any of these lads and ladies?

He shook his head. "Nah. My grandparents kept this faith but it was burned with their Plague-ridden bodies."

Each devout wore one of three simulacra representing their patron: a gear for the Timescribe; a hammer for the Worldscribe; a claw for the Lifescribe. It made Grimshaw shiver.

They keep only their most holy relics on the first level. A stone from the Worldscribe's mountain. Flask of oil that dripped from the Timescribe. Hair from the living pages of the Lifescribe's book. Down here are their extras.

Grimshaw chuckled. "How does it feel to know you're not as important as a rock?"

Chernyl curled the fingers on his hand, dragging Grimshaw's two good fingers across the rough stone.

Door on your left, he said.

Grimshaw grit his teeth and walked faster. The door was unlocked.

The chamber opened up and down, left and right, like a bubble at least as large as the upper portion of the Church. A thin stairway led down into darkness, past the reach of Grimshaw's light.

Chernyl whistled.

"I hope you know where to look."

And I hope your legs aren't tired. Let's get moving, buddy.

ᛟ

Grimshaw wove in and around piles of what could only be called garbage. Stacks of moldering paper dripping with fluid from broken canopic jars. Soiled habits half-buried in rubble piles. Towers of torn paintings. He raised the candle above his head, but the light was swallowed by the massive cavern. Agoraphobia threatened to infiltrate his mind, squeezing it with an icy claw.

Calm down. I know the way back better'n any compass.

Grimshaw took a deep breath and started walking again.

"How far in is your head?" he asked.

Feels like it's near the back wall.

"Great."

The walk wouldn't have been so bad if it had been in a straight line, or if drops of cold water didn't fall down the back of Grimshaw's shirt, or if the growling would stop.

It's at the center of the next pile, Chernyl said. Grimshaw looked around, but all he could see was what could only be called a mountain of paper, each page dense with characters.

"In there?" Grimshaw asked, pointed.

Yessir. Feels like five feet up and straight through to the heart.

Grimshaw picked up a handful of sheets. Dense scrawl, not unlike Chernyl's, packed every page, but it was nonsense. Random combinations of verbs, nouns, and adjectives.

"Break library cold running rat vase falling," Grimshaw read. The words began glowing.

Drop those pages! Chernyl yelled in his mind. Grimshaw let them flutter to the ground and watched as the paper deformed, crumpled, tried to create what he had read. Rats, books, vases tried to push free of the page, their silhouettes looking like objects trying to press through cotton sheets.

The commotion stopped, though, as the paper was ripped to tatters by the competing words.

"What in the blackened name of the Fiend was that?" Grimshaw asked, stepping back.

Me head's where the base of me power is. It musta contaminated the rest of this paper.

"What are you?"

An arm and three fingers. Now get digging, buddy.

Grimshaw shook his head and looked at the mountain of paper once more. It stretched into the darkness above him. No way could he dig through the entire pile, searching for a single sheet among the rest. Then an idea struck him.

He used a tooth to reopen the wound on his thumb and wrote "crumble" on Chernyl.

What'a doing?

"Trust me, buddy."

Grimshaw tore the strip off and set it on the pile.

"Crumble."

The word glowed white, and then broke into smaller pieces. Grimshaw's stomach flopped as he watched; nothing else seemed to happen. Then, the paper underneath the scrap turned to dust, and the sheets touching that piece turned to dust, and then the reams touching the sheets touching that piece turned to dust.

Chernyl grabbed Grimshaw's thumb, welling blood onto his own finger. With deft motion, Chernyl wrote "Stop" on his shoulder, and tore the scrap off. He crumpled the scrap into a ball and tossed it as high as he could.

"Stop," Grimshaw said and didn't say. His mouth moved, forming the words, but it wasn't his voice that came out. It was a low and raspy voice.

The ball of paper burst into a fine paper mist and settled on the crumbling mountain.

Don't do that again. Now go get me head.

Grimshaw was at a loss for words. He could see the distinct yellow-brown of Chernyl's skin sitting on top of what was left of the mountain and started to scramble up the side to get it. His feet slipped on paper and slick dust, but he managed to ascend the pile.

Chernyl's head looked more like a cowl with eyeholes. It was large enough to cover Grimshaw down to the shoulders.

Grimshaw picked it up and started walking to the edge of the mountain when he heard the soft noise of bare feet on stone. He dropped to his belly and extinguished the candle.

Moments later, a dozen Scribes armed with pikes and feuerglas lanterns walked out from behind a mound of rusting iron.

"I heard something," one of the lantern-bearing Scribes said.

A larger Scribe with a pike snickered. "I'm sure you did. The garbage in here shifts constantly."

"But the door was open."

"True, but it may have been open for months. Nobody comes down to the lower levels."

Grimshaw moved back from the edge.

What're we going to do? Grimshaw thought.

Simple, buddy. Put me head back on.

Out of the question. We're waiting till I can get us back to a controlled environment.

Chernyl laughed. *Controlled environment, buddy? When'll you learn?* Chernyl pushed hard on the mound, sending a cascade of papers down toward the Scribes.

You have no control.

"Up there!" the lantern-bearing Scribe said, pointing.

You've killed us both.

I can't be killed, but you can. Now, buddy, put me head on and I'll get us out of here.

Fiend be damned, tell me how.

The Scribes were nearing the bottom of the mountain, their voices raised in excitement.

You're a thick git, ya know buddy? We've been together months now and ya still don't know? A child coulda guessed by where ya found me.

Grimshaw thought back. Thought back to the lock and legends. The realization broke on him like a cold tide. His good hand shot into the air, waving frantically.

No. No. I—I can't let you. I won't.

"Over here," he said, before fingers clasped his throat, taking him back to the ground.

Sorry, buddy. Can't let you do that. Not yet. It's been so many years. So many sharp quills scratching my skin. Stories of love and death, shop inventory, children's sums, even a ransom note, all bleeding into me and me bleeding back. Not anymore, buddy. Can't do it anymore. Chernyl slammed a palm into Grimshaw's nose. The bone crunched and blood began to flow. His eyes crossed and he forgot where he was for a second, but a second was all Chernyl needed. His yellow-brown hand snatched the cowl and threw it over Grimshaw's head.

"Together," said the raspy voice. The word glowed white and Grimshaw went away as it felt like all the blood between his ears was sucked into the cowl. He could still see, could still feel, but it wasn't him anymore.

Chernyl stood up and stretched. One of the lantern-bearers threw his lump of feuerglas onto the top of the mountain. It tumbled to a stop near Chernyl's foot. Even as smoke began to rise as the feuerglas ignited the mountain, a collective gasp went up as the light touched his parchment-bound arm, and their eyes followed the yellow-brown trail up past, elbow, shoulder, neck, to the ink-stained skull. The Scribes fell to their knees and bowed their heads.

Chernyl smiled and ran a thumb through the blood flowing from his nose. In quick, precise strokes he wrote three words on his chest.

"The Inked Man," he said, and his whole body began to glow white.

From the Heart
By Kella Campbell

Lola knew exactly where she was—again. The teal-and-gold tiles under her cheek belonged to the VIP men's room upstairs at the Club; achy stiffness and a gummy feeling around her eyes and mouth suggested that she'd been lying there a good few hours. *Oops. Again.*

A dusty early light crept in through crimson-draped windows, gleaming on the balcony railing and the brass poles down onstage. *Right through till morning, even.* Lola staggered down the stairs, fumbled her way backstage to the dressing room and her locker—it'd be a bit much to go across to the Coffee Cave quite as she was, barely covered by a few bits of sequin and rhinestone—and where the hell had her corset gone? Pasties left on overnight would be adhesive-welded in place, so she didn't bother trying to remove them, just tugged yesterday's T-shirt overtop, with the faint hope that not too many people would notice the heart-shaped outlines. *Again.*

Her lower back ached and stung as she zipped up her skirt, and she wondered if she'd fallen and scraped herself on something.

❦

Chad at the Coffee Cave eyed the heart shapes with a smirk as he took her money.

"Rough night?"

It would have taken too much energy to even roll her eyes in response. Embarrassingly, her hand shook as she lifted the coffee mug from the counter, and she heard Chad snicker as she turned away. Near the front of the coffeehouse, a skinny, homeless-looking guy mopped the floor, pale hair in a ragged ponytail, clothes hard-worn under the Coffee Cave apron— obviously from the Neighbourhood Work Initiative, doing chores in exchange for a meal. *You'd think a coffee place that participates in the NWI would have staff a little more respectful of alternative lifestyle choices—at least I can feed myself and have a roof over my head.* God, it was good coffee, though.

Behind her, Chad called out, "Nice tramp stamp, Barbie Doll."

The fuck? Did I get a tattoo last night?

Head high, refusing to acknowledge the comment or reach around to feel her back for evidence, Lola stalked toward the door, smiling slightly as she heard Chad's outraged, "Hey, that's a for-here mug!"

"I'm only going across the street; I'll bring it back when I'm done, hipster boy."

The NWI mop-man shrank back and hissed at her as she passed.

The tattoo was a flower, maybe a rose, no bigger than a silver dollar, with a few delicate leaves and thorny tendrils curling to either side. *So sue me for my drunken lack of originality —it could as easily have been some dumb unicorn or emo skull art, stuck on my skin for all eternity.* The dark design stood out against tender angry skin, inked in black or maybe a dark-singed crimson; Lola couldn't be sure as she twisted and squinted in front of the mirror, trying for a better look. *Does it matter?*

She gave up, and scrabbled at the bottom of her locker until she uncovered a bottle of extra-strength Aleve and a flask of unspeakable hooch she'd apparently not found the night before. *Hair of the dog...* She splashed some into the remains of her coffee and washed down the Aleve.

Eventually she felt well enough to stagger the few blocks home, where her roommates shook their heads and made her put some Bacitracin on the tattoo before she fell into bed.

"You ought to eat something," said Chad as he poured her coffee.

Lola shrugged. "What do you care, hipster boy? You get a raise if you sell enough sandwiches?"

"Nah." He turned away, wiping the counter until it shone. "You're just... you look..." He sighed. "If you're dieting, you don't need to. If you're broke, I got some day-old muffins back here waiting to go to the NWI center, and maybe you need 'em more than they do."

"I'm not hungry." She slapped some coins down on the counter. *See? There's more than enough, and I'm not even going to count it or ask for change.*

Chad stopped her with an awkward touch to her wrist when she would have turned to go, and she saw reluctant concern in his eyes. "I know it's none of my business and all, but you shouldn't spend all your money adding to that tattoo, m'kay? You gotta eat."

She jerked her arm away. "I'm just not fucking hungry!" Hearing the crazy-lady shrillness in her own voice, she bolted for the door, glancing back as she realized she'd abandoned her coffee—and in that instant, in the doorway, she crashed full-speed into the NWI mop-man just coming into work. His lean frame was more solid than she would have guessed, and she rocked backward, only saved from falling by his firm grip on her upper arms. "Oh, God! I'm so sorry."

"S'all right." His voice was soft and raspy, as though he weren't used to talking much. He released her.

Feeling too many eyes on her, Lola stepped away from him, back to the counter to collect her coffee. "I'm not a charity case," she told Chad in a voice that came out a little too loud. "I have a job—even if you're standing there judging me for it. And I don't spend my grocery money adding to a tattoo that I didn't goddamn want in the first place."

As the words left her mouth, she thought of the mop-man standing behind her, and she turned to see how his face had closed up, his eyes gone like stone. *Charity case. Oh, hell.* But it couldn't be unsaid.

⋁

There was a rosebud next to the rose now, a sprouting of new leaves, another tendril of thorns dipping down toward the base of her spine. No sign that she'd had fresh ink done, this time, no redness to the skin. *Maybe it was always…?* But Lola felt uncomfortably sure there had only been one blossom before, and nothing that dipped below the top of her jeans.

She hitched her waistband up and tightened the belt another notch.

⋁

"You're going to have to take a break from dancing, hon."

She'd known it was coming, this moment, but it still hurt. "I… I'm fired, Morgan? For real?"

"Call it sick leave, okay? Maybe you need to lay off the partying, take care of yourself a little better." The Club manager had always been a blunt talker, and met her eyes squarely. "Burlesque is about flesh and curves, Lo, you know that— guests don't want to look at a dancing skeleton, now, do they? Eat some donuts, sit in the sun a bit; you'll be back before you know it."

Tears stung. Lola blinked them back. But they didn't do hugs and cups of tea at the Club. She pulled the corners of her mouth up, working at a smile. "D-do I need to clear out my locker?" She couldn't bring herself to ask about turning in her key to the stage door, but it came to the same thing.

"Not right away. But if I have to hire a new regular…"

"I know. You'll need the locker for her. How long do I have?"

But Morgan only shrugged, half turning away, conversation over— nothing more to be said. "I'll wait as long as I can, Lola." And that was as much sympathy as she'd get.

⋁

Lola grew paler, weaker, sicker. And the rose rambled over her back and began to wrap its thorns around her sides, sneaking up toward the curves of her breasts, its color now definitely a rich wine red.

♥

She squinted at the overcast and drizzling sky out her bedroom window. The walk down to the post office seemed a long way and a lot of effort, but she needed a stamp to mail Aunt Nancy's birthday card, and anyway she was flat out of bourbon, not to mention anything much edible. *Hello, credit card.* She avoided thinking about the growing mountain of debt.

At least it's not sunny out. She'd Googled sun allergy and solar urticaria and polymorphic light eruption, and thought of going to the clinic, but she figured they'd commit her to the psych ward if it came out that she thought her tattoo was growing and changing color. Easier just to stay in and sleep on sunny days. *It's not like I have anywhere to be.*

On the doorstep, she nearly turned back. Steeled herself against overwhelming weakness and the lure of going back to bed. *I'll just go as far as the Coffee Cave, treat myself to a latte. Then we'll see.*

♥

Lola saw him there as she approached: the mop-man, lounging against the brickwork outside the Coffee Cave, partially sheltered from the rain by the overhanging roof. *Awkward, much?* She'd avoided him since that day when she'd spoken too loudly about charity cases, even resorting to convenience store coffee instead of going in if she saw him there through the window.

But this time he was outside, his eyes already on her, and in any case she felt too ill to do anything but move forward, with an uncomfortable nod for him as she turned in at the doorway.

"Excuse me, ma'am," he said, his voice the same soft rasp she remembered, his face stiff with reluctance. She looked about, but he could only mean her. "May I ask where you got your tattoo?"

Could there be no greater shame? "I—well, uh, I was drunk. So I don't know. I… woke up with it," she choked out, feeling her face flame with embarrassment.

He bit off a frustrated expletive. "Can't be helped, I suppose. Sorry to have troubled you." And he turned away, her cue to go on into the coffeehouse. *But why did he want to know? Why would he care where I got it done?*

Lola tried to put it from her mind, but couldn't. At the counter, she found herself asking Chad if he knew what the mop-man liked to drink. "Ian? He's the herbal tea kind. Lemon-ginger, usually. Puts honey in it."

Damn, going to have to do this. "Okay, I'll get one of those as well. To-go cups for both."

"Hey," Lola said. When the mop-man—Ian—turned, tense and wary, she held out the steaming cup to him. "Here."

"Kind of you, ma'am, but I don't drink coffee."

"And you don't take charity. I know. But it's the lemon tea Chad says you like, and it's not charity. It's… I owe you an apology. Consider the tea an apology." She drew a deep breath. "I don't like to be judged over being a dancer; I had no business judging you."

He nodded, a gracious inclination of the head, and took the cup. "Thank you, ma'am." Was that a trace of a Southern accent? He sipped his tea, observing her, waiting. Not making it easy.

"You… you asked about my tattoo." She paused, hoping that he'd volunteer something, but only the merest lift of his eyebrow encouraged her to continue. "There's something… I mean, God, you'll think I'm insane, but—"

"But you aren't," he said.

"Oh?"

"Yes, it's growing. Yes, it's getting redder. Yes, it will probably kill you if you do nothing."

"How—"

"I have one too." With an almost angry jerk, he stretched the neckline of his T-shirt down just far enough to show the head of a dragon on his shoulder, and skin horribly scarred by fire. "You, ah, don't want to try to burn it off or cut it out. It's rooted too deep; you'll only mess yourself up."

"Christ!" Lola took a steadying gulp of her latte, tried not to visibly shudder at the burn scars or gasp with relief when he covered them again. Tried not to think about what he must have done.

"Ma'am, I've got to go inside about now. Earn my supper." He grinned, half rueful and half challenging. "But you need to know some things. Would you meet me after? That is, if you don't mind being seen with a dude who lives in his car."

He looked shabby and poor, maybe even a little bit dangerous, and every learned prejudice came rushing up inside her. But then she thought of all the times she'd been called a slut and a tramp, the sneers and condescension given, the assumption that all dancers were whores.

"Call me Lola," she said. "Where and when?"

They sat on the hood of his beat-up Volvo station wagon, eating orange Creamsicles in the last rays of the sun. *No booze to take the edge off the awkwardness.* He'd shaken his head at the suggestion, so she'd bought the frozen treats from the gas station instead, unable to face the conversation with nothing in her hands for distraction.

Lola's T-shirt was knotted up under her breasts, and Ian had taken his off altogether, apologizing and turning his scarred side away from her. "You want to get as much sun on it as possible," he'd said. The sunlight on her back stung and itched, but he told her not to mind it, that it would get better as the tattoo lost its strength.

"So what is this… thing?" she asked.

"I, ah, think it's somehow vampiric in nature," he said, watching her with wary eyes, waiting for her to doubt, to laugh. "You got weak, didn't you, like you were losing blood?"

"True." *Like I'd just given blood, only worse, all the time now.* Drained.

"And the only food that sounds anywhere close to good is rare steak?"

She stared. "Yes. Though even that… when I actually go to eat it…"

"And you've been avoiding sunlight, and sleeping all day, haven't you?"

She shuddered. "You said… it would probably kill me if I did nothing. Can it turn me into… I mean…"

"That, I don't know." He sucked the last bite of his Creamsicle off the stick. "But you'll be fine. I've had mine four years, and I've kept it from growing more'n a quarter-inch. You just have to live a little carefully, fight its grip. Lots of sun. No alcohol or caffeine."

"Shit," said Lola.

"Yep." An oddly companionable silence settled between them; for the first time in ages she felt herself free to just *be*—neither judged and found wanting, nor up on a pedestal of lust. The sun slipped below the horizon. "I've been tracking the bastard tattoo artist who did this for four years," he said as the dusk drew in. "Living out of my car. Taking odd jobs, busking, kindness of strangers and all that. Out west for a long time, up and down the coast. Started moving eastward 'bout a year ago. And then I followed him here, and lost him."

"Well, it might not be much help, but whoever did this has got my corset." She laughed, caught between indignation and the absurdity of it. "He took my best fucking corset!"

With the sun gone, the air had cooled. Ian picked up his shirt and pulled it over his head, but when Lola made to unknot hers, he held up a hand. "Wait a moment, sugar, there's one more thing—" He boosted his long body off the hood and popped open the car door, reached under the driver's seat to pull out a small plastic deli tub.

Crushed garlic. Lola gagged.

"Whoops—sorry! Should've warned you. Breathe through your mouth; I'll be quick." He scooped out a handful and mashed it against her lower back.

She came around to a lemon-disinfectant smell as something wet slid over her lower back.

No garlic?

Lola opened her eyes to find herself inside Ian's station wagon. The rear seats were folded down to make a flat bed, and she lay face down on a neatly spread sleeping bag, with Ian kneeling over her, antiseptic wipe in hand.

"Damn, sugar, you gave me a bit of a fright there." He gave her back a final swipe, and disposed of the towelette in a small lidded garbage pail. Even in the fading light, it struck her how clean and orderly the car was—not at all the rat's nest of clothes and trash she'd expected—and the sleeping bag had the dryer-sheet scent of a recent washing.

"What happened?" she asked, rolling onto her side.

He grimaced. "You blacked out. The first dose of garlic sends the tattoo-thing into some kind of shock, I guess, but it never knocked me out. Yours must have gotten an awful strong grip on you. I, ah, I'm sorry I waited so long to—"

Lola waved his words away. "Not your fault. I didn't exactly give you a chance…"

And then she noticed how dark it had become, grew acutely aware of his hand where it rested on her hip. *And I'm lying on his bed.*

His indrawn breath and a sharpening intensity in his gaze warned her that he felt it, too.

I should be scared. He's still a stranger. He lives in his car, for fuck's sake!

But she tingled all over with anticipation, and she realized that she found him attractive.

One corner of Ian's mouth curved upward in a slow smile. "Am I right in thinking you might be giving me a chance now?" he asked, his voice deep and thick with sensuality. *Waiting for permission.*

"Oh, hell, yes," she gasped, reaching up to draw him down.

In the morning she suggested he come back to her place for a shower.

Her roommates blinked at him and giggled and offered breakfast, shooting curious and significant looks at her—she'd never been one for mornings-after. Or maybe his untrimmed hair and threadbare clothes made them nervous. *Somehow Ian makes it easy to forget about those things, once you know him.*

She saw in the mirror that her tattoo was darker, less red.

"I'm no one's girlfriend," she told him. "I do my own thing." Refusing the urge to ask when she'd see him again.

"S'all right," he said. "I don't like labels and boxes either." But his hand stroked hers with affection.

Garlic capsules from the Vitamin Shoppe had no smell, and seemed to work—at least, Lola found herself wanting to eat again. Her energy picked up. The sun bothered her less. Her tattoo didn't shrink—perhaps the inky spread could not be reversed—but nor did it grow.

Ian conceded that taking garlic internally was a good idea, though he still argued that it should be applied to the surface as well. A couple of times a week, she'd let him mash the nasty stuff on her, and it no longer knocked her out.

Chad at the Coffee Cave started calling Lola "Barbie Doll" again.

"Oh, go pleasure yourself, hipster boy," she snapped back in high good humor, having run into Morgan outside the Club. "I'll have a cherry Danish with my latte, please." She'd be dancing again in less than two weeks—on probation at first, but she wasn't concerned.

Her days now felt like vacation, not desperation.

Ian hunted for the tattoo artist methodically, single-mindedly, with maps and notes, and hours spent online at the library. Lists of tattoo parlors, artists' websites, some sort of data analysis program he carried on a memory stick. He scoured reviews for hints of oddity. Compared names for similarity to those used in previous cities. Measured distances from the Club, as the last known point of contact.

Lola just walked. On every sunny day, in the skimpiest possible tops and tiny shorts—so the tattoo would have nowhere to hide—she walked miles of sidewalk, showing off her re-emerging fine self and flipping the bird at disapproving stares. Always looking, searching. Following her impulses. *He has my damn corset, and I swear I'll find it.*

And yet, when she saw it on a mannequin in the window of the Devil's Ink Tattoo Emporium, she could hardly believe she'd found it. *Probably just looks a bit like mine. Couldn't really be...* But the sequined hearts were the same, and the beaded fringe that had cost a goddamn fortune.

She called the Coffee Cave. "Hi Chad, this is Barbie Doll. Is Ian there?... Yes, it is a fucking emergency, or I wouldn't bother. Please?"

After an agonizing pause—so long that Lola began to wonder if Chad had forgotten altogether about her being on the phone—Ian's voice came on the line, rough with concern, asking, "What's wrong, sugar?"

"I, erm..." With the moment at hand, she wasn't sure how to say it, especially when he would have Chad and customers around him, listening. "I found my corset."

"Ah, I thought Chad said you—never mind. So it wasn't taken that night, then? You'd just misplaced it?" His matter-of-fact tone didn't quite hide the disappointment that their one clue had fizzled.

"No. Ian, I *found my corset*. In the display window of a tattoo place."

Silence. *Shock?* Then, "Where are you? I'm coming."

"Kensington Market. I'm in that coffee place on St. Andrew. But... you're working, aren't you?"

She heard him chuckle over the phone—maybe the word "working" wasn't the right choice, exactly. "Doesn't matter. If we've found him, for real,

I can—oh, Lord, I can go back to... I..." He cleared his throat. "Stay where you are. Please. I'm coming."

Efforts to peer through the windows came to nothing—the Devil's Ink attracted passersby with tattoo-painted mannequins, posed in front of atmospheric velvet curtains that looked like theatrical window dressing but effectively concealed the shop's interior. A sign on the door indicated that it wouldn't be open for another hour.

"D'you suppose the artist really is... something satanic?" Lola blurted out before she could censor herself. "Not that there's such thing as a devil, but..." *But if tattoos can grow and drain our blood, what else might exist?* Broad daylight on a busy public street mocked her.

"I have no idea what's in there, natural or unnatural," Ian said, a grim set to his face, "but I have no intention of waiting around for an hour to find out." He fished a set of thin picks from his pocket. "Stand close in so no one can see my hands."

"You... you're..." Discomfort washed over her. She hadn't suspected he'd be criminally inclined. Still couldn't quite believe it, despite the evidence in front of her.

He shot her a wry grin. "Sugar, I've never taken anything that wasn't freely given, but I've sure met a lot of, ah, interesting people on the road. Learned some useful tricks." And the lock clicked open.

No one waited in the front room—in the dim light filtering in from the front door, the place looked like any other tattoo parlor, with black vinyl benches to wait on, boards of designs on the walls and more in binders to flip through. A faintly medical-antiseptic scent drifted through a curtained archway to the back area, and Lola shuddered. *Surely I'm only imagining the smell of blood?*

To Ian's credit, he never asked her to wait outside or tried to keep her behind him, though she thought perhaps he might want to do just that. "Going in," he murmured, nodding toward the archway. But there were no surprises behind the curtain, only empty cubicles, sterile equipment.

And then they found stairs going down, of course. A basement.

◊

Red eyes glowed at them in the moment before Lola found the light switch. And she felt her tattoo prickle in recognition.

Then the fluorescent strips blinked on overhead, and beside her Ian cursed, but it wasn't in fear. *Poor damn thing.* An emaciated adolescent figure lay bound to a filthy cot, wrists and ankles blistered raw from silver chains. A handful of drained rat corpses had plainly been her only recent meals.

"I... ah... think we can assume you're not our 'artist,' ma'am?" said Ian.

"No. He made the last one turn me. He takes my blood, to make his evil ink," the girl whispered, her voice a broken scrape of wire on stone. "Please... let me go."

Lola gazed in horror at the soiled sheets, the festering sores under the shackles. "We have to let her go, help her get away," she said to Ian. "Even if she is a..." *No. Saying that word would make this too real.* "Even if she's... not like us... no one should be kept this way."

"I don't think she means to escape, Lola," Ian said. "It's more a shuffling-off-this-mortal-coil kind of thing, I believe. Ma'am?"

The girl nodded, an almost infinitesimal movement of a head too weak to hold itself up. "Please. I'm... too weak to run. I want to be... beyond his reach."

The scrape of a footstep echoed on the stairs beyond the door.

Ian drew a switchblade from his pocket. "Silver blade," he muttered, popping it open. "I'll be quick."

"Bless you." The words were barely audible, but the heartfelt gratitude unmistakable.

Lola looked away, tried not to hear the wet puncture sound, the momentary thrashing of weak limbs. She felt an odd, vanishing prickle over the tattoo on her back, like a heartbeat winking out. And then there was nothing left of the birdlike girl but a double handful of ashes crumbled on the foul bed.

❦

Afterward, Lola had trouble piecing the next sequence of events together.

She remembered surprise that the tattoo artist looked so ordinary: heavyset bodybuilder's physique under a Devil's Ink T-shirt, shaved head with a knotted bandana, neatly-trimmed soul patch on his chin. She remembered Ian circling him, wet-red blade in hand, and her own voice shrieking, "Don't kill him, Ian! You don't want to go to jail, or have to run from it!" Though what she'd thought would happen when they went after the tattoo artist in the first place, she wasn't sure. She remembered jumping back against the wall as the two men lunged and dodged and grappled.

She never could picture exactly how the tattoo artist ended up out cold on the floor with Ian's knee on his neck, though Ian later told her—and gently demonstrated—the jujitsu moves that had brought the man down. What stuck in her mind was the moment of stillness afterward, and Ian breathing hard, saying, "Now what?"

Unconscious dude. Basement room that had obviously held a hostage or victim of some sort. Somewhere on the premises, equipment to draw blood, and contaminated tattoo ink. "We call 911," Lola said. "This nasty creep has obviously been putting blood and God knows what else into his tattoo ink, which is pretty much assault on unsuspecting customers, right? And I'd think this room points to kidnapping or worse."

❦

As the men in blue removed him from his erstwhile business premises, Elliot Pugmann—Caucasian male, 49—did not help his case by proclaiming himself an artist and genius, and shouting that they'd no right to destroy his blood source.

The tattoo still covered most of Lola's back; delicate leaves and thorny tendrils rambled outward from the original silver-dollar rose at its heart, but they no longer grew, and the ink stayed solid black. For all Pugmann's skills as a biochemist and tattooist, he hadn't found a way to keep the blood active past the demise of its donor. *Psychopathic egomaniac, but at least the artwork's good.* And she wondered how much of its beauty had come from the artist's hand, and how much had blossomed from the dead girl's heart.

She'd never get the corset back—it was likely in a police evidence locker somewhere, and asking for it would draw too many awkward questions—but she was rethinking her stage wardrobe anyway to go with her new inked look. *A little less old-time glam, a little more rock 'n' roll.*

Morgan liked the idea and was eager to have her back onstage.

They sat at a window table in the Coffee Cave. He held her hand under the table. Nearby, a ragged young woman from the NWI mopped the floor. *Too young to be living on the street.*

Ian had paid for their lattes out of his first real paycheck in four years—as doorman and security at the Club. His jujitsu skills had given Lola the idea, and a hands-on interview won Morgan over. "It's only until I can update my skills and get back into programming," he'd said at first, but readjustment to a life he hardly remembered came hard, and the Club was a good place for people who didn't like to be boxed in.

Lola sipped her latte and looked out the window, across the street to the daytime-closed front of the Club. The marquee lights wouldn't go on until dusk, but it felt right to see her stage name up there once again. "You know I'm going to keep dancing," she said to Ian. "Not because I have to. Because I want to."

"S'all right," he said. "I'll probably keep living in my car a while. I'm, ah, used to it now."

Lola grinned, thinking of his car and that first morning-after, when she'd taken him home for a shower and breakfast. "You can shower at my place anytime, love."

Sideponytail
by Lily Hoang

Charlotte is into role-playing. She wouldn't call herself an addict or anything severe like that, she doesn't have a *problem*—that's what Carson said, "Girl, you've got yourself a *problem*," but he's all drama so whatever, what's the point in having a platonic male friend if not for fireworks and flavor?—it's a *hobby*.

Everyone has hobbies.

◆

Yesterday, over mimosas and crab-cakes, he said, "But you were into it," something between a scientific fact and incredulity.

She shouldn't have said anything. Like, it's fine when Carson rattles about his *bitches*, but she says one little thing and he's all interrogation detective. The way he asked her, shame was braided into the rhetoric and she was guilty, better put her on the sex offender registry, snap snap.

"It's, like, a big part of girlhood. Like, dolls are supposed to be real babies that you cradle and burp and come on, Disney?"

Carson tipped his champagne glass towards her, "Jesus, of course. You're so predictable."

◆

Charlotte skims the woman's file. She wants to be patient, but she only allots one get-out-of-jail free card, that's it. Just one.

"What about my kids?"

The only thing worse than a convict is one who uses her kids easy as trading cards. "You should've thought about them before using." Charlotte aims to look intimidating: sharp black suit, glasses that slide down her nose to make her glare hint at menace.

"It ain't right, Miss Anders, swear it. Just must be it's still in my system. I haven't used in months, honest." The woman crosses herself. "Swear to God Himself." She shakes her head, but it's more like thrusting, no control.

The woman must think she's a fool, like it isn't her job to sieve lies, like this woman is something special, no, she's just another tick for recidivism and Charlotte's the one who's going to have to do it, this woman should be taking care of her kids, not going back to prison for dirty piss. It's stupid. Charlotte hates the woman, hates all the ones who make her do it, and this woman is no different, they're all the same: they beg, they always do, and bargain and threaten and lie, a bunch of goddamn liars.

Charlotte picks up the phone and the woman is cuffed.

She was lying, of course. Charlotte doesn't feel remorseful, not even when the woman spits *bitch* while she's being led out, like one cruel word might give her freedom, like there's no such thing as culpability or rightness or justice. Charlotte wishes the woman *had* been telling the truth, but she's not some amateur at her job: she knows exactly how long it takes a body—a *female* body—to synthesize every drug, how long it takes a body to eject every drug, how to read the numbers. When she started the job, she thought of herself as an advocate. Now, her coffee is cold but whatever, it still works fine enough.

♦

"What about whores?"

His eyes were open, his hands pushed her hips down hard.

"Sad cases, most of them."

"How many men have you fucked tonight?"

It was kind of like his dick belonged to some monstrous thing, like he asked the question and her whole body became smaller. And they'd *been* having sex. She knew how things should fit, this was something else. "Six."

Freddie made fists around her tits and pulled. He whispered, "Do I get a discount for being the lucky seven?"

Charlotte's one of the girls who thinks up the perfect comeback right off beat, it's an issue of timing.

She just about threw up finishing him, not—like—in a bad way. She'd blown him before, plenty of times, plenty of other guys too. This, she understood, was recess, the bell rings and the teacher releases the kids to play. Afterwards, they slept the way they did every time she spends the night: him on his back, arm hooking her waist, her head already asleep somewhere along the brawn of his chest.

\)

"It doesn't even matter why, okay? I'm fine with it."

Charlotte didn't want to lie. Or, she didn't want to be exposed as a liar. It's just that he was being all accusatory, like there was something *wrong* with her.

Carson downed his mimosa. "No," he said, the glass was still touching his lower lip, challenging. "You're not *fine* with it at all, you little tramp." The glass, with its slender funnel and the pressing New Orleans humidity, filled and emptied at every word, his sass collected in small condensations. "You like it." He stood up. "Round three is on me, hussy." Before Charlotte, Carson had sex with all of his female friends, which accounted for something or other she figured, so he made up for it by pretending he was gay around her. Because they weren't having sex. Well, they *were* having sex and it was kind of a big deal, when Charlotte told him she was sort of really into this other guy, and Carson didn't take it well but then he changed his thinking or something because at some point, Sunday brunch became tradition and him acting compensatorily gay and her confessing things about her sex life that she didn't tell her closest BFFs became tradition too.

Some buskers started up. They were all soul and beat, probably around the corner but their music carries and keeps. Part of her hoped that buskers could save her from her Midwestern lines, corn and apple trees in simple lines, line after line, gridded rules, and buskers bent and shook and quivered. They lived.

"Okay, real talk," Carson said, "and be honest with me, okay? How freaky does it get? Like, I'm imagining you're Bella, but the real question is: is he an Edward or a Jacob?"

This time, she didn't miss her shot. "Both," she'd aimed right at Carson's annoying man-complex and blasted it down. Maybe it was mean of her, but she knew, fake gay or not, he hated that she didn't choose him. Carson wasn't in love with her or anything, obviously, but it was a pride thing, the easiest tackle. Then, relenting, she said, "Jesus, Carson, I'm not twelve, I don't fantasize about vampires and werewolves, okay?" She felt suddenly insulted, probably because he was right. "You of all people should know that."

"Oh," he said all exaggerated, "I get it." The trumpet was trilling off wild. Charlotte wished she knew how to play, maybe she should start up lessons, she was jealous of her friends growing up, the ones with decent parents because they cared or something. They learned music. It was like a way of talking that she couldn't even understand. Her parents gave her money and bought her the newest gadgets and after all that shit in middle school, they were decent enough to put her in private high school—*fresh start*, they'd said, or, no, they didn't say it. As in they didn't speak the words, they were in Galapagos or wherever, or her mom was there on business, who knew!?, she got it on her pager, this cryptic message, *fresh start*, and so it was, a fresh start and all without music. "Charlotte."

"Yeah?"

"So am I right or what?"

"About what?"

"I don't know why I bother."

"Stop being a prima donna, Christ."

"I was just saying that I was wrong."

"About what?"

"Whatever, girl, you've got yourself a *problem*."

"Well, I guess the moment of humility was really just a moment."

"Humility? Why would I need to be humble? I'm not one of your felons, dig? I was wrong, you got that one right, but only because I got the roles confused. There's no way you'd be Bella. You'd make him be Bella. You're all vampire empress, totes. I bet you make him beg." Carson's voice got louder, heavier, it pushed the music out and away. "I bet you emasculate him, take away his dignity—not that you'd be with a man with dignity, you always choose weaklings you can dominate and own, am I right? Poor Freddie, so effete and fragile! So *feminine*—and that's when you do it, fanged out machetes and I bet you're so into it you actually lick the blood right off his neck."

With all her fancy education, she shouldn't be a probation officer. Every day, she wonders why she's doing it. It's not for the money, that's for sure, her parents didn't give her attention or hugs—they were busy, she gets it and doesn't—but the fact is, she doesn't need to have a job, much less a *profession*, but here she is, looking at the clock, looking at the files, looking at people she's responsible for getting cuffed and carted away. Her desk is confusion, like how a kid shuffles cards before he knows how to shuffle, loose papers in puddles and mounds. Charlotte takes a stack and tries to at least align the edges. It's nearly five, and Freddie won't be free until eight. She has three hours to get ready, minus the commute.

In middle school, Charlotte saw something terrible. She was in English and her school was trying out some stupid new program that separated the girls from the boys in AP classes. Her parents—both of them—had to go to a big deal meeting about it. They went out for Italian food after. Charlotte can't remember anything about the meeting, just that her mom had a grilled chicken salad and her dad had spaghetti and meatballs but with white sauce and she had lasagna and they shared a tiramisu and pear gelato. Charlotte was in eighth grade. It was 1995, a month before summer break, and

Charlotte's biggest worry in life was whether she liked Tommy more or Peter more, Tommy was supposed to be a phenom pitcher but it's not like baseball players score really high on popularity points—*although*, he was already a freshman, which meant that next year, she'd start school with a boyfriend who was already established, and that'd make it easier for her, *probably*—but Peter was way hotter but he was in her grade and he was into computers and nerdy stuff like that *and* he didn't know that he was way hot so it was like he'd worship her or something, which would be kinda nice. Charlotte was trying her best to imagine what her first kiss would feel like with each of them, it was important, a moment to be remembered, one's first kiss, she wanted it to be sudden and unexpected and romantic like in the movies, and she wasn't paying attention, even though she liked the class, because this was like big picture stuff and she'd already read *Pride and Prejudice* like ten times, and she almost missed it. It wasn't until Maggie started screeching out cusswords that Charlotte was kicked out of daydreaming. There was a man, Charlotte didn't recognize him because he had his back to the students, he was holding Miss Salerson's arm, talking into her ear. And then he shot her, Charlotte hadn't even seen the gun, or she doesn't remember it, but she must've seen it because it was a rifle and really big and he shot her right under her neck and then he aimed at the same spot on his own body and fired.

♥

Her parents had wanted her to stay in town for college—her dad was the dean of something or other, which meant she'd go for free, or maybe he was a provost, she really didn't care—and Charlotte wanted away, anywhere, and she had her choice of her top choices and she picked Tulane arbitrarily, because New Orleans seemed like an exciting place. Also, it was far, a whole different world and culture from South Bend, like it was a place that actually had difference and culture, and Mardi Gras and boats and cafés. She didn't have anywhere to go after she finished school, so she stayed.

Being a probation officer is totally not what she thought she'd be doing when she left the Midwest. Sometimes, she imagines what eighteen year old

Charlotte would think of thirtysomething Charlotte, she'd be disappointed, for sure, at her future self, that this is the sum of her life, she hadn't just squandered it, she flat gave up, didn't even try, thirtysomething Charlotte: she's a paper pusher. Her social life is the kind of joke without a punch line. She's pretty sure Freddie's cheating on her or something. She's pretty sure something isn't right. But the worst of it, she's on the wrong goddamn side.

Eighteen-year-old Charlotte was a radical, a feminist, an ankh tattooed on her ankle before ink was mainstream; she was hardcore in that way that only privileged kids can be. Nor is thirtysomething Charlotte just a passive cog in *the system*—eighteen year old Charlotte would've balked at that too, hard to say which one she'd think of as worse—no, she's an active participant, every day she sees people who started life fucked and no one bothered to teach them any different and it's her job to teach them but it's like she doesn't even have control over what she can teach, because there are all these rules. Like there's no such thing as positive reinforcement. Doing good means her *students* get to stay free. It's like she can't even praise them, but bad behavior earns immediate punishment, she's a terrible teacher, the whole operation is a failure, just like she is, that's exactly what eighteen year old Charlotte would say, and then there's all that business with Freddie and the role-playing, which was all her idea, she'd scripted it out and everything, because she'd been there before, that moment when sex gets stale and she uses role-playing out of desperation, to keep her man, because let's face it, she is pathetic, unlovable, someone who deserves a hypothetical teenager's mockery.

❦

Truth is: Carson *was* wrong, but only because he chose the wrong vampire.

Charlotte picks out a tangerine tank, low-cut and cleavage needed, a blue plaid shirt, and denim shorts that aren't nearly short enough. If Carson knew her at all, he would never have chosen *Twilight*, she's not into that amorous longing stare and she doesn't own stock in star-crossed stupidity. If Carson knew her at all, he would've known that if she were going to role-play any vampire story, it'd be *True Blood*. She doesn't watch it for plot, it's the raunch she's after. Charlotte takes a pair of scissors to her shorts. She's never cut denim before. She usually buys her costumes. She can't control the lines, they diagonal and fall in tiers: irresistible.

◈

The problem with Freddie is that he's a gentleman.

He opens car doors and all doors and he knows what wine pairs best with what meat.

He pays his bills on time.

His house is always clean, his bed is always made.

His towels—all of them—match.

His hair is always in place, even when it seems impossible.

He has business cards.

He is a replica of her father, at a quarter his salary, which doesn't break any deals.

Like walking into a swarm of gnats, that's how Charlotte feels with every opened car door and every bottle of wine and every check he writes and on.

Charlotte thought there was no way he'd go for it. But right around the time she told Carson she was kinda into this other guy, she handed Freddie the script. He had just come home from work, hadn't even had the time to undo his shoes. Either he played or she would end things, he was a nice guy and that was the problem. Charlotte had a fucking problem.

"What's—"

Charlotte kneeled.

◈

She showers and shaves. She doesn't know if she should wash her hair or not. Sometimes, Sookie rocks that day-old low-sideponytail look, and that's what Charlotte wants to imitate. She towels off, makes pouty lips at herself in the mirror. Her cheeks are too high, otherwise, she could pass for Anna Paquin. She's always been pretty but unremarkably so. There's just nothing to her that's special. When men, even Freddie and Carson back in the day, praise her, they use vague words like *hot* and *sexy*, sometimes a rare *beautiful* sneaks up in there, but no one points to one specific thing—her smile, her eyes, her legs, her ass—that makes them wild, just wild, she's pretty enough to be pretty, she doesn't want *pretty*, she wants to be arresting, she wants to arrest men. She laughs at her pun, apropos but without the wit of humor.

※

Yesterday, over dessert and really tossed, Carson asked her, "Why him?"

She knew the issue would come up sooner or later, Carson was a catch and he knew it. He's handsome and successful and they watched British comedies in bed together. And the guy's name is Freddie, for Christ's sake, what kind of man goes by the name *Freddie*?

"I know," she said. "I tried calling him Fred for a while, see how he took to it, tried Rick too, but that was way weird." Charlotte knew she was avoiding his question, it was obvious, caught in the air like there was never any music, just sourness and champagne.

She waited, hoping he would relent.

In those extending, flexible seconds, the clouds fell low and tight. The sun slipped through in straight banners, majestic, cinematic even. It was all so artificial.

Carson let loose a laugh, and sound and time and everything else too came at Charlotte at full force. It was like spilling a whole tray of drinks. She felt—fine.

Finally, with resolve, he said, "Girl." The word had a million elastic exaggerated syllables. "He's not the only one who'd be all freaky freak with you." The violinist soloed in ragtime, her up-beat swinging, her down-beats crumpled fenders, easy. He blushed. "I'm just saying that you didn't even ask me, like, if that was some deciding factor, you didn't even ask me."

Freddie rolls whatever it is around the glass. It clings. "Char, I can't."

"Sookie," she corrects.

"Charlotte." His firmness is uncomfortable.

She pushes her lips towards a pout, trying to be sultry. "Bill Compton, aren't you just ravaged?" She bends her neck to the right, tosses her blond hair. At the last minute, she just had to give it a washing and conditioning and rehydrating and drying and curling. "Can you smell my temptation?"

"Look, Char," Freddie loosens his tie, "I mean, this is fun every once in a while."

She tries, "Like once a full moon?" It's pathetic. Beggarly. She's so pathetic.

"Seriously, okay? Just look at you. And this!" He pours the *drink* into the sink. It comes out in curdles. "What the fuck is this?"

"It's—"

"No. I don't even want to know and I for sure don't want to know how much time you wasted on this shit."

Hours.

Charlotte had spent hours.

Jello and food coloring.

Blood isn't strawberry.

"I'm not saying that it isn't fun because it is. And I'm definitely not saying that I'm not into it because I'd be lying, it's just, you can't expect me to do this every single night. I'm not playing dress up just so you can get off, okay?"

"Me? You think this is about me?"

"Oh, so this is about me."

"I didn't—"

"All you do is blame other people. If you like doing this kind of shit, fine. I'm cool with it. I'll play along. Just not every night, okay? I'm tired. I work."

"Fuck you, Freddie, like I don't work or what?"

"Can't we have just one night where we pretend to be an actual couple?"

"What the—"

"Like just pretend we're in a real relationship, cook dinner and watch a movie and not even fuck, I don't even *want* to fuck, I just want to cuddle up and touch your skin and maybe we can bake some cookies or eat ice cream in bed and set our alarms and drink coffee together in the morning. Do a boring goddamn crossword together, I don't know, normal shit."

"Normal shit."

"Yeah, like, I'm almost forty."

"That's so irrelevant."

"Stop it. Just stop, okay? I'm almost forty and I want a normal boring life. I want to come home from work and know that you'll be here and that you're not going away because you find me too boring. Char, don't you get it?"

"No, I don't."

"Let's get married."

⁂

Charlotte was too busy dreaming about her first kiss. She hadn't heard him, but he'd proposed, too, and when her teacher said no, he pushed the barrel tighter on her skin, offered a chance to reconsider. He was a stranger. They didn't know each other. That's what the newspaper said, all news reports too.

It wasn't really the type of story to deserve national—or even regional—attention, but that didn't mean that it wasn't important.

Charlotte almost never thinks about it. It was so long ago and her recollection of the events is underwhelming at best. At the time, though, she must've been devastated. Miss Salerson was handily her favorite teacher, everyone's, she was smart and she wore the coolest threads and like all of her other teachers were so yesterday—more like three decades back—and a snooze, whereas Miss Salerson made books and reading seem cool, like totally cool.

When Charlotte actually thinks about the event though, she recognizes that there had to be some sort of consequence, for her, to her. It should have been a turning point, a moment that she revisits and spins in her head, but there was no impact, barely even a residue, the memory shaped more through news and gossip than memory.

According to her best friend's kind of boyfriend, he wasn't a stranger though. The news got it all stupid, he saw the two of them necking in the Martin's parking lot, or, at least it looked like her hair—and he could recognize her from behind, *easy*—but it was for sure him.

According to her other best friend, he was her high school sweetheart. According to Jessie, who Charlotte *hated* because she knew everything about everything and everyone, he'd been following Miss Salerson around for years—in fact, she only moved to the Bend to get away from him—and she was scared of him, like really really scared. Jessie was the reason she started going by Charlotte in high school, the truncation of her name plus *ie* was too close to *Jessie*, not that she could recall any specific reason for her hate, girlhood doesn't work that way.

Neither does memory.

From that year, the most important memory should be Miss Salerson's shooting, but there's only the lack of first kiss and Jessie.

She had wanted to explain everything to Carson, but he wouldn't get it, there was no way he would've understood. She doesn't even understand.

Undressing, Charlotte forgives her parents for their negligence, stops being mad at Jessie for no reason at all, wishes Carson could just get it already. She fingers a few strands of loose hair along her neck, their loneliness.

Bill Compton will keep them company.

When he bites down, her skin releases.

His Face, All Red

by Gemma Files

"You're up very late, my dear," the old man said, when Leah came over to hand him a menu and pour some complimentary water. It was 3:37 a.m. by the clock above the range, and the place was pretty much deserted—just her, him, and Amir and Gue back in the kitchen.

She shrugged, indicating the sign in the front window. "Twenty-four hours. Means somebody's always gotta be up all night, and that's me."

He turned to study it a moment, quizzically, like he hadn't even realized it was there, even though he must've passed right by it to get to the front door. Then replied, without much surprise, or interest—"Oh, well, yes."

The old man had one of those crazy accents, prissy and kind of hot at the same time, every vowel struck like a bell—sounded like Gandalf, basically, or maybe Jean-Luc Picard. Leah couldn't begin to reckon his actual age. Also, the nearer she got to him, the more she saw how his skin was kind of… flawless, creepily so. Eyes like blue glass, narrowed by smile-lines; perfect teeth, too, and wasn't that weird, for an English dude? When he smiled, he looked like everybody's favorite librarian. But he was wearing a decrepit, faded Lamb of God T-shirt that'd seen better decades and a pair of bright pink sweatpants, both much too big for his hawk-slim frame, with a cracked and battered set of Crocs Leah swore to God she could see his (slightly overlong) toenails through.

"What's with the clothes, sir?" she asked, trying to make it sound funny, charming even—but she had to guess it probably didn't sound like either of those things, because his good cheer faded on contact; he frowned slightly and looked down, studying the outfit like (again) someone had stuck it on him without his noticing.

"What is with them?" he repeated, genuinely baffled. Then: "Oh, these aren't mine; I found them in a trash-bin, I think. The one at the end of that alley beside your fine restaurant, with 'Twister Relief' written on its side."

"I don't think that stuff is meant for... somebody like you," Leah began, immediately feeling even sillier; now it was the old man's turn to shrug, however, giving her an excuse to change the subject. "What was wrong with what you were already wearing?"

"Oh, it simply wouldn't have done at all, my dear, not for a public venue. For one thing, my suit was almost completely covered in blood. And for another, I had been wearing it a good twenty years already, at least."

Leah only realized she was staring at those amazing teeth of his—so white, so straight, so sharp—when he snaked his tongue out, unexpectedly, and licked them, like an animal. Completely out of left field, and gross, too; perverted, somehow, or at least profane. For anybody that age to be getting such an apparent charge out of being hungry, breathing in deliberately, holding it like a mouthful of weed-smoke... tasting the air itself, sensually, as though it were a steak he longed to take a bite out of...

"'Covered in blood,'" she hear herself mimic as he stood up, seemed to almost eddy forward, near enough to touch. "'C—covered in—'"

"Yes, dear. Just like that."

"Whose... blood was it?"

"Oh, I don't believe I ever got their names; professionals, you see. No element of friendliness about that transaction, I can tell you. Not like you and I."

"...can't move."

"No, of course not. That's what the hypnotism is for, you see."

Perfect teeth, so straight and white and shiny. She felt a tear streak down one cheek, and thought, He's such an old man, and I'm not. I could—I should—

But she didn't, of course, for far too long. And then there was a sudden, terrible pain, a tearing just above her collarbone, quickly followed by nothing at all.

V

When Leah came to again, everything hurt: her eyes, her guts, her skin. It was bright outside, enough to make her wince and flinch at the same time, cowering back, shoving herself as far underneath the table the old man'd been sitting at as geometry would allow for. Thank God, though, the two women standing in front of her seemed to have already figured out they should probably close the blinds before she woke, or lose their only witness to spontaneous inhuman combustion...

(What?)

...and oh, such an additional pain, so sharp and coring, to even think—let alone voice—that name. The one she was now forbidden access to, forever.

I don't know where this is coming from, any of it, Leah realized, suddenly sick. Or how I know it... what I think I know, even...

Eyes flicking first left, then right, as though bracing herself for further attack; hands fisting so hard she could hear her nail grate on the floor beneath, scratching the linoleum, like claws. But the vertigo that immediately welled up made her want to put her head between her knees and moan, like a poisoned dog, so she did, while the women—sisters, they were definitely sisters, she could smell it on them—simply stood there and watched, the taller one projecting an aura of quiet authority and genuine sympathy even as the smaller simply rocked back on her bootheels, her sniper's gaze never wavering from Leah's face and one hand sneaking behind her back, feeling for some kind of weapon.

Better put me down quick, bitch, you want to keep me there, the unfamiliar mind-voice (that doesn't sound like me) whispered in her head, gleefully sly, all its worst instincts pricking up in anticipation of slaughter. Better not let me get a good jump in, 'less you want to be wiping little sis's blood off the wall...

Leah shook her head again, just once but sharply, to dismiss it. And made herself look back up, trying her level best to not only look harmless, but be so.

"That old man... is he still here?"

The taller one shook her head, blonde braids swinging. "Long gone, I'd say. Given the temp on your friends."

"Gue—Amir?"

"That's what their badges said, yes. And you're Leah, right?"

Leah nodded, sniffed, eyes blurred and stinging. But when she put up a hand to wipe away the tears, she drew it away smeared with red.

"Oh Jesus," she said, staring at the result, no matter how the word hurt to use. "Oh God, oh Christ. What happened to us all?"

The taller woman sighed, and took a moment, like she wanted to choose her next words carefully. In the meantime, Leah found her eyes drawn to the tattoos she could suddenly see crawling up along the woman's arms, weaving underneath the sleeves of her shirt to climb the sides of her long neck like vines. They were snakey, deep-carved things, some of them roughly keloided as though self-inflicted, a strange contrast with the woman—girl, really, Leah now understood—herself, who seemed gentle, almost sad. I want to help, her gray eyes seemed to say, though they both knew that was impossible.

(Yes, yes we do)

(How, though? Why?)

"His name is Maks Maartensbeck," the tall girl began, reluctantly. "Professor Maartensbeck. Highly respected, in our field; did a lot of good, once. Saved a lot of lives. But he hasn't really been that man for a very long time, now."

"Then... what is he?"

"Oh, Leah, come on. You've seen the movies. He came in here at night, put you to sleep with a look, drank from your neck, then ripped your friends apart. So if you just let yourself think about it for a minute, I kind of think you already know."

(Running her tongue along the inside of her lips, across her teeth, and feeling skin part, seamless. Knowing without even having to check how they would shine just as brightly as the old man's, now; white-sharp like the new moon. Her empty stomach contracting, and the rush and pulse of blood—not her own—rising in her ears, more beautiful than any remembered song.)

The smaller woman was visibly tensed now, biceps gone hard beneath the sleeves of her many-pocketed East Coast gangsta parka; she had thighs like she pumped prison iron, so cut Leah could see definition even through her jeans. Such a tough little cookie, with her narrowed brown glare and her dirty blonde Boot Camp haircut, and Leah felt herself beginning to fairly long to see what exactly she was reaching behind her for, the roots of all Leah's brand new dental accoutrements set aching at once. With the bad voice whispering yet again, up and down the dry rivers of her veins, Yeah, go on ahead and whip it out; get it over with, 'cause I'm tired of talking. Sun's up, my head hurts, and better yet, I'm—I'm just, just so, so—damn—

(hungry)

But: This is NOT ME, she told herself. Not while I can still refuse to let it be.

Then added, out loud, like she was arguing the point, "That stuff's not real, though, is it—not outside of... True Blood, and whatever? It just doesn't happen."

The taller woman cocked her head slightly, neither confirming nor denying—though one tattooed shoulder did hitch just a tick, automatically, a movement perhaps only kept from blossoming into a full shrug by some arcane version of politeness.

"Not usually," she agreed. "But sometimes. This time."

"But... "

Now it was the smaller woman's turn to shake her head, punchtuating it with a snort. "Just skip the counselling, Sami," she told her sister. "You were right the first go-'round—she gets it, just doesn't like it, 'cause who would? Now get your whammy on, and let's do what's gotta be done."

"Dionne—"

"Samaire." Turning to Leah, she said, "You got a bad case of the deads, kid, and it stops here, before you start treating the next diner's staff like your private buffet. Nothing personal."

"Dee, Jesus."

"What about him? Oh, that's right, not here. As usual." The thing behind her back was a machete, carving fluid through the air, already nicking Leah's throat; Leah felt the creature inside her leap, vision red-flushing, and knew her teeth must be out, lips torn at their corners. But Dionne didn't flinch, barely turning to yell, over her shoulder, "DO it, goddamnit, 'less you wanna be doing me next!"

(Yes yes and FAST do it FAST)

Something caught Leah then, square in the back of the skull, like a hook; it lifted her up and soothed her slack at the same time, a novocaine epidural. She was sewn tight, paralyzed, unable to fire a single nerve—the voice, the hunger, all drained away, replaced by a smooth, warm feeling of peace. Behind Dionne, she saw Samaire's long fingers flicker, drawing symbols on the air. Her many tattoos were glowing now, right through her clothes, each too-black line somehow rimmed in vitriolic green and sulphur yellow-touched at the same time, like light reflected off a shaken snake-scale.

I didn't ask for this. Yet even as she willed her lips to shape the words, failing miserably to bring them to completion, she already knew Samaire could hear them anyhow. And thought she heard, in reply—echoing, as it were, from another part of her too-full head entirely—

No. No one ever does.

Seeing the cores of the tall girl's eyes twist sidelong, little black swastikas at the center of two pearl-gray pools. And letting her own drift shut, letting go of everything at once; barely feeling the pain as Dionne's blade slashed through her spine, severing her new-made vampire head with one quick, expert blow.

☥

Take the night shift and lose your life, maybe your freaking soul; wake up with a killer hangover and a cannibal thirst, catapulted into a world where the best you could hope for was somebody like Dionne and Samaire

Cornish to put you down before you did the same to anybody else. That was their cross to bear in a nutshell, Dee knew: the family curse, spelled out coast to coast in monster-blood and mayhem, still-live warrants for prison break and felony murder notwithstanding. But at least they could trust the Maartensbecks to use all that career vampire-killer money of theirs to cover their tracks for them this time, supposedly, so long as they returned the favor...

She stepped back just in time to let poor Leah's skull fall one way and her body the other, neatly avoiding the tainted geyser of blood spraying out every which-way, cellular-level desperate to find something else to infect before its time ran out. But Sami was already twitching the diner's blinds up again, letting in enough sunlight to crisp that evil shit to ash so fine it wouldn't register on any CSI test. Of course, they could've just taken the former waitress down that way in the first place, but it was messy, to say the least, and beheading was a clean, relatively painless death. So saving the daylight exposure option for body disposal suited both Dee and Sami fine.

No time for much more than starting to think *Good work, little sis...* before Dee found herself stopping short again, machete automatically whipping back up, as an all-too-recognizable voice drawled, from the diner's conveniently propped-open doorway—

"Hmmm, messy. Not s'much as the old boy I just did somethin' similar to, 'course, but that's probably 'cause practice makes perfect. Y'all truly do know your stuff when it comes to supernatural creature disposal, you two."

Oh, you have gotta be fucking kidding me.

Both of them turned together, then, to see well-known holler witch turned cellblock pimp Allfair "A-Cat" Chatwin standing there with both hands buried wrist-deep in her hoodie's front pocket, large as life—which really didn't work out to be too damn large at all comparatively, though grantedly bigger than Dee—and twice as skanky. Her bush of malt-brown hair was jammed down under a backwards-turned trucker cap so gross she might've rolled an actual trucker for it, and Dee was amazed (yet not, somehow, surprised) to note the crazy bitch was still wearing her prison jumpsuit, albeit with the shucked top hung down like shirt-tails, so it probably read to the uninitiated as nothing more than a particularly heinous set of bright orange parachute pants.

Had a big book tucked under up one arm, too. Bible-heavy, though Dee didn't have to see Sami's nose twitch to know it probably had a very different sort of stink to it.

Sami would claim they owed 'Chatwin something for helping in the escape from Mennenvale Women's Correctional, Dee believed, if pressed. For herself, Dee was pretty sure all they owed her was a quick put-down, an unmarked grave and the promise not to piss on it after, but she'd long since had to reconcile with the fact that whenever Sami's highly flexible conscience was involved, things didn't always go her way.

"We should talk, that's what I'm thinkin'," Chatwin suggested, black eyes glinting with ill charm and a touch of sly humor both, like she could read Dee's mind right from where she stood. And hell, maybe she could—Dee'd seen Sami do something similar enough times to not bother counting anymore, using the half-demon blood she and Chatwin shared, supposedly from the same source. That was if you could trust Chatwin on that one, which Dee very much didn't, having watched her calmly lie about the sky being blue in her time (metaphorically speaking) for the express purpose of messing with both their minds, not to mention seeing how far she could slip inside Sami's pants while doing it.

Moriam Cornish's sin made flesh, Dee's dead Daddy would've called it, they hadn't already shot his veins full of poison for killing her over lying down with the Fallen. She'd only done it to help him fight a crusade she apparently felt worth sacrifice, but that sure hadn't saved her, once he found out. It was the key event of both their childhoods, Sami's birth out of their Mama's useless death—the thing that'd sent Jeptha Cornish to jail and both his kids into different degrees of foster care, kept them separated 'til they were both adults and well past the age of consent when they'd made their own pact together, a vow to take up the reins and keep fighting their parents' Anabaptist crusade, with that solemn troth plighted on Moriam's grave and sealed since in a hundred different variety of strange things' blood.

Dee'd already started up where Jeptha left off, wielding rote-learned knowledge and home-made weapons she would turn to her sister's service, playing knight to her reluctant sorceress—just as Sami had committed on her own to Moriam's path, though without the shamefaced layer of secrets and lies that had eventually dragged her down. Had already taken the first few steps along it back when Dee turned up at her university dorm room's door, in fact, so long since. When she'd opened it gingerly, scratching at the first few raw, hand-scribed lines of Crossing the River—the Witches' Language, Jeptha'd called it, a foul tongue good for nothing but spell-work and bindings on things too awful to force the thousand names of G-slash-d to touch—she'd just inscribed along her left wrist, and squinted down at Dee from under floppy blonde bangs, asking, Can I help you?

Samaire Morgan? I'm Dionne. Cornish.

Morgan's not my real name.

I know. Can I come in?

Standing there in her fatigues with a stolen sawed-off full of salt-cartridges in her backpack, and looking shyly 'round at the detritus of a life she'd never once thought was possible to achieve, on her own—track-meet photos, scholarship documents, the tricked-out laptop with all its bells and whistles. The friends, grinning from half a dozen frames—one in particular, familiar from various news stories and police reports.

Heard about Jesca Lind, she'd offered.

Did you. Wouldn't've thought that'd've made the papers, over in Iraq.

Well, I got it from your Mom, actually, when I was tracking you down—Mrs. Morgan. She said you guys went to prom together, picked out the same university, all that. As Sami nodded, slowly: Yeah, that's a damn shame, losing somebody you love so young. A beat. She really possessed, when she died?

She was something, all right—and she didn't just die. Why do you ask?

You know who I am, Sami?

I'm—starting to get an idea; Mom showed me coverage of the trial, when she thought I could handle it. You're Jeptha Cornish's daughter.

Your sister.

That's what it said on the birth certificate. So, Dionne… you here to kill me, or what?

They looked each other over a moment, taking stock; Sami was bigger but lankier, and Dee was fairly certain she hadn't had a quarter of as much training, not physically. Then again, if she took after Moriam the way Jeptha'd thought she would, she wouldn't need it.

I'm your sister, Sami, she repeated. How you think you got out of that trailer, in the first place? I picked you up and I ran 'til I couldn't run anymore. Never looked back, no matter how hard he yelled at me to. So hell no and fuck you, 'cause I ain't him.

That familiar/unfamiliar gaze—Mom's eyes, Dad's unholy calm. That set mouth, lips gone just a shade off-white, asking, But you know, right? What I am.

Sure. You're blood.

Only half. Half-human, too—by family standards.

To which Dee'd simply shrugged, throwing four hundred solid years' worth of witch-hunting genes to the winds, at least where it concerned one witch in particular—and not giving all too much of damn, as she did it. Because: How many relatives did she have left, anyways, in this frightful world? How many did she need?

Good enough for me, she'd said.

And Sami had nodded, eventually, once she saw she meant it. Then slipped her sweater off to show the rest of what she'd been doing to herself, all up and down and every which-way, penning the forces she had no choice but to know herself capable of wielding carefully back inside her own skin. Tracing marker with razor, then rubbing the wounds with a gunk made from equal parts ink, salt and Polysporin, 'til the result began to heal itself out of sheer contrariness. Lines of power digging themselves down deep from epidermis to dermis, burrowing inwards like worms of living light, sinking 'til they could sink no more.

Help me, then, she'd told Dee, a hundred times calmer than she'd had any good reason to be, given the circumstances. You see my problem, right? 'Cause long as my arms are, I just can't seem to reach my back.

And she'd handed Dee a blade, and Dee had taken it. Said, I got you. And...

...that was it, slang become fact. It was done.

In the here and now, Dee hiked her eyebrows at Chatwin, trying her best to project every ounce of contempt she had across five feet of space, without moving more than those thirty tiny muscles. "Team up again, uh huh," she replied. "'cause that worked out so well, last time."

"Still outta jail, ain't you?" Continuing, when neither of them answered, "Naw, just listen—not exactly like I want to, ladies, given the acrimonious way we parted, 'cept for the fact that it sure does appear we're workin' the same case for the same people, from suspiciously different ends. An' if yours told you the same pile of bull mine told me, might be we should throw in together regardless of past conflicts, just to keep ourselves all upright for the duration."

"Pass," Dee started to snap back—then sighed instead, as Sami waved her silent.

"I want to hear," the big idiot said, stubborn as ever.

"The shit for, Sami? She dumped your ass in the woods, left me stuck inside a wall."

"Didn't expect that to happen, just t'say," Chatwin pointed out. "Neither a one."

"Not like you tried all too hard to stop it, when it did."

A shrug. "Well, in for a penny."

Sami rolled her eyes. "Look," she told Dee, "you were already sure the Maartensbecks couldn't be trusted in the clinch, considering who we're chasing. And it strikes me A-Cat probably knows a dirty deal when she hears one—better than us, given we're not exactly social."

Dee had to smile at that, since it was nothing but true; hell, even Chatwin knew it. As they both watched, she sketched a little bow, shrugged again, tossed her head like a hillbilly beauty queen. And drawled back, without any more or less malice inherent in the words than usual—

"Well, ain't you sweet, still. Princess."

When most people talked about the Maartensbecks, they concentrated on their twinned academic prowess and charity-work, not to mention their storied genealogy—elliptical mentions of them stretched all the way back to the Ninth century, when Holland separated from Frisia to become a county in the Holy Roman Empire, and a man named Auutet from Maarten's Beck ended up qualifying as a student of the Corpus Iuris Civilis at the newly-founded University of Bologna. For those in "the life", however, the name carried a very different sort of weight.

"They're Dutch, and all they hunt is vampires," Moriam Cornish had told her eldest daughter one night, during a Hammer Horror movie marathon. "Sure, they don't use a 'Van' when they sign anymore, but you do the math."

Though not rich in a conventional sense, their consistent ability—and willingness, even when it cost them bad enough to denude whole generations—to tackle the Rolls-Royce of monsters head-on had produced a wide-flung funding network of grateful, financially liquid patrons. And with the foundation of the Maartensbeck Archive in 1968, they'd begun to amass a vault full of magical artifacts other people wouldn't touch with a literal ten-foot pole: grimoires, cursed objects, holy weapons, all of which the family's surviving members either caretook or banked accordingly, loaning them out at a fair rate of interest to anyone in search of a way to kill the unkillable who could afford to pay their late fees.

Occasionally, someone would be dumb enough to think they could go full supervillain with whatever it was they'd borrowed, then find out better once the Maartensbecks came to retrieve it; Dee had seen photos, and the results weren't pretty. These crafty stealth badasses might have multiple degrees and class out the wazoo, but they sure weren't fussy about coming down hard on whoever they considered evil, a category whose boundaries sometimes appeared to shift at whoever was currently heading the Maartensbecks' boardroom table's will.

For the Cornishes, who'd received their initial email while recuperating after the M-vale break in a motel Sami swore up and down didn't even have WiFi, contact had been made in the well-preserved person of matriarch Ruhel Maartensbeck, legendary Professor Maks's only granddaughter. She was a silver fox of a woman with Helen Mirren style and Vanessa Redgrave pipes, turning up to their highly public first meeting—at yet another all-night roadside greasy spoon, somewhere on the Jersey Turnpike—dressed all head to toe in retired teacher drag so good Dee would've pegged her for a civilian, at least from across the room. Then she drew close enough to sit down, revealing sensibly low-heeled lace-up shoes with enough tread for a high-speed chase, a no-grip Vidal Sassoon crop, and the discreet lines of a high-calibre pistol packing modified rounds under one arm. The overall effect was of a stretched-out Dame Judi Dench, voice almost-accentless and tartly crisp, as she slid her long legs under the plastic table and opened by saying—

"Congratulations on your recent return to circulation, my dears. Believe me, I'm not usually one to interrupt a celebration, but... well, the truth is, my family finds we have a problem that requires an outsider's touch, albeit one educated in very—specific ways. I know you'll understand what I mean, given your background." A pause. "Beside which, we've heard such good things of you both, it seemed a pity to look anywhere else."

Dee had to bite down on the urge to laugh, hard. But a quick glance Sami's way told another tale; she had a look on her face that read as partly stunned, part wistful. This was civilized talk, Mrs. Morgan-grade, of the sort that hadn't come her way in years—not since that last phone call, when Dee'd tried not to let herself overhear as Sami told her former "mother" how she not only wasn't gonna make it for Christmas, but wouldn't be able to tell her where to get in touch with her anymore. 'cause yes, what those cops had told her was true, to a point: they had just killed a bunch of people in a Beantown bar, deliberately and with premeditation, just like the charges said. But only their bodies, because the things inside those bodies weren't the people they were claiming to be at all, what with the whole tempting transients down to the basement, then killing and cooking them routine they'd gotten into recently... let alone the additional part about feeding the remains to their customers as a Tuesday Night Special, afterwards.

Thing was, when stuff'd already gone that far, that was pretty much the point where prayer and a 911 call stopped being any sort of use at all, and white magic against black took over; magic plus a bullet, or a load of cold iron buckshot mixed with salt. 'cause just as Jeptha'd always said, Exorcist movie franchise aside, sometimes the Power of Christ alone wasn't up to compelling shit.

And: Oh God, Samaire, she could remember Mrs. Morgan crying, tinnily, on the other end. I told you it was a bad idea to take up with her. Told you that nice as she seemed, she was probably just as psychologically disturbed as that man, her father... oh baby, and you were doing so well, too, even after Jesca! My smart, smart girl. Where's it all going to end now?

Good enough question, back then; even better question seven years on, parade of victories balanced against the occasional defeat or not. Though it wasn't like Dee really had the first or faintest idea of an answer, either way.

Ruhel Maartensbeck had come equipped with two fat files, that night. One was full of background stuff on them, which Dee found creepy, enough so to mainly skip over, but she'd seen Sami studying it off and on since, apparently fascinated by how the Maartensbecks had managed to trace the exact moment where the long-defunct European Cornîches had broken off into their only slightly less so Americanized brand, after a younger brother of witch-finder Guillaime Cornîche converted to Huguenot Protestantism, fleeing France for Quebec in the wake of the St. Bartholomew's Day Massacre. The other file, meanwhile, was about Miss M.'s "little problem" itself, a crisis forty years in the making—one that'd started all the way back in 1971, with Professor Maks's tragically quick and surprisingly unheralded passing, from Stage Four prostate cancer...

... except, well, that turned out to be a bit of a face-saving fib, on the Maartensbecks' part: i.e., for "prostate cancer," read "undeath."

"'Vampire-hunter turned vampire, no news at eleven,'" Dee'd commented, munching a fry. "Understandable, right? I mean, that's really gotta rankle."

"Somewhat, yes."

Nodding, Sami said, "Be hard to cover up, though. Unless—oh, tell me you didn't."

"Didn't what?" Dee'd demanded, watching Ruhel Maartensbeck nod, sadly. But then the penny dropped, with an almost audible clink—'cause while she might not've been able to get much schooling beyond what her Spec-4 called for (high school equivalency, plus some Engineering Corps courses and a whole two years of Explosive Ordnance Disposal training), no one could accuse Dionne Cornish of being completely unable to follow things through using plain old logic.

"You stuck him in the vault," she said, out loud. "'Course you did. 'cause given that place is like a toxic dump, 'cept for magic crap, there must be some real full-bore sons of bitches trying to slip in there—and a live-in vampire? Best security system money can't buy. Don't even have to feed him, just let him keep what he kills, long as he doesn't actually turn any of 'em… "

"Well done, Miss Cornish the Elder." Ruhel sighed. "Yes, that was the plan—his idea, actually, a contingency protocol decided on long before it happened, which he made me swear to honor, if and when. Imprison him in there and wait for the vampire who killed him to come free him, as a trap. But it never showed up, and after a certain amount of time, I simply ceased periodically dropping by to check on… that thing."

"Not like it was really your grandpa, anymore."

"No, of course not. You understand: everything I know I learned from him, and it knows everything he did, so it knows not to even bother claiming to be him. Vampires aren't people; not the people you hope they are, anyhow."

Sami, taken into care far too young to remember Jeptha and Moriam's bedtime stories, raised one eyebrow. "So what is it, then?"

"A demon wearing my grandfather's skin which says horrifying things to me in a beautiful voice, such as 'oh, you're pregnant—it's a boy, how lovely. Babies taste so good, or so I've heard.' Not to mention one entirely capable of biding its time, fashioning an escape plan and just waiting, as such things can, until I'm too old to do anything about it."

Said without rancour, so far as Dee could tell. This swank old lady had killed a thousand similar monsters in her time, probably—more than she and Sami'd ever seen—but when it came to emotional weaknesses, everybody had their something; if she wanted to contract hers out, Dee could certainly relate. No different from any other job, long as the money was good.

"We're still wanted," Sami reminded her. "Sticking around in the States wasn't part of the plan."

"Oh, no doubt. But you'll need new identities, won't you, to cross the border into Canada? Unless you're planning on using magic, that is—and that does leave a trail."

"Not one the FBI can follow, far as I know."

"Ah, yes. But what of Miss Chatwin, your former partner in escape?" Here Ruhel had tapped the second file, lightly. "Turns out, there's a fair deal of historical linkage between her family and yours, above and beyond the sad fact of both your mothers having decided to initiate, ahem, intimate contact with the same member of the Goetic Coterie—"

"Careful," Dee said.

"I'm always careful, Miss Cornish; so should you be. Especially since I know you both know that Allfair Chatwin remains fixated on her half-sister, for... various reasons, all of them toxic. A dangerous woman."

Dee shrugged, reluctant to state the obvious. But it was Sami who answered, anyways.

"Look," she said, "I don't think we have any problem with hunting your grandfather down, per se. But what is it you want us to do with him, exactly, once we find him?"

※

"So she give you a phone too, huh?" Chatwin shook her head, grinning. "Can't say they ain't a canny lot, them Maartensbecks. Particularly like her usin' me as a threat, too, to light a fire under your asses."

Dee snorted. "'Threat,' Jesus. Annoyance, maybe... "

"Now, now, Lady Di. No need t'be insultin'."

"Just shush it, both of you," Sami broke in. Then asked, of Chatwin, "So who'd you talk to? Ruhel again?"

"Naw, they sent me a pretty little brown gal in undercover cop slacks and a Kevlar neckerpiece, tough as nails. Said her name was Anapurna Maartensbeck, so I'm thinkin' she's probably this generation's granddaughter, but she didn't say nothin' 'bout her great-great-great… whatever. Just how there'd been a break-in at the vault, some big black books took, an' now they needed somebody t'get 'em back, an interested third party knew enough of what magic smells like t'sniff 'em out."

"They sent you after books." Dee shook her head. "The fuck."

"Funny, that's what I thought; them books weren't the only things stunk, by a long shot. Most 'specially so 'cause when I did track 'em down, they turned out t'be mainly no great shakes—I mean, sure, I guess if you never seen a grimoire in your life, you might get all het up. But really: Agrippa, Paracelsus? The Petit Albert? They're the Time-Life series of black magic—ten a penny, find a copy any damn place. Hardly worth the lockin' up, 'sides from this… "

Bitch meant what she had under her arm, of course—that squat, thick tome, more folio than book at closer examination, ill-bound in sticky-pale leather. She flourished it forth at Sami with a little half-bow, running her thumb along the embossed title, which Sami read out loud. "Of The True Hierarchy of Hell, or Pseudomonarchia Daemonium, blah blah blah. Greatest Magical Hits bullshit, like you said."

"Uh huh. Now flip it open."

Sami did, gingerly. And Dee watched Chatwin grin even wider, so much so it was like the top of her skull was in danger of falling off, as her—their, shit on it all—half-sister's eyes widened, when she saw what was written inside.

"Clavicule des Pas-Morts," she said, amazed. "This is… this was burnt. Wasn't it?"

"Oh, more'n once, from what I heard. Then again, those might've just been rumours put 'round by whoever had it at the time, to throw everybody else lookin' for it off the scent. 'cause once you got a copy of this bad boy, you probably want to keep it just as long as possible, don't ya think?"

Dee looked at Sami, the resident expert. "Okay," she said, "I'll bite. Why?"

"Because whoever has the Key of the Not-Dead can cure vampirism," Sami replied, eyes still firmly riveted to the thing in question. With a slight tip of her head towards Chatwin, she asked, "How'd you find it?"

Chatwin shrugged. "Easy enough. Miss Anapurna give me a box of forensic samples, said they took 'em at the crime-scene—I whipped up a trackin' spell, but didn't get more'n one trail and that gone cold hours back, 'cause it looked like the old boy who made it was already dead. Odd thing was, though... "

"He was still moving?"

"Mmm. Just like old Professor Maks, I'd bet—or like that gal he left behind here would've been, you hadn't performed an emergency head-ectomy."

"So you figure out he's a vampire, kill him, grab the book...and? Maartensbecks are the ones who lied to you, why aren't you takin' it up with them? How'd you even know where to find us?"

"Aw, now you're drainin' all the fun out of it." Chatwin waited for Dee to rise to the bait, then sighed when she didn't. "Well—as it ensues, Princess here was always gonna be my next stop already, but let's lay that by, for the nonce. Given Mister Book-Snatcher didn't look like he'd been undead too long, I decided t'use his blood and see how near the one'd turned him was, just in case it decided to come lookin'; that's what brought me this-a-way, though I guess I'm runnin' a bit late in terms of catchin' up with the head monster-maker himself. Imagine my surprise, though, when I snuck up t'peek through the diner window and saw the two of you standin' there, all large as life, 'bout to cut yourself some fresh new vampire's throat!"

"Like Christmas," Sami agreed. "Or Hallowe'en."

"Six of one, darlin'. And now... here we are."

A pause. Sami looked away, tapping two fingers against her lips and cogitating so furiously Dee could almost smell the gray cells burning. Chatwin took advantage of her distraction to run a frankly admiring look up and down Sami's frame that made Dee long to knock her into the middle of next week, thinking, Eyes front, bitch. I got a cold iron knuckle-duster in one pocket and a shaker full of salt in the other, both with your name written allll over 'em.

"Okay," Sami said out loud, interrupting Dee's reverie. "Professor Maks is a vampire, been one since 1971, and Ruhel still seems pretty cut up about it—so if they have the Clavicule, why don't they use it? 'cause... "

"'cause—they didn't know they had it," Dee answered, slowly. "Not until it was already banked. Only thing that makes sense."

"Yeah. They take the cover at face value, then find out they were wrong. But by that time, it's already inside the vault, with not-Professor Maks guarding it."

A-Cat frowned. "Just a second of enlightenment here, ladies, for all those who ain't in the biz...wouldn't havin' a vampire squattin' over your stuff put a kibosh on the Maartensbecks' whole magic item-loanin' sideline?"

"Oh, I'm pretty sure they could negotiate with him to get him to send things out, considering how dependent on them he'd be," Sami replied. Give him extra blood, maybe even donate their own... but they certainly wouldn't tell him about the Clavicule, because he'd know what they wanted it for."

"Granted," Dee agreed. "So—how they did want to get it back out?"

"Arrange a break-in. It's pretty much the only way."

Dee frowned. "They must've known he'd get out, though."

A raucous snort, from over Chatwin's way. "Known? Lady Di, I'll stake my box they was bettin' on it."

They both turned to look at Chatwin, who nodded, almost to herself. Then added, for clarification, "Yeah, just before I told that old boy to put the book down and step back, I recall he was goin' on about how he didn't understand why 'the money people' hadn't shown up yet. In fact, I think he kinda thought I was one of those people."

"Why'd you want him to step back?" Dee asked.

"Oh, that was so's none of him'd get on the book when I opened the door t'let the sun in, basically. 'cause one way or another, I knew I was gonna need it, later on."

That smile again. Sami looked anywhere but, while Dee met it straight on, glaring extra-hard. *You're gonna get yours, Chatwin, and sooner than you think. That's if I got anything to say about it.*

Would she, though? This was starting to be the baseline problem, whenever Sami and Chatwin got in close proximity. There was no denying the witch could be useful, in her way, but Christ.

She's evil, Sami, Dee tried to signal her sister. *And you, no matter what happened, 'fore you had me help you cut those binding tattoos into your skin—you're not. Don't matter how much blood you share; you and me must share the same amount, right? And human trumps demon, or should...*

But it wasn't like Sami could hear her, anyways. At least—

(—she didn't think so.)

Chatwin was leaning forward now, hand raised tentatively, like she actually thought she was going to try and lay it on Sami's shoulder in mock-sympathy, or some such shit. If she did, Dee thought, it was more than likely she—Dee—would respond to that unbearable provocation by leaning forward herself, and stick her vamp-killin' blade so far through the part of Chatwin's wrist that didn't connect with Sami's flesh she might succeed in severing both bones at one chunk.

Luckily for everyone concerned, however, it didn't prove necessary, after all.

"We need to get to Professor Maks first," Sami said. "Then hold him, 'til his relatives show up. After which we can discuss all the people they've let him kill so far just to get a chance at turning him back, not to mention whether or not we were supposed to be three of them."

Dee sighed. "There go the spankin' new IDs."

Chatwin laughed at that, heartily. "Oh, Lady Di," she said, "that's precious. You should'a heard what they promised me, to get me t'deal myself in."

No I shouldn't, Dee thought.

Dee left the magic shit to Sami and Chatwin, just like last time, when they'd ended up using a spell called the Sator Box and a scrap of dead girl's soul stuffed in an aspirin bottle to bust themselves out of M-vale. Just sat there and listened to them hash out how to use blood from two of old Prof. Maartensbeck's spawn and that goddamn book a whole bunch of people who'd never heard of him had all paid so much for to locate where he was right now, then drag them towards it, like iron filings to some tainted magnet. She was trying to remember everything Jeptha and Moriam had ever told her about vampires, which wasn't much, aside from don't get within grabbing range but only thing really works for sure is the head comin' off, so...

(And here she had a clearish image of Jeptha shrugging, somewhat baffled by his own contradiction. Shooting Moriam a smile as he did and seeing it returned, softly, yet with interest.)

Thinking, They did love each other, once. Just like Sami and me. That's the fucking pity of it.

Then remembering a little further on, the last time she'd seen him, after the date'd finally been set and all his appeals wrung out. Sitting there across from a man she barely recognized anymore, listening to him rant about how if she ever found out where her little sister was he was counting on her to finish the damn job, this time, sentiment aside. You hear me, Dionne? To which she'd just shook her head and answered no, on no account, no fucking way—you hear me, Dad? Just goddamn NO.

They'd sat there a minute, glaring at each other with the same fierce eyes. Because she's my sister, and I love her, no matter what. You do remember how that goes, right? Family is family, that's what you always said... up 'til the night you decided it wasn't, anymore.

Think I didn't love your Mama, Dee? he'd answered, finally. I did. Still do. But—

—sometimes, that didn't mean as much as it should, in context. Sometimes it couldn't. Not when civilians were involved. And she knew that, too.

Britishisms aside, the Maartensbecks had to "understand" it just as well, if anybody did.

(Civilians like Jesca Lind? that voice at the back of Dee's mind asked her, though, its tone also Jeptha's, as it often was. Not that that likeness was ever enough to keep her from ignoring it.)

I made my choice, Dee thought, giving her machete a last quick, sharpening scrape. And tuned back into the conversation still going on to her right, even while stowing the whetstone away in one of her jacket pockets.

"Now, you got to keep a tight hold, this time, Princess," Chatwin was warning Sami. "Don't wanna go spinnin' off all unexpected-like, not given the forces we're playin' with, here… "

"You just make sure we all arrive together—me, you and Dee," Sami replied. "Because if I come out of fugue and find her gone again, first thing I'm gonna do is put a thrice-blessed iron cross-nail right through your Third Eye."

"Witch's lobotomy? Perish the thought."

Dee stood up, tucking the machete out of sight. "All that mean we're good to go, or what?" she demanded, eyes firmly on Sami, who sighed. Replying, as she did—

"Good as we'll ever be, I guess."

Things contracted, then there was some old-fashioned Appalachian hair-knotting and a bit of hemoglobin fingerpaint action, followed by a three-way handfasting and widdershins footwork on three, two, one. Seconds later, with a pitch-black spacetime rip through a wormhole where only Sami's lit-up tats showed the way, they stumbled like one clumsy, six-legged animal into the parking lot in front of one of those weird new airport motels with the courtyard inside the building, six stories of glass-fronted apartments looking only inward, where a sunken fountain-pool combo and some scattered built-in couches lurked.

Those apartments were all vacant now, though not exactly empty, their redly hand-printed vistas giving only the impression of drawn blinds, or maybe a fall of particularly virulent-colored cherry blossoms. While down in the pit sat Professor Maks Maartensbeck, leant back in the now deep-dyed fountain's bowl with his equally-scarlet eyes half-shut and his long legs delicately crossed at the ankles, frankly luxuriating, dyed head to toe in unlucky moteliers' blood.

He'd swapped his Twister Relief dumpster outfit for what looked like the remains of a security guard's uniform, along the way. Still slightly too big for him, but a far better overall impression.

"Well, ladies," he called up to them as they stood rooted in the doorway, ridiculously polite voice anti-naturally resonant, some distant silver key dragged over ice. "Two witches, both demon-blooded, both by the same sire—and one full human, by the same dam; hmmm, let me see. The fabled Dionne and Samaire Cornish, I presume, here to chastise me for my many sins… but who, pray tell, are you?"

Chatwin shrugged, then sidled in crosswise and sauntering, though Dee could tell even her hackles were up, under that don't-care prison swag show. Calling down, "Allfair Chatwin's my name, sir, thanks for askin'. But you can feel free t'call me A-Cat, you find yourself so inclined."

"Ah, yes. Descended from the fabled demoiselles de Chatouye, I'd wager, whose village was burnt by none other than these two's equal-distant genetic author, Witchfinder Corniche. Voulteuses of great power, all, as I'm sure you must be yourself, to find me so quickly… especially once one takes into account your—other connections."

"Too kind, Professor. Just a humble holler-worker out of Black Bush, that's all."

"Oh, hardly."

They're fast, too, Moriam'd said, that long-ago night, so don't forget it—and holy shit was that ever true, what with all that fresh Type Whatever jacking up Maartensbeck's system. Because all it took was a blur of movement, a single tiny eyelid-flick, and there he was, right up in all three of their faces at once and smiling horribly, a highly-educated human shark with blood-breath sporting a manicure that—now you saw it close on—read halfway between Fu Manchu and full-on ten-fingered raptor.

"You see, modesty truly does ill-become creatures such as we, my dear," he told Chatwin, who stood there frozen for once, while Sami and Dee both shifted a half-step back into automatic attack-stance. "Why quibble terminology? Be proud, whatever you choose to call yourself."

Chatwin breathed out, visibly smoothing her face back into its usual smarm-charm lines. "No argument from me, on that one," she replied, lightly. "In fact, you'll find monster pride's pretty much my middle name, under most circumstances... unlike some I could mention."

He smiled, gore-mask crinkling. "Well, then. Since you've mentioned her—" Switching over, he said to Sami, "What a very decorative object you've made of yourself, Miss Cornish, to be sure. Can those be binding sigils? In Crossing the River, no less?" She nodded. "One would think they'd make it rather more difficult to summon your power, even when faced with imminent threat. And yet one can only assume you thought that a desirable outcome, when you carved yourself all over with them."

Dry: "Uh huh."

"Why?"

"Less people get hurt, this way."

Dee saw one stained yet elegant eyebrow tic up in disbelief. "Ah yes," the Professor replied, with fine contempt. "Morality."

"Kinda heard you had a thing for that, back in the day," Dee couldn't quite keep herself from snapping, though she knew it'd turn him her way—but hell, she was ass-tired of things like this supercilious old fuck always talking around her, just 'cause her Daddy wasn't the one with horns. So when Maartensbeck's blood-charged gaze met hers, she just smiled: not as sharp as him, but sharp enough. Only to be more surprised than she'd expected to be when, a moment later, he did the same.

"Little soldier," he called her, with what rang like a gross parody of affection (though for all she knew, he actually might've meant it). "How you remind me of Ruhel, at your age... "

Then threw back over his shoulder without turning, diction still crisp, yet tone gone melting, "...or you, of course, Anapurna—is that the correct pronunciation? What a joy! I still remember what your father's heartbeat sounded like, in Ruhel's womb. You also have his smell."

Dee looked up, and found herself locking eye-lines with what must be Chatwin's recruiter: little, yes—small as Dee herself—and definitely a shade darker than the Maartensbeck norm, curly beech-brown hair drawn back in a tightly practical French braid, though her Bollywood movie-star eyes were as blue as his once must've been, or her grandmother's still were. Had a modified flare-gun in held in a two-hand grip (white phosphorus? That would've been Dee's call) trained between the Professor's shoulder blades, with the famous Kevlar gorget peeping from her silk blouse's collar. Much like Ruhel, she had her game-face down pat, given that was undoubtedly who she'd learned it from. But—

It's different, when it's one of your own. Always.

"Great... great-grandfather," Anapurna Maartensbeck said, finally.

"Oh, that does seem a touch over-formal. Do call me Maks."

"I've—always wanted to meet you."

"And I you." Cornish sisters and Chatwin apparently equally forgotten in the face of this long-desired reunion, the Professor turned his back on them and took a pace forward, chuckling when he saw Anapurna's finger tighten on the trigger. "But where is my pretty girl, my dear-beloved granddaughter? Where is my Ruhel?"

"Here, grandfather. On your nine o'clock."

"Excellent. You never disappoint."

So here they all were, weapons either out or on the verge of being so, with the walking corpse of Professor Maks playing monkey in the middle. To her right, Dee had Anapurna, gun-barrel still levelled; to her left was Ruhel, having materialized out from behind what used to be the motel's front desk, toting what looked like ether the world's biggest Taser or a high-tech portable flamethrower scaled down far enough you could hide it under your coat, like a shotgun.

Must be nice to get paid corporate rates, Dee thought.

"I'm sorry to have lied to you, at least by omission," Ruhel Maartensbeck told them, voice only slightly shaky, "but I needed that book, as well as my grandfather's location, and I needed whoever brought it to me not to know why. So while I must admit that Miss Chatwin turning out to be able to recognize it took me somewhat by surprise—"

Chatwin shook her head, trucker-hat bobbing. "Tch. Why does everybody assume just 'cause I never got my GED, I must'a stopped readin' for pleasure altogether?"

Dee could sympathize, not that she was going to say so. "Well, it's here now, one way or the other," she told Ruhel, instead. "It, him, and... about twenty dead bodies I can see plus six more floors of ones I can't, plus whoever else he might'a happened to kill, on the way over... "

"Plus the team you sent in to get it," Sami added, "up to and including the only guy he didn't gut right then and there, the guy A-Cat got your book from. Plus Leah, the waitress, who didn't even know what was happening to her, 'til Dee cut her damn head off. Her, those two guys in the kitchen, a couple more people who came in before Maks here was finished, just looking to get a midnight snack... "

The Professor threw back his head and hooted, delightedly, while Ruhel's mouth trembled. "Please," she said. "I know what we've done must seem—excessive, to an outsider—"

Dee rounded on her. "'Scuse me? We're hunters, lady, just like you—that's how you fished us in, in the first place. So no, I don't give a shit how nice he used to be, or whether or not you can maybe make him that way again. You let your granddad eat people, real people. The kind we're supposed to save from things like him."

"Be polite," Anapurna warned her, voice chill.

"Or what? How old are you, man? You don't even know him!"

"True enough. But I know her—when my Mum and Dad died, she's who took me in. So—"

"—she tells you he's worth however much collateral damage it takes, then that's what goes, huh?" Dee didn't quite spit, but it took effort. "Yeah, well—know what my parents told me? How you people were heroes."

At this, the Professor laughed so hard he had to bend over just a bit, bracing himself, before finally trailing off. "Oh," he said, "that was delightful. Do you know what a hero is, my dear? As much a killer as anything he kills, but with far better public relations."

"That what the guy who made you this way told you?"

"Amongst other things." The Professor sighed. "Ah, and now you've made me sad. I did think, you know—he and I having been nemeses for so long—that if I only caused a long enough trail of damage once I finally got on the other side of those five-foot-thick walls, he might hear about it, and come join me." A hapless shrug. "But... as you see."

"Men," Chatwin commiserated, deadpan.

"All that effort, and all for nothing," the Professor continued, as Sami and Dee shot each other a quick glance behind his back while Anapurna's eyes slid over to her grandmother, who was starting to look queasy. "I'd discorporated him five times already, throughout my career, which I now suspect he took as a variety of flirtation. But then I was old, and one night I dreamt he appeared in my bedroom, telling me he'd slipped some of his blood into my food. You will change either way, Maks, but if you meet me directly, if you let me do as I please, I can keep you from harming Ruhel, at the very least. I agreed, naturally enough—"

"—because that was the sort of man you were," Ruhel broke in here, desperately. "Because you were good."

"No, child: because I was a fool. Because I didn't know, then, how little I'd care about hurting you at all, once the deed was done." If he heard her little gasp, horror-filled and breath-caught, he gave no sign. "So I went out past the point where my home's protective wards ceased to work, and I bared my neck to him. Even thoroughly infected, I had time to make my peace and write out instructions before falling into a trance; when I woke, Ruhel had already prisoned me inside the vault. Of course, I understood why he wouldn't try to free me himself—I'd designed it, after all. A dreadful place, and booby-trapped, to boot. But still I warmed myself over those intervening years with the idea that if and when, he'd surely be bound to come and meet with me, at last—just drop by for a little look-see, no social obligations assumed. No... pressure."

"So you could kill him," Anapurna suggested.

"Oh no. So I could thank him."

Ruhel gasped again, the sound deeper this time, more of a half-sob; Anapurna jerked a bit, as if face-slapped. Then said, with an optimism she didn't seem to feel, "But we have the book, yes? The Clavicule. So we can put it all back, the way it should be. The way you should be."

"And how's that, exactly?"

"Human. That was... the whole point, of all of this."

"Oh, dear. My poor, sweet girl, really—why on earth would you think I would ever want that?"

And there it lay, at last, between all seven of them: the gauntlet. Dropped like it was proverbially hot, like a mic, or a fuckin' bomb.

"Well, there you go," Dee heard herself observe, ostensibly to Anapurna, who she almost thought she saw give a tiny little nod, in return—before Ruhel jumped in on top, crying out, "But you can't possibly mean it, grandfather—you, who taught me to always keep fighting, no matter what! This isn't your fault, for pity's sake. You have a condition, but it's curable, and with the book's help, you'll be exactly the person you were again, before all this... oh God, why are you still laughing?"

Because he doesn't give a shit? Dee wanted to blurt at her, to grab and shake her, bodily—anything to keep her from abasing herself in front of this goddamned ghoul, this sacrilege, just because it wore a rough approximation of the person she'd once loved best in all the world's face.

But—

"Well, one never does know 'til one's in it, so to speak," Professor Maks explained, grotesquely reasonable. "But the fact is, I may have told you a bit of a fib, my darling, without meaning to—because so far as I can tell, I am exactly the same person I was before, right now. I know what I've done. It's just, as I've already said, that I simply can't seem to bring myself to care."

Oh, we got trouble now, Dee's brain told her, stupidly. As though it'd somehow convinced itself they hadn't had any, before.

Out of the corner of one eye, Dee saw Chatwin reach to slip her hand in Sami's, brazen as ever—and Sami, with no other alternative, close her fingers on it, hard. Saw those sketchy sigil-letters start to light up all up and down her arms, hair haloed and lifting; saw the trucker hat pop straight off of Chatwin's asshole head, as her own mane did much the same. And felt the power they were both suddenly funneling into her start to light her own medulla oblongata up like a bulb, switching her over to full berserker mode without her even asking. The machete's blade glowed horizon-flash green as she struck out, burying it hilt-deep through the Prof.'s long-dead bicep;

he whipped 'round snake-quick, all fangs, but Dee managed to dodge and slip anyhow, steering him straight into a twinned blast of arcane witch-juice from Sami and Chatwin's upraised, fisted fingers that sent him reeling, almost flipping back into the fountain.

At almost the same instant, Anapurna pulled the trigger, firing into his side. White light bloomed, taking half her great-great-grandfather's ribcage with it; he gave a shriek, spinning sidelong, then shrieked yet again when Ruhel discharged her own weapon, half-harpooning him with a species of grappling-hook that chunked in deep and sizzled as she juiced him hard: once, twice, three times, 'til his hair stood straight on end, smoking, and his eyes rolled up white in their sockets. But did he fall?

(No.)

Sharp teeth set and grinding, Maks Maartensbeck clambered grimly to his feet once more, shook himself like a wet dog, throwing off sparks. And began, by slow, tug-of-war degrees, to pull the cable between them ever tighter, reeling her steadily in.

Though Ruhel fought him all the way, it was a foregone conclusion; Anapurna scrabbled in her vest for another cartridge, tore her palms reloading, but his claws were already closing on her grandmother's throat—so she threw a glance Dee's way instead, too angry to beg, and Dee found herself punching Sami's arm, gesturing at the book Chatwin still clung to. "READ IT!" she yelled.

Sami's brows shot up, startled by the very notion... just as Chatwin, predictably unpredictable, flipped the folio open one-handed, and started to do exactly that.

"O judge of nations!" she yelled out. "Ye who threw down Bethsaida, Chorazin, Sodom! Ye who raised Lazarus up, whose voice spoke out of the head of the tempest! Ye who made the bush of the Hebrews burn!"

"Lift up this carrion flesh, and make it clean!" Sami chimed in, scanning the page over Chatwin's shoulder. "Ye who made wine of Your own blood and bread of Your own meat, heal even this mortal wound! Ye who harrowed Hell, put fear into this black and fearless heart!"

At the first few words, a shudder straightened the Professor's spine, whip-cracking him erect. His mouth squared in pain, "You—" he began. "You, I—stop it. Damn you! Stuh, stuh—stop—"

Not likely, motherfucker. One more time, Dee glanced at Anapurna, who nodded, and whistled at Ruhel: a three-note phrase, very definite, clearly some signal. Still vainly fighting against the pull, Ruhel reached inside her jacket for a glass ampoule of some red liquid, which she broke open with her thumb and deftly tossed, splattering its contents across her grandfather's deformed face. The bulk of it landed straight between those snapping jaws, sizzling as it went down; Maks Maartensbeck coughed smoke, then retched outright, bringing up a rush of hot, black, stinking mess. His hands slipped off the Taser's cable, letting Ruhel leap away even as Anapurna jumped forward, landing a vicious kick to the small of his back that sent him crashing further down, face against the floor.

"Adjuramus te, draco maledicte!" Sami told him, every word a blow, under whose impact Dee watched him writhe. "Exorciso te! Humiliare, sub potente manu Dei!" To which Chatwin added, without any apparent shred of irony, "For my God is frightening in His holy places, since all places are those He has made, and thus it is His name before which all terrible things must tremble."

The Professor looked up, punished face-skin starting to darken and tremble, almost to melt and run—and was it just the light in here, or did his squinted eyes suddenly look less red, more blue? "Whah wash thah?" he demanded of Ruhel, then spat yet more black, before continuing: "Ih fehlt… blashphemous."

"Communion wine, blessed by the Pope. The literal Blood of Christ."

"Buh ohny a priesht—"

A sad smile. "You told me yourself, grandfather: we have an indulgence, because of what we do. Who we are."

Yeah. 'cause Sami and her, they were just itinerants like Mom and Dad, riding 'round from town to town in a series of stolen cars, dodging Feds and killing things out the back. But the Maartensbecks were Templars, for real, Vatican giftbags included… and for all Dee'd found herself thinking must be nice, earlier on, maybe it wasn't, so much. Not the way Ruhel made it sound.

"Sympathetic magic," Sami murmured, to which Chatwin snorted.

"Or some-such," she replied. "Ain't religion grand?"

They looked up to find Anapurna glaring at them both, eyes wild enough to make Dee automatically reach for her drop-piece, the little .22 she kept holstered up one sleeve. Hissing, as she juiced the Professor twice more, in quick succession, "Did she tell you to STOP?"

"Do not keep in mind, O Lord, our offenses or those of our parents, nor take vengeance on our sins," Sami replied, not skipping a beat, while Maks Maartensbeck—him, increasingly, rather than the terrible force that had driven his frail form hither and yon these forty-plus years, gulping down anything stupid enough to come near—shuddered at her feet. "Lift this sufferer like Lazarus, out of the grave. Bring him forth, whole once more."

"Restore him," Chatwin agreed. "Change his gall for blood, corruption for health. Set him free."

"This we pray: liberate him from the mouth of the Abyss, ex inferis, in nomine patris, et filis—"

"—et Spiritus Sanctii," they all chimed in on this last part, seemingly without premeditation: Ruhel, Ana, Dee. Who glanced down herself as she said it, eyes drawn back to the sheer spectacle of the Professor's—Jesus, who knew, at this point—salvation, ruination. One out of the other, out the back and right back in, straight on through 'til morning...

Saw his lips move, whitening, firming. Saw his wounds begin to bleed, first clear, then red. And heard him gasp as the pain came rushing in, at last—a torrent of it, others' as well as his own, deferred almost half a hundred years. The pain, so long forgotten, of being merely human.

"Ruhel..." he managed, just barely, but she heard it; fell to her knees in the mess at the sound, all uncaring of her lovely suit, and hugged him so hard he screamed. Exclaiming, as she did, "It worked, oh God, you're cured. I knew it would. Oh, grandfather..."

Anapurna, boot still on his back and her gun leveled between his shoulder blades, seemed unconvinced, but Ruhel laughed and wept like a child; Dee wanted to look somewhere else, but was sort of starved for options.

The Professor, meanwhile, took it just as long as he could before gingerly shifting back, the Taser's cable dragging painfully between them. And—

"No, Ruhel," he managed, lips twisting wry over a mouthful of newly-blunted teeth. "It... simply won't do, you know."

"Grandfather?"

"Oh my girl, you know it won't. Look around you. Someone has to pay for... all this."

She shook her head, shamed, dumb. Put a hand up to stop him speaking only to have him print a kiss onto her palm, so light and sweet it made her groan out loud, then fold to sag against him, sobbing against his frail, torn chest. He patted her awkwardly with the arm that wasn't left hanging, Dee's blade still stuck through it, and addressed the others over her shoulder, head turning in a short half-circle to them in turn—Sami and Chatwin, Dee, Anapurna. "Ladies," he began, visibly exhausted, "there is... so much I must leave unsaid, and for that... I apologize, most of all for how quickly I must discard this gift you've bled to grant me. The last thing I wish is to seem ungrateful. But... blood sows guilt, as we Maartensbecks well know. And I..."

Gaze left steady on Anapurna alone now, she stepping back, regarding him for the first time as anything but a threat. Those fine blue eyes, both sets of them, shining with unshed tears.

"I understand," she said.

"I have... been damned, all this time, utterly. But what they did saved me..." Nodding down, as Ruhel continued to cry, "She saved me, as she always said she would. I was the one who... tainted it. Do you understand that?"

"I think so, sir."

But she didn't move, and neither did he—gaze holding steady while hers slipped sidelong, supplicant, almost. Pleading. For what?

Dee wondered, but only momentarily.

"You want to die, again," she said, out loud. "For real, this time. But you can't pull the trigger—damn yourself all over, if you do. That right?" The Professor didn't answer, but didn't object. Dee nodded at Anapurna. "So you want her to kill you, instead."

"'Want' would be a... strong word."

"For her too, given she fights monsters and you're not one, anymore. Plus, you're family."

(I know a little about that.)

Anapurna stiffened, gun jerking back up, as though challenged. "Never said I wouldn't," she snapped, to which Dee shrugged, making a placatory movement: Peace, lady. Managed to get this far without shooting each other—let's go for the gold, huh?

"Just think maybe it'd go better if it wasn't either of you," she said, mainly to Maks. "'cause when you're bent on doing good, doing bad—no matter why—don't ever seem to help."

He didn't bother to nod, but Anapurna did it for him, so... good enough, Dee guessed. Pressed tight to her granddad's clavicle, Ruhel covered her eyes with both hands and wept on, bitterly. And Dee reached into her sleeve, for real, this time—not knowing if Sami was watching, but sure as hell not wanting to check, either. Hoping Chatwin was, though, and attentively, as she cocked back and dug the the barrel into his fragile, rehumanized temple.

Been dead a long time, she reminded herself. "I'm sorry," she heard herself tell him, nevertheless. To which he merely smiled, answering, with amazing self-control—

"I'm not."

(So thank you, dear girl. Thank you.)

Over his shoulder, she saw Anapurna not quite close her own eyes because somebody had to stay on point, and thought, Damn, if you didn't get the exact same training I did. We could've been friends, maybe, if not for this.

But that's just me, right? Always the bad cop.

"Okay, then," Dionne Cornish said, to no one in particular, as she pulled the trigger.

In the motel battle's immediate aftermath, nobody but the surviving Maartensbecks was greatly surprised to discover that Allfair Chatwin had used the Professor's death as distraction and run off while the getting was good, taking the easy-to-sell-for-travelling-cash Clavicule des Pas-Morts with her. Since Ruhel—icy veneer firmly back in place—was already on the phone arranging cover-up plus retrieval for her grandfather's corpse, however, now finally set to occupy the tomb bearing his name at last, Anapurna was the one who offered the Cornishes a ride to the Canadian border, along with those fabled clean new IDs.

"Chatwin'll be our next project, if I have any say in it," she promised Dee, too.

"Good luck with that," Sami replied, crossing her arms, not quite allowing herself to shiver.

Later yet, as the miles were eaten up beneath them and Dee stared at the back of Anapurna's head, rubbing fingers still a little bruised from the recoil, Sami leant over to assure her she'd done the right thing—"the only thing, Dee, under the circumstances. He knew it. You do too."

"Do I?" Dee shook her head. "Don't feel that way. More like... well. Kinda—"

"—like it sets a bad example?"

A pause. "There is that," Dee eventually agreed, so quiet she could barely tell herself what she thought about it.

CANADA: ONE HUNDRED FEET, the next sign said. Above, the moon hung high; Anapurna Maartensbeck tapped the wheel as she drove, beating out some tune Dee couldn't identify. "So who's this guy your—the Prof. kept on talkin' about?" Dee asked her, falling back on business, for lack of better conversational topics.

"Juleyan Laird Roke," Anapurna replied, not turning. "Wizard first, then graduated to vampire at the moment of his execution, during the Civil War—ours, not yours—through some spasm of ill will and sciomancy. Helped that he was a quarter fae on his mother's side, with ten generations of hereditary magic-workers on the other... a rancid bastard, too, from all accounts. Doesn't surprise me a bit that he left poor old Maks to rot, once he'd had his way."

"Uh huh. So tell me, Miss M.—is some holler witch you barely know really at the top of your list, with this guy still on the loose?"

"Perhaps not."

"Good luck again, then. Twice over."

"And let's hope the chase ends better for me than it did for my grandfather? Why, Miss C., I'm touched." An expert swerve took them into the express lane, where Anapurna slowed to an idle. "Enough so to wish you the same, in fact, on your journey. Since, after all… "

But here she broke off, maybe thinking better of finishing the thought, considering how Sami was sitting right there all extra-large as life, listening. Or how she already knew Dee had a gun.

Because: Some hunt monsters, Dee thought, and some become monsters, in their turn. But some are just made that way, with no say at all in the matter—collateral damage, already born fucked, just waiting for the worst possible moment to fall down.

Family as destiny, its own little ecology, forever struggling forwards, forever thrown back. But… it didn't have to be a foregone conclusion, was what Dee believed, at the end of the day. What she had to make herself believe, to keep on going.

What's the difference? she wondered, knowing there wasn't much of one—that there couldn't be, for any of it to work. And reached out, in the darkness, to take her sister's hand.

Editor Biography

Shannon Robinson's work has appeared or is forthcoming in *Iowa Review*, *Gettysburg Review*, *Nimrod*, *Joyland* and *Joyland Retro*, *New Ohio Review*, and has been anthologized in *New Stories from the Midwest* and *Specter Spectacular: 13 Ghostly Tales*. She holds an MFA in fiction from Washington University in St. Louis, and served as Writer-in-Residence at Interlochen Center for the Arts in 2011. Past honors include the Katherine Anne Porter Prize in Fiction, a grant from the Elizabeth George Foundation, and a Hedgebrook Fellowship.

Author Biographies

BARBARA A. BARNETT is a writer, musician, graduate student in library and information science, intern in an orchestra library, Odyssey Writing Workshop graduate, coffee addict, wine lover, bad movie mocker, and all-around geek. Her short fiction has appeared in publications such as *Beneath Ceaseless Skies*, *Fantasy Magazine*, *Intergalactic Medicine Show*, *Shimmer*, *Daily Science Fiction*, and *Wilde Stories 2011: The Year's Best Gay Speculative Fiction*. Barbara lives with her husband in southern New Jersey and can be found online at www.babarnett.com.

MEGAN LEE BEALS lives in Tacoma, Washington with her husband and one-eyed cat. She drinks coffee late at night and has three drawings tattooed on the skin of three people. None of which depicts a fly. You can find her online at www.beehills.wordpress.com.

RACHEL CAINE is the *New York Times* and *USA Today* bestselling author of more than forty novels, including *Prince of Shadows* and the *Morganville Vampires* series in young adult, and the *Weather Warden*, *Outcast Season*, and *Revivalist* series in urban fantasy. She lives and works in Fort Worth, Texas with her husband, fantasy artist R. Cat Conrad.

ADAM CALLAWAY's Lacuna stories have been reprinted in *The Year's Best Dark Fantasy and Horror*, nominated for the Million Writers Award, The Shirley Jackson Award, and named to the Locus Recommended Reading List. He lives in Superior, Wisconsin, with his wife and two dogs. You can find him on his website at www.adamcallaway.net, or on Twitter @Sensawunda. He is currently working on a novel set in Lacuna.

KELLA CAMPBELL is the nocturnal alter ego of someone who sits behind a publishing desk by day. She can usually be found in Vancouver, Canada. Her writing almost always has romantic/emotional/relationship elements, sometimes expressed as speculative fiction, and she's drawn more toward exploring the edgy side of things rather than the sweet side. She's on Twitter @kellacampbell and links to her blog and other places are collected and sorted at www.kellacampbell.com or about.me/kellacampbell.

GEMMA FILES, former film critic and teacher turned award-winning horror author, is probably best-known for her Hexslinger series (*A Book of Tongues*, *A Rope of Thorns* and *A Tree of Bones*, ChiZine Publications). She has also published two collections of short stories (*Kissing Carrion* and *The Worm in Every Heart*, Wildside Press) and two chapbooks of poetry. The characters of Dionne and Samaire Cornish and A-Cat Chatwin have previously appeared in *Black Bush* (Arcane, Nathan Shumate Books) and *Crossing the River* (Mighty Unclean, Dark Arts Press). She is currently hard at work on her fourth novel.

JOSHUA GAGE is an ornery curmudgeon from Cleveland. His first full-length collection, *Breaths*, is available from VanZeno Press. *Intrinsic*

Night, a collaborative project he wrote with J. E. Stanley, was recently published by Sam's Dot Publishing. He is a graduate of the Low Residency MFA Program in Creative Writing at Naropa University. He has a penchant for Pendleton shirts, rye whiskey and any poem strong enough to yank the breath out of his lungs. He stomps around Cleveland where he hosts the monthly Deep Cleveland Poetry hour and enjoys the beer at Brew Kettle.

LILY HOANG is the author of four books. She edited the anthology *30 Under 30* with Blake Butler, and with Joshua Marie Wilkinson, she is currently editing *The Force of What's Possible: Writers on the Avant-Garde and Accessibility*. She serves as Editor-in-Chief at *Puerto del Sol* and Editor at *Tarpaulin Sky*. She teaches in the MFA program at New Mexico State University and can be found virtually at HTML Giant.

SANDRA KASTURI is a writer, book reviewer and Bram Stoker Award-winning editor. She is the co-publisher of the World Fantasy Award-nominated and British Fantasy Award-winning press, ChiZine Publications. Her work has appeared in various magazines and anthologies, including *ON SPEC*, *Prairie Fire*, *Taddle Creek*, *Shadows & Tall Trees*, several of the *Tesseracts* anthologies, *Evolve*, *Evolve 2*, both volumes of *Chilling Tales*, *A Verdant Green*, *Star*Line*, and *80! Memories & Reflections on Ursula K. Le Guin*. Sandra managed to snag an introduction from Neil Gaiman for her poetry collection, *The Animal Bridegroom* (Tightrope Books). Her second collection, *Come Late to the Love of Birds*, came out in 2012. Sandra is working on a mythological noir novel and her third poetry collection. She likes red lipstick, gin & tonics and Michael Fassbender.

NANCY KILPATRICK, award-winning author, has published 18 novels, about 200 short stories, and has just edited her 13th anthologies. She also published the non-fiction book *The Goth Bible: A Compendium for the Darkly Inclined* (St. Martin's Press). Her two most recent titles are (as editor) the anthology *Danse Macabre: Close Encounters With the Reaper*, and her sixth collection of short stories, *Vampyric Variations* (both from Edge

Science Fiction and Fantasy Publishing). She lives in Montreal with her cat Fedex, but travels frequently. Check her website for updates: nancykilpatrick.com, and join her on Facebook (Nancy Kilpatrick, Writer and Editor).

CARRIE LABEN is originally from New York and now lives in Missoula, Montana, where she recently obtained her MFA from the University of Montana. Her work has previously appeared in such venues as *Clarkesworld*, *Apex Digest*, *Camas*, and anthologies including *Fantasy: The Best of the Year* and *Shades of Blue and Gray*. When not writing, she can usually be found staring at birds or enjoying the local microbrews. Her father once saw a tree struck by lightning, but no one in her family has ever been attacked by vampires.

CHRISTINE MORGAN works the overnight shift in a psychiatric facility and divides her writing time among many genres. A lifelong reader, she also writes, reviews, beta-reads, occasionally edits and dabbles in self-publishing. Among her most recent novels are *Murder Girls*, about college housemates who decide to become serial killers, and *The Horned Ones*, in which a disaster traps tourists in a scenic show-cave. Her stories have appeared in more than two dozen anthologies, 'zines and e-chapbooks. She's been nominated for the Origins Award and made Honorable Mention in two volumes of *Year's Best Fantasy and Horror*. Her husband is a game designer, her daughter was published in a zombie anthology at fourteen and plans to major in psychology and film. A future crazy-cat-lady, Christine's other interests include gaming, history, superheroes, crafts, and cheesy disaster movies. Lately, she's discovered a love for Viking-themed horror and dark fantasy, with several such stories already written and a blood-soaked novel called The Slaughter in the works.

DANIELS PARSELITI has been writing fiction and non-fiction for the last fifteen years. He holds a BA in philosophy for Wesleyan University and an MFA in fiction from Washington University in St. Louis. His fiction has been published in *The Brooklyn Rail* and his nonfiction in *The Subway*

Chronicles: Scenes from Life in New York. Dan grew up on the east coast, but now calls St. Louis his home. He pays the bills working in the wine business, and reads philosophy in his spare time.

CAT RAMBO lives, writes, and teaches by the shores of an eagle-haunted lake in the Pacific Northwest. Her 200+ fiction publications include stories in *Asimov's*, *Clarkesworld Magazine*, and Tor.com. Her short story, *Five Ways to Fall in Love on Planet Porcelain*, from her story collection *Near + Far* (Hydra House Books), was a 2012 Nebula nominee. Her editorship of *Fantasy Magazine* earned her a World Fantasy Award nomination in 2012. For more about her, as well as links to her fiction and information about her online classes, see www.kittywumpus.net.

MARY A. TURZILLO's novel *An Old-Fashioned Martian Girl* and Nebula Award winning novelette *Mars Is no Place for Children* are recommended reading on the International Space Station. She has been nominated for the Rhysling, the British Science Fiction Association Award (*Eat or Be Eaten, a Love Story*), and the Pushcart (*Your Cat & Other Space Aliens, vanZeno*). She has recent and forthcoming work in *Asimov's*, *Paper Crow*, *Analog*, *New Myths*, *Strange Horizons*, *Bull Spec*, *Magazine of Speculative Poetry*, *Ladies of Trade Town*, and *Stone Telling*, plus an authorized Philip José Farmer sequel story, *The Beast Erect*, in *The Worlds of Philip José Farmer 2*, Meteor Press, 2011. Her latest book, *Lovers & Killers* (Dark Regions), has been nominated for both the Stoker and the Elgin.

PAUL WITCOVER is the author of the novels *Waking Beauty*, *Tumbling After*, *Dracula: Asylum*, and *The Emperor of All Things*. A fifth novel, *Eternity in Love*, is forthcoming. He is also the author of a short-story collection, *Everland and Other Stories*. His work has been a finalist for the Tiptree, Shirley Jackson, World Fantasy, and Nebula awards. He lives in Brooklyn, NY.

EVIL GIRLFRIEND MEDIA

WWW.EVILGIRLFRIENDMEDIA.COM

Look for the big red heart to find new favorites in the Sci-Fi, Fantasy and Horror genres!

ALSO AVAILABLE IN EBOOK AND PRINT:

The Heart-Shaped Emblor
by Alaina Ewing

Witches, Bitches & Stitches
A Three Little Words anthology

Roms, Bombs, & Zoms
A Three Little Words anthology

Made in the USA
Charleston, SC
05 January 2015